I have recently been reminded that although all Christians do not agree on all aspects of biblical doctrine, most of us are united in these beliefs: the sanctity of life and the evils of one human believing they have the right to own another. I've seen proof of this from a man who, by an act of Providence, was our guest. In his possession was a note from a preacher who has dedicated his life in service to God and showing God's mercy to all. This note helped convince our guest that saving a child's life is worth more than what this world has to offer. Mercy's song.

Prudence Willard
December 20, 1857

SECRETS OF WAYFARERS INN

SECRETS OF
WAYFARERS INN

Mercy's Song

CANDICE PRENTICE

Guideposts

New York

Secrets of Wayfarers Inn is a trademark of Guideposts.

Published by Guideposts Books & Inspirational Media
39 Old Ridgebury Road
Danbury, CT 06810
Guideposts.org

Cover and interior design by Müllerhaus
Cover illustration by Greg Copeland, represented by Deborah Wolfe, LTD.
Typeset by Aptara, Inc.

Printed and bound in the United States of America

10 9 8 7 6 5 4 3 2

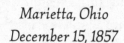

CHAPTER ONE

Marietta, Ohio
December 15, 1857

Prudence Willard wrapped her wool shawl tight against the winter weather. Ice pellets beat against her face as she fed her chickens. *God have mercy on anyone out in this.*

Patience, their imperious white goose, pecked her leg. The goose's behavior was unusual, and it added to Prudence's anxiety. She'd felt as if eyes watched her ever since she found what looked like a partial boot print in the mud around the back of the coop.

Her husband, Jason, had looked at the print, shaken his head, and suggested perhaps the cold had heightened her imagination.

Back inside, Prudence made dinner and enjoyed the warmth of the house and the presence of her husband. After they ate, Jason read out loud from the Bible, and then they sat quietly, meditating on the verses he'd chosen.

Prudence wanted to mention her uneasiness again but was reluctant to disturb their peace. Then Jason's chin fell to his chest, and he began snoring through his nose.

She drifted off too. But she awakened when she heard a thump. She glanced at Jason. He still snored. His Bible had slipped to the floor. Had that been what she'd heard?

She picked up the sacred book, concerned for the fragile pages, but they hadn't been hurt. Then she cocked her head to listen. She heard nothing. *Imagination, Prudence.*

She touched Jason's arm. He stirred and opened one eye.

"Thee has been asleep." Prudence smiled.

"Thee should have awakened me before now." He pretended to frown, but his eyes were warm. "And do not say that I was snoring."

"I will not. However, I will say that thee was dreaming out loud of sawing wood."

Jason chuckled and stretched.

She lifted the black book in her hand. "I thought I heard something outside, but I think it was thy Bible slipping to the floor."

"I'll go check. From the sounds of the ice on the roof, another armful of wood won't hurt."

A cold draft blew through the house when Jason opened the door. He quickly shut it, but it flew open again a moment later.

"Prudence, come quickly!"

She hurried to his side. "What is it?"

Jason pointed to the front porch. A man lay there. Quiet. Still. Skin so white, she wondered if he was dead.

Two thoughts occupied LuAnn Sherrill's mind as she stepped out of Jeremiah's Coffee House with two lattes and a breakfast wrap. The first was the Marietta Christmas in History Home Tour, for which she'd recently been asked to step in as chairwoman.

The second was the imminent arrival at the Greyhound bus station of one of her favorite past students, Jerri Carrington— the person for whom LuAnn had bought breakfast.

LuAnn hummed "Silent Night" as she walked to her car. Abnormally cold wind buffeted her head. Christmas wreaths hung on the lampposts, reminding her of the finishing touches on the Christmas decor still left to complete at her home and business, Wayfarers Inn.

She glanced at her watch. Normally at this time of day, she was at the inn, working the breakfast rush along with her best friends and co-owners, Tess Wallace and Janice Eastman. They had graciously covered for her so she could pick up Jerri.

"LuAnn, wait!"

LuAnn turned. Fern McPherson, one of the Christmas tour committee members, hustled up the sidewalk toward her, plump legs churning and heels clomping on the cement.

"Good morning." LuAnn gritted her teeth as a burst of arctic air blasted past her.

Fern stopped two feet in front of LuAnn, reached into her purse, which was the size of a shopping bag, and pulled out her leather-bound notebook, waving it in the air.

LuAnn backed up in surprise.

"I've made a new list," Fern said.

"About what?" Making lists was one thing she and Fern had in common, but Fern took list making to a whole new level. As she swirled her notebook in the air like some sort of conductor's baton, LuAnn couldn't help but notice the exquisite floral tooling on the cover.

"I'm checking on the people whose homes are part of the tour. Yesterday afternoon I went to see the Bickerton sisters to check on their progress. They wouldn't let me in the house."

LuAnn's gaze snapped back to Fern. "You what? Uh, they are, uh—"

"Eccentric." Fern waved her notebook again, eyes glinting. "I'll be checking in with the Aldriches today. I assume Wayfarers Inn will be prepared for the tour, and I won't need to check it."

LuAnn eyed Fern with concern. "At the previous meeting we agreed that I would check in with everyone later this week, after the final committee meeting."

Fern shrugged, hitched her purse strap closer to her neck, and squinted at LuAnn. "I wasn't at the last meeting or the meeting before that, and no one consulted me. Besides, one person shouldn't be running the whole show."

LuAnn struggled to find words that might take some of the fire out of Fern's eyes. "None of us is solely running the show. We're working as a team."

Fern sniffed and ignored LuAnn's comment. "In addition, I'll be at the final committee meeting tonight to protest this ridiculous idea of non-paying participants."

"We discussed the idea at the meeting two weeks ago. Everyone voted to approve. I handed out fliers to local businesses to advertise. Surely you saw one of those. After the main event on Saturday, the host houses will be open for two hours on Sunday afternoon so people from the community can look at the decorations and lights. But desserts and lectures won't be included. It's a good community outreach."

Fern slapped her notebook on her free hand. "I should have been consulted."

LuAnn shivered, and she hoped the lattes weren't going cold. "The notes from every meeting are emailed to every committee member. You received a copy. You never replied with any objections." She drew in a deep breath, but it only served to make her throat close against the cold. "Let's discuss this further at the meeting tonight," she croaked.

"Oh, we will." Fern whirled on her practical black pumps and stalked toward Jeremiah's.

LuAnn hurried to her car and reached inside to place the lattes in the cupholders. She slipped into the driver's seat, shut the door, and turned on the car, willing the heater to start immediately. Then she took a deep breath and closed her eyes. The confrontation was unexpected, even from acerbic Fern McPherson.

When the original chairwoman of the Marietta Christmas in History House Tour had delivered her baby two months early, the committee had gone into a semi-meltdown, and several of the stronger personalities threatened to derail the camaraderie that the group had enjoyed up to that point. LuAnn had been chosen to fill in as chairwoman by anonymous vote, but she did so reluctantly. The vote hadn't been unanimous, and the confrontation with Fern was a reminder of that fact.

LuAnn bowed her head. *Father, please help me handle this situation. I don't understand why Fern is so upset.*

She reached for the gearshift just as her phone buzzed with a text notification. She pulled it from her purse. It was from Jerri.

We're going to be on time—any minute.

On my way. LuAnn texted. *Picked up a plain latte for you and a breakfast wrap.*

Perfect. See you shortly. Can't wait.

LuAnn put her car in DRIVE and headed up the road, quickly covering the scant mile from Jeremiah's to the bus station. As she drove, her anticipation over seeing Jerri grew. LuAnn hadn't seen her old student in years. They'd communicated intermittently, mostly through social media. Because Jerri's sister Michele lived in Marietta, they'd anticipated seeing each other at some point. Now the time had arrived. But there was one niggling question in the back of LuAnn's mind—why had Jerri asked LuAnn to pick her up rather than ask her sister?

The bus arrived just as LuAnn parked. She exited her car to wait. When the willowy woman stepped down the bus stairs,

LuAnn felt unexpected tears in her eyes. Jerri looked different from the thin, intense girl who had walked into LuAnn's classroom so long ago, yet LuAnn would have known her anywhere. She remembered Jerri's brash, even abrasive personality, the result of insecurities brought on by the death of her father and a mother who spiraled into drug abuse after her sister was born. Making matters worse, Jerri's mother ended up in prison, leaving her daughters to finish high school while they lived with their grandmother.

"Miss Sherrill!" Jerri's voice could have been heard a block away. LuAnn smiled. That hadn't changed either. Jerri hurtled toward LuAnn, arms outstretched, ignoring her suitcase that had been unloaded from the bus.

LuAnn barely remained standing, surprised by the intensity of the greeting, especially since Jerri didn't like hugs. "I'm LuAnn now, remember?" Her words were muffled in Jerri's coat-clad shoulder.

"I didn't realize just how glad I'd be to see you," Jerri murmured into LuAnn's neck before she took a step backward.

LuAnn smiled even while she choked back tears. "It's certainly a greeting I'll never forget. But you'd better go get your suitcase before someone else claims it." She pointed behind Jerri.

"Yes, ma'am." Jerri's laugh lingered in the air as she retrieved her bag.

When they'd settled into LuAnn's still running car, they grinned at each other. Jerri's dark eyes sparkled with life, despite the deep circles under them.

"Latte?" LuAnn held up Jerri's cup. "It might be lukewarm, but it's caffeine. And here's your breakfast wrap."

Jerri took both, laid the wrap on a napkin in her lap, and sipped the latte. "So good." She sighed and looked at LuAnn. "I remember the first time you brought me a hot drink—hot chocolate."

"I remember," LuAnn said softly.

"Then you got permission for me to study in your classroom after school."

"So I did." Memories flooded LuAnn's mind, making her feel weepy in a good way. She hoped she wouldn't spend the whole of Jerri's visit on the verge of sentimental blubbering. "And look at you now, working on your doctoral dissertation. You've come such a long way."

"I owe a lot of that to you, teaching me how to concentrate and study. Here's hoping I do you proud." Jerri lifted her drink.

"I'm sure you will." LuAnn lifted her latte, and they tapped the tops of their cups.

"I was sorry to hear of your grandmother's recent passing," LuAnn said. "I would have come to the funeral."

"I know you would have." Jerri picked at the paper around the breakfast wrap. "I didn't feel like I could ask you since I hadn't remained in real close contact with you. Besides, it was just a tiny affair at her church."

"I would have come, no matter what."

"I know."

LuAnn sipped her drink. They hadn't moved from the parking lot, but she didn't mind. She wasn't in a hurry.

"I miss Granny." Jerri pulled the paper from one end of the breakfast wrap and took a bite.

"She always did her best by you."

Jerri nodded and chewed. "She did. I appreciated that more as I got older." She paused, and her lower lip trembled. "Her death was a loss, for sure. But as I was cleaning out her attic, I found the papers that led to the research I'm doing for my dissertation. It was as if she left me one last gift. I can't wait to show you. It's so cool. I think it's proof that one of my relatives came through Ohio on the Underground Railroad."

"And we can help you find more information." LuAnn put her latte in the cupholder and faced Jerri. "I'm curious about why you didn't have Michele come and pick you up."

Jerri put her wrap down. "I figured you'd ask me that. I'm embarrassed to say that I wanted you with me when I see her. We haven't been on the best of terms. We talk on the phone, but it's awkward and superficial."

"Does she know you've arrived?"

Jerri looked at her phone, forehead wrinkled. "I texted her and then tried to call her when the bus arrived in Marietta, but she's not answering. She might still be at work. She had one job scheduled for early this morning." Jerri glanced at LuAnn. "If she's not at home yet, she said her neighbor has a key. I'll get that, and maybe you and I could talk for a while until she arrives?"

"Of course. I set aside the whole morning for you." LuAnn put the car in DRIVE and headed out of the parking lot.

"Thank you." Jerri smiled, but tension pinched her mouth and eyes.

"You look tired. It's a long trip from Georgia."

"It is, but it's not the trip. I managed to sleep, thanks to earplugs, but I'm worried about Michele. She wanted me to come as soon as possible. When she called me last week, she sounded nervous."

"You mentioned that when we talked. She had some concerns about her job?"

"Yes, but two hours ago she called me to make sure I was really on my way. She sounded scared. And now she won't answer the phone."

LuAnn frowned. "That is odd."

"I'm torn between concern and irritation." Jerri clenched her fists. "Here I am, making a last-minute trip that I wanted to take next spring, traveling on a bus overnight because I didn't want to deal with the airports this time of year, all because she begged me to come. And she isn't answering my calls or texts. I would have thought she'd be waiting for me. Unless something is wrong."

"Perhaps she's just so excited you're coming that she forgot to turn her ringer on. Let's go find her. She's still on Charles Street, right?"

"Yes, she is."

LuAnn turned onto the Byway, driving past Marietta College.

Jerri ate more of her breakfast, then faced LuAnn. "I call Michele every week, mostly because my grandmother used to make me, and now I do it out of habit. The conversations are short. 'I'm fine. You're fine. I like my dog.' It's as if she doesn't want me to be part of her life. Do you remember that she used to be into some drug stuff?"

LuAnn nodded.

"As far as I can tell, she's been totally clean for a couple of years now. She has new friends. She even started going to church." Jerri sighed. "For some reason I've always brought out the worst in her. Sibling rivalry, maybe? Like she had to compete with me."

"I remember some of the issues you two had when you were young."

"Apparently the issues haven't changed, but the way we handle them has. We no longer fight. She avoids talking to me about anything important. And I just try not to think about her much."

LuAnn ached at the bitterness and hurt in Jerri's voice.

"Anyway, I was surprised when she suddenly called me out of the blue and said something was wrong. She needed me. She was afraid of something. It reminded me of the past when she was scared as a little kid." Jerri's voice sank to a whisper. "I really had no choice. I had to come."

Jerri, always the rescuer of her little sister. LuAnn reached over and patted her arm. "I did try to contact Michele after I moved here, but she didn't seem interested in seeing me. That was over a year ago. I didn't want to be a pest, so I haven't contacted her for a while."

"Probably because she associates you with me and doesn't want to get close."

LuAnn glanced at Jerri. "That could be. But maybe this visit will be the very thing that brings the two of you together.

After all, it is the Christmas season. Jesus' birth. God's mercy in the flesh. His plan to reconcile humans to Himself."

"Yeah, I guess."

LuAnn felt a wall go up between them. Jerri turned her head to stare out the window. The skepticism she'd had as a teenager about the things of God hadn't changed. The little girl who had gone to Sunday school and church with her grandmother had disappeared somewhere underneath the hard shell of a struggling adult.

Jerri finished her breakfast wrap and crumpled the paper just as LuAnn rounded the corner onto Charles Street. She almost skidded to a stop. Red lights blinked ahead of her.

Jerri leaned forward. "Is that an ambulance?"

"Yes, it is." LuAnn saw someone being loaded onto a stretcher.

"That's Michele's house! I recognize it from pictures. Is that her they're loading up?" Jerri jammed her latte in the cupholder.

"It might be. I'll park so we can get out." LuAnn pulled along the side of the road.

Jerri jumped from the car and ran toward the scene. LuAnn followed.

A small crowd had gathered in front of a small blue Cape Cod, clutching their coats close to their bodies, breath coming out in steam.

Jerri shoved past them. "That's my sister! What's happened?"

A short older woman, whose full head of textured dyed red hair stuck out in all directions, moved closer to Jerri. "Michele was upset. I yelled out the door for her to be careful, but she wasn't paying attention. Down she went on a patch of ice. I told the county they needed to do something about it." The woman pointed to ice on the cracked cement sidewalk.

A tiny, scrawny terrier mix, leash dangling on the ground, panted and whined next to the stretcher. Jerri tried to get closer, but a medic stopped her.

"Ma'am, we have to get her to the hospital. She's had a nasty knock to her head."

"But she's my sister!" Jerri cried. "I want to go with you. I'm her only family here."

"Sorry, ma'am. No can do. I sympathize, but I need you to please step aside and let us do our job."

LuAnn touched Jerri's shoulder. "I'll take you. We'll follow them, okay?"

"Yes, okay." Jerri nodded.

The back door to the ambulance slammed shut. The paramedics jumped in the front, and the vehicle drove away, lights flashing, siren wailing.

The terrier barked and whined. LuAnn grabbed the leash just in time to keep the little dog from following. The crowd dispersed, heading back to their houses.

"What do I do about the dog?" Jerri glanced around in a panic. "She loves that dog."

The red-haired woman stepped up and reached out for the leash. "I'll watch her for you. I'm Mrs. Brewster. I live just next door." She pointed to a house that was a mirror-image of Michele's. "I take it you're Jerri?"

Jerri nodded.

"Michele told me you were coming."

LuAnn handed the leash to Mrs. Brewster. "Thank you."

A tall man wearing shiny cowboy boots joined her. "I can always walk him if Mrs. Brewster can't."

"Thank you both," LuAnn said.

"Um, okay." Jerri glanced at the two of them with confusion and turned to LuAnn. "All I really care about right now is getting to the hospital. Let's go."

CHAPTER TWO

Two hours later, LuAnn pulled into the parking lot of Wayfarers Inn and turned off her car. She closed her eyes for a moment and leaned back against the seat, letting the watery winter sunlight coming through the windshield hit her face. The events of the morning tumbled through her mind. Fern. Jerri. Michele's fall. At least Michele was alive and being treated for head trauma. Jerri would give LuAnn updates later.

Judging by the number of cars in the parking lot, the lunch crowd had gathered. She took a deep breath to nudge herself into hostess mode. Then she grabbed her purse and phone, exited her car, and headed inside.

Local residents, as well as a number of their overnight guests, were eating soup and breads in the café. Two of those guests, an older couple named Merrill and Carleen Boycraft, looked up and waved. She waved back. Their daughter and her husband were part of the Marietta Christmas in History House Tour, and they had come to help. The couple always wore matching clothes. Today's outfits included blue jeans and sweatshirts covered with bells and Christmas trees.

Tess stood by one of the tables, talking to a guest. She nodded at LuAnn as she crossed the room.

Janice and Tess had been busy in her absence, putting some finishing touches on decorations. Wayfarers Inn had been chosen to represent the Civil War period for the Christmas tour. LuAnn spied greens on the windowsills and tabletops. Brass candelabras that the Bickerton sisters, Irene and Thelma, had given LuAnn the year before, looked perfect among the greenery. A Balsam Christmas tree, decorated in homemade ornaments, including strings of popcorn and cranberries, sat in a corner of the café. In keeping with the time period, the decor was understated and very different from the decorations LuAnn had put up last year.

Janice came through the swinging kitchen door and passed LuAnn, carrying a tray laden with bowls. "It's good to see you. We've been praying for Michele and Jerri."

"I appreciate the prayers."

Janice went to deliver the soup, and LuAnn headed for the kitchen. Life at the inn had continued as normal while she and Jerri had waited for the doctors to decide what could be done for Michele. The hospital had been a stark reminder of LuAnn's distant past, when her fiancé had died suddenly. As she pushed against the swinging doors, she felt overwhelming gratitude for the mundane and vowed not to take things for granted, including her friends.

In the kitchen, heat from Big Red, their massive stove, filled the room, along with the delicious scent of soup and baked goods. Winnie, their cook, stirred the contents of several large pots.

"Hi, Winnie." LuAnn's stomach growled.

Winnie turned and waved a wooden spoon in LuAnn's direction. "My lands, LuAnn! I heard your stomach clear across the room. You'd best get some food inside you before you do anything else. Otherwise you might fall over."

"Time for eating after work is done," LuAnn said, even though she wanted nothing more than to sit at the table and scarf down some food. Breakfast seemed a long time ago.

Winnie clucked her tongue, shook her head, and muttered under her breath.

LuAnn reached for her apron just as Janice, followed by Tess, came back to the kitchen.

"You look about done in," Janice said.

"Put that apron down," Tess ordered. "You're going to sit and eat something."

"Just what I said," Winnie harrumphed. "She won't listen."

"I feel guilty doing that while the rest of you work. I've been gone since before breakfast. We do have a full house, you know."

Janice wrapped an arm around LuAnn. "Relax. We can handle it for ten minutes more while you eat."

LuAnn's shoulders relaxed. "Thank you."

Winnie grabbed a bowl. "Sweet potato soup today."

"That sounds marvelous, but you don't have to wait on me." LuAnn spied a cake cooling on the counter. Her mouth watered.

"Just sit," Winnie ordered.

LuAnn dropped heavily onto a chair and rested her apron on her lap. She didn't dare object to any more of Winnie's directions. The woman was relentless once she made up her mind.

"When you texted us from the hospital, we wanted to come and join you," Janice said, "but one of us had to be here. Besides, we figured until the doctors took care of Michele, we'd just be in the way. So instead, we put finishing touches on the decorations."

"Thank you for doing that. They're perfect."

Winnie slipped a bowl of soup in front of LuAnn, along with a fresh roll.

LuAnn lifted a spoonful to her mouth and then sighed. "This hits the spot."

Tess began rinsing dirty dishes in the sink to put in the dishwasher. "You gave us a scare when you first said you were at the hospital. We thought you'd hurt yourself on a patch of ice."

"Thank you for caring. It has been a morning." LuAnn felt another rush of gratitude for the women in the room, and she whispered a "thank-You" to the Lord. "Michele is in the ICU. She had some bleeding on her brain. They did a simple operation to relieve the pressure."

"Oh my," Janice said.

"Is Jerri okay?" Tess asked.

"Yes and no." LuAnn glanced at the counter. "Is that another Mary Todd Lincoln White Cake?" The previous week, Winnie had made a sample of the cake they intended to serve during the tour of their inn. This one was even prettier.

"Yes indeed." Winnie laid her hand next to the cake on the counter. "We can test it after lunch. I want our dessert to be the best of the tour."

Janice went back out to the café to check on guests.

Tess followed with a full coffeepot. "We're enjoying the full house," she said over her shoulder. "Remember last year when we were worried about not making the bills?"

"Things have definitely improved." LuAnn smiled. "Wayfarers Inn is becoming the bed-and-breakfast that we dreamed of."

When the lunch crowd had thinned, LuAnn rinsed dishes in the kitchen sink while Winnie put the food away. Tess and Janice saw to the last of their guests and cleaned the café then joined LuAnn and Winnie in the kitchen.

"You ready for cake?" Winnie plated large slices without waiting for an answer, then set them on the table.

"I guess so." Janice chuckled as she took off her apron and rubbed her hips. "I can feel them growing between Christmas cookies and all this cake."

"No kidding." Tess pulled at the waistband of her pants. "I think we'll need to do some serious post-holiday exercise."

"Winnie, since we're having cake, why don't you sit with us and have some too?" LuAnn asked. "You need a break too."

"I think I will." Winnie grabbed another plate and joined them.

Janice took a big bite. "Oh my. This is as wonderful as the first one."

LuAnn bit into the cake. "Perfection."

Winnie chewed thoughtfully. "It is. Now that I know how many people will be here for the tour, I'll calculate how many cakes I need to make, and I'll give you a list of ingredients."

"Sounds good to me," LuAnn said.

"You're awesome." Janice sighed and ate more cake.

"I am, aren't I?" Winnie grinned at them.

They all laughed.

Winnie looked at LuAnn. "That young woman who hurt herself goes to my church."

All three of them swiveled their heads toward Winnie.

"Really?" LuAnn asked.

"Mm-hmm. And our guests Merrill and Carleen Boycraft have family who go to my church too."

"The Paglinos," LuAnn said. "Rosemary and Frank. Their home is part of the Historical Tour."

Winnie nodded. "That's them."

"I heard the Boycrafts mention their daughter when they signed in, but I didn't know the connection to you," Tess said.

"That's really sweet of them to come help their kids," Janice said. "They're such a nice couple."

Winnie set her gaze on LuAnn. "Is Jerri still at the hospital with Michele?"

"Yes." LuAnn leaned back in her chair. "This morning we picked up a rental car for her to use while she's here since she hasn't been able to ask Michele's permission to use hers."

"What's Michele's prognosis?" Tess asked.

"As of right now they're keeping her sedated. They said she could be home within a week if all goes well, but they hemmed and hawed about the long-term effects on her brain."

"I took the liberty of telling Stuart what happened," Janice said. "He might stop by and see if Jerri has any questions he can answer." Janice's son was a local doctor, and the women relied on him for medical advice.

"Good idea," LuAnn said. "Thank you."

"How did it happen?" Tess asked.

"According to her neighbor, Michele slipped on a patch of ice outside her house when she was walking her dog. Went and smacked her head on the corner of a cement step."

Janice put her fork down on her empty plate. "We need to make sure we keep our sidewalks clear."

Tess finished her cake and put her chin in her hands. "LuAnn, you mentioned before that Jerri and her sister didn't really get along."

"Yes. Sibling rivalry continued into adulthood, maybe? I'm not sure what's really going on, but it's from both sides. I'm praying things get resolved."

"You wouldn't have known there were problems from the way Michele talked about her sister," Winnie said. "Like Jerri was the cat's meow or something."

"Really?" LuAnn asked.

Tess furrowed her brow. "But you said that Michele suddenly called Jerri and asked her to come early and to stay with her. Why the change?"

"That's why the request was so odd," LuAnn said. "Michele begged her to come. Something about her job, but she refused to explain. Then this morning Michele called to make sure Jerri was on her way, and Jerri said she sounded frightened."

"I wonder why," Tess said.

"Jerri has no idea. Just that it had to do with her work."

Winnie crossed her arms. "When Michele started attending our church a couple of years ago, she was just out of rehab. She was troubled at first, but she really started turning her life around."

"Gracious," Janice said. "I hope she hasn't had a setback."

"Jerri doesn't think it has anything to do with the past or Michele's old habits. I'm sure the hospital will be running a million tests, and anything out of the ordinary will show up." LuAnn looked at Winnie. "What did Michele do for work?"

"House cleaning. Through some service, I think. And maybe some other things. I don't know details. I wasn't that close to her. But I know that girl would've given you the shirt off her back."

"Hopefully Michele will be able to explain everything soon," Tess said.

Winnie stood and covered the cake.

"Is Jerri still coming to dinner tonight?" Janice asked.

LuAnn nodded. "As far as I know, she is. And please remember she isn't normally an affectionate, huggy kind of person. She never was."

"So that means we don't force affection on her?" Tess asked.

"Read her body language and judge for yourself. It'll be pretty obvious."

"Okay," Janice said. "I'll keep that in mind."

"She'll be working on her dissertation while she's here?" Tess asked.

"She will be. She found some sort of paper that led to a relative who might have passed through Marietta on the Underground Railroad, so it's possible her relative came through the Riverfront House. We'll take her on a tour through the basement and the tunnel."

"I wonder if our Prudence knew her relative," Tess mused.

"That's one of the things Jerri wants to find out."

Tess stood and picked up everyone's empty plates. "I assume the committee meeting will go on as expected tonight?"

LuAnn's stomach lurched. "Yes. And I need to warn you. I ran into Fern this morning. She's upset." LuAnn told them about their confrontation. "She wants to address the committee tonight about her concerns, and she's resentful that she wasn't notified of any changes."

Tess raised a brow. "Didn't she get the previous weeks' emails with committee meeting minutes?"

"I sent them to her. Whether or not she looked at them is up for debate. I've never seen her so hostile."

"Oh dear." Janice sighed. "I suspected she was a little upset. I watched her face as the committee asked you to step in. I wonder if maybe she's jealous."

"I'm not sure, but I'd gladly turn the whole thing over to her if it would take care of her anger."

"Even before you took over as chairwoman, I'd noticed some changes in her behavior," Janice said. "From tolerably crabby to 'best to avoid her' testy."

"I noticed that too," LuAnn said. "Now she's as good as accused me of trying to control everything. She also stopped by the Bickertons to check on their decor. Thelma and Irene refused to let her in."

"She must have been pretty pushy. They don't normally act like that. They love company."

Winnie snorted from the counter. "Those two! If they don't like something, you'll know about it, sure enough."

"Very true. And I'll find out more when I stop by their house tomorrow." LuAnn stood. "Is there anything that needs my immediate attention around here? I'd like to go to my room, freshen up, and check my to-do list. I appreciate you guys covering my duties today."

"Laundry is done for the moment," Tess said. "Rooms are cleaned."

Janice nodded. "All our guests seem happy."

Winnie cleared her throat. "I do have one thing I want to talk about before I leave for the day."

The three of them faced her.

"I think we should have fresh, individually wrapped Christmas cookies available for our guests in the evening. Perhaps two cookies per package? Out in the big room?"

LuAnn glanced at Tess and Janice, who both nodded.

"Good idea. It'll help make their stay more home-like," LuAnn said. "Tess, how many are staying through Christmas?"

"Several of them, including the Boycrafts."

"That's right." LuAnn nodded. "I remember Carleen said she recently lost her mother. This trip is a gift from her husband to help her recover by being near their daughter." LuAnn's mother passed away over a year ago, and she understood the need for a change of scenery.

"Well, I need to head out." Winnie pulled a piece of paper from her apron pocket and slid it to Tess. "Here's the grocery list for cookie ingredients. Marcus said he'd pick them up as soon as you order them."

Winnie's grandson Marcus delivered most of the supplies for the inn.

Tess looked it over and laughed. "You already assumed we'd say yes to fresh cookies?"

Winnie took her apron off and hung it inside the storage closet. "I figured you'd agree with me that our guests are important." She pulled her coat on and left, singing "Onward Christian Soldiers."

"I think she feels like she owns this place," Janice said.

LuAnn laughed. "She probably does, but the reality is, we wouldn't be able to do what we're doing if she weren't here."

CHAPTER THREE

In her suite, LuAnn dropped onto her recliner. Huck, their little dog, bounded into her sitting room, greeting her with enthusiasm. She petted him until he settled at her feet. Tom the cat entered at a more leisurely pace. He hopped into her lap, pressing his head against her chin. Then he settled in the space between her thigh and the arm of the chair.

She felt exhausted, and it was only after lunch. But the tiredness was strange. Her body was weary, but her emotions felt taut, like guitar strings wound too tightly. She stroked Tom's head and felt some of the stress seep away.

Seeing Jerri again brought back many good memories, but those had been overshadowed by Michele's accident. The young woman was in good hands, medically speaking, but no one knew what the outcome was going to be. That left Jerri in a quandary. Michele had called Jerri, so frightened that she begged her to come, even though they were semi-estranged. And now Michele was sedated, and poor Jerri was here, not knowing what was going on with Michele, medically or any other way. And she was without family to help her make decisions.

The upcoming tour also loomed heavy on LuAnn's mind. The responsibility was a large one. Although local town officials weren't formally part of the committee, they were watching from the sidelines. And Fern could potentially irritate the tour hosts, affecting the tour. If LuAnn was honest, she felt irritated herself. With a full inn, Christmas around the corner, and now Jerri's visit, she had enough on her plate without having to deal with the disgruntled Fern.

She pulled her Bible from the table next to the chair and tapped her pen on her lips. There were so many things going on, and LuAnn could do little at this point except pray.

Except pray. LuAnn smiled toward heaven. That was the most important thing she could do.

She bowed her head and began, but the heavens felt like the proverbial brass. She tried again. Nothing changed. "What's going on, Lord?"

An image of Fern's face came to her mind, and she realized what God was trying to say. She was irritated at Fern and needed to let it go. She flipped her Bible open to a well-read portion, the Gospel of Matthew, and one of her favorite parts. The Beatitudes. *"Blessed are the merciful, for they will be shown mercy."*

"Mercy," LuAnn whispered. "Thank You for the reminder, Father. Especially now, in this season that represents Your mercy for people. Please, grow my capacity to extend mercy to everyone, including those who irritate me, like Fern. And I do forgive her for her hostility toward me."

There. That felt better. LuAnn went on to pray for Jerri and Michele.

When she was done, she checked her notebook where she kept her to-do list to make sure she wasn't forgetting anything. As she put it in her lap, she rubbed her finger over the cardboard cover and thought about Fern's exquisite notebook cover, with leather the color of cinnamon and dark tooling of flowers and leaves and twining vines.

She felt a brief stab of envy. Then she caught herself with a tiny chuckle. "Father, I'm sorry. I'm on the verge of coveting. My notebooks do just as good a job of keeping lists as one with a beautiful cover."

With that, she opened her notebook, grabbed a pen, and ran down her list. If the past few days were any indication, the lunch rush would continue to be busy. They should verify that they had all the ingredients Winnie needed for the meals she'd planned. The holidays had brought visitors into town, not to mention residents who were out and about, doing things for the season. Then there were the normal inn chores. Checking on the guests. Cleaning rooms. Doing laundry.

Tonight, Jerri was supposed to come for dinner at five. Tess was making lasagna. And at seven thirty, LuAnn, Janice, and Tess would host the final meeting of the Marietta Christmas in History House Tour committee. The event itself was on Saturday. This evening, the group would finalize details. Tomorrow she had to pick up an order from the printer, as well as begin to visit the other three host houses to make sure they had everything they needed—or, as Tess said, checking to ensure the hosts had decorated their homes like they'd agreed to, without appearing as if she was checking up on them.

Then there was the matter of Fern. She'd be there tonight, and given the conversation today, her presence might present a challenge.

Her phone buzzed with a text notification. It was Brad Grimes, nephew of Thelma and Irene Bickerton, as well as a good friend of LuAnn's.

How is your visit so far?

Briefly she texted what had happened.

Wow. I'll be at the meeting tonight. I'll expect to hear more then.

LuAnn thanked him for asking and put her phone on her lap. Knowing Brad was on the committee and coming this evening made her feel better in general.

She leaned back in the recliner and closed her eyes, thanking the Lord for all the blessings He'd given her. Good friends. This inn. Good health. She drifted off to sleep only to be startled back awake by the ringing of her cell phone. It was Jerri. LuAnn quickly answered it.

"Hello. Funny you would call. I was praying for you and Michele just a few minutes ago. How are you? How is Michele?"

In the awkward pause that followed, LuAnn was reminded once again that Jerri didn't believe in the power of prayer like she had when she was young.

"Michele is sedated. I'm okay. Tired. And back at Michele's house for a little while. I feel like a snoop. Here I am in her house with all her stuff. Everything I do, every cupboard I open, is getting into her business, and she doesn't even know." Jerri sighed. "And I picked up her dog from the neighbor, Mrs. Brewster. I have no clue what to do with it. I don't even like dogs much. At least I don't think I do, but I wouldn't know because I've never had one." She sighed again. "From what I understand, this is a house dog, not a backyard dog. I don't even know how many times a day I'm supposed to let it out."

LuAnn smiled at Huck, still sleeping at her feet. "Dogs are good at telling you when they need to go out. Some of them dance around or go to the door. And since that dog is an adult, if you regularly let her out three times a day, you should be good."

"All it wants to do is be with me. I've been exploring the house, and every time I turn around, it's right behind me. It stares at me all the time and even follows me to the bathroom."

LuAnn chuckled. "You keep calling her 'it.' I think the neighbor said she's a female?"

"Umm, let me check." LuAnn heard shuffling through the phone speaker. "It's a girl. No boy parts."

"Does she have a name?"

"Yes. The neighbor called her Diesel."

"Diesel?" LuAnn laughed. "With a name like that, I'd expect a big, stocky male bulldog, not that little scrawny thing. Well, I'm sure Diesel knows something is awry. She was there when Michele fell. And she saw them take her away."

"You really think dogs feel stuff like that?"

"They know when things are different and their people aren't there anymore."

"Oh. I never thought about that before, but if that's true, then she might be upset. I guess I should be extra nice to her. And I need to see if there's dog food here."

"Good idea."

LuAnn heard Jerri rummaging around.

Finally, Jerri spoke again. "I found dog food. And based on Diesel's reaction, I think she's hungry." The sound of dog food hitting a hard bowl came through loud and clear on LuAnn's phone. She held it away from her ear until Jerri was done.

"Wow. She's eating like she's starved. Thank you for helping me with that. But what I really called about is that I found Michele's art books and her planner...I guess you'd call it a planner. Some people might call it a bullet journal. It not only contains her schedule, but it also has random notes and lots of little drawings. All of them are like artwork. She loves to sketch."

"I remember that, now that you said something." LuAnn returned the back of her recliner to a sitting position.

"When she was a kid, I could tell what kind of mood she was in by her doodles. When she was happy she'd fill pages with round things, like hearts and flowers. Positive words. When she was upset, the pictures were jagged with sharp edges, like squares and triangles. And she'd sometimes write angry words. A psychiatrist would have a field day with all of that, I'm sure. I always figured it was just a good outlet for her. Some people exercise to let off steam. Other people do art and stuff."

"Is it possible to determine from the planner why she asked you to come?"

"I'm not sure yet, and I feel even more like a snoop looking through her personal notes. I'd be mad if someone looked at mine. But this is an emergency, right?"

"I'd agree with that."

"Okay, good. So I flipped through it, and many of the recent pictures are jagged. She had lists of school stuff to do.

And appointments, but only initials, not names. Like P.A. or M.P. And there are some words scrawled around the edges. Anyway, I need to read through it more thoroughly. It might help me figure things out. I could just kick myself for not insisting she tell me more."

"Would you like me to come over?"

"No. You don't need to do that. I need to be a grown-up and deal with all of this. Including Diesel. Oh, and I'm still coming to dinner tonight, if that's okay."

"Good. Tess and Janice are looking forward to meeting you."

"I'm looking forward to meeting them as well. I just wish the circumstances were different."

"I do too," LuAnn said.

CHAPTER FOUR

Jerri arrived at the inn at exactly five. The circles under her eyes had darkened since the morning, but her smile was bright. "You Ohioans certainly know how to do a cold snap."

LuAnn laughed. "This has been a particularly brutal couple of days. Hand me your coat."

Jerri shrugged her arms out of the sleeves and handed it to LuAnn, who hung it up.

"How are you tonight?"

"I'm about as good as you'd expect, probably. Tired and worried." Jerri glanced around the room. "This place is outstanding."

"It really is. We're honored to own such a marvelous piece of history."

"I'm looking forward to learning more about it. How amazing that this was a stop on the Underground Railroad. Even more so now that I suspect one of my relatives passed through Marietta, possibly even this inn." Jerri pointed at the tree. "Your Christmas decorations are simple yet beautiful."

"The decor this year is much different than last year. Last year I went all out. I even blew a fuse with all my Christmas lights. This year the inn represents the Civil War in the Marietta

Christmas in History House Tour, so we researched and decorated in a way that we felt represented the period. Do you think we accomplished what we set out to do?"

"Yes, I do. People would have used what was handy, like you did. Greens, things from nature, from foods like popcorn and dried fruit. They even made little dolls from nuts."

"That's good to know. Thank you for the confirmation. The tour is this Saturday. I'm the committee chairwoman."

Jerri swiveled her head back to LuAnn. "A historical tour sounds like something I'd love, given my degree."

"It's a ticketed event, but you're welcome to attend as my guest. The folks staying at the inn will be attending as well."

"If Michele is doing well by then, I will." Jerri made a circuit of the large open room, to the fireplace, the piano, then back to where LuAnn stood. "It's peaceful here. I feel like my tensions are smoothing out. I would love to stay here sometime."

"You're welcome to stay anytime. I'd be glad to put a hideaway cot in my suite for you. We've asked God to make Wayfarers Inn a place of refuge. Although we're not in the business of helping escaped slaves on their way to their new homes, we are in the business of helping people find some solace and peace when they're away from home."

Jerri's gaze slid around the room. "Where do you guys eat?"

"We have a small kitchen in our living area on the fourth floor. Come on, I'll show you. Tess is making lasagna for us tonight."

They rode the elevator up to the fourth floor.

When the door opened, Jerri took a deep breath. "It smells good."

"It does." The scent of Italian spices made her mouth water.

They walked down the hall to the common area. Tess was at the counter cutting thick, cheesy pieces of lasagna.

"Our guest has arrived. Jerri, this is Tess Wallace."

Tess smiled. "Jerri, welcome. We've heard a lot about you recently, and we're so glad you've joined us tonight."

"Thank you. I'm glad to finally meet LuAnn's friends."

Tess had set the table with a pretty cloth and dishes, along with pitchers of lemonade and water.

Janice walked into the room with a grin. "Hello there!"

"This is Janice Eastman."

"I'm so happy you're here," Janice said.

"You're the mom of that nice doctor who came by the hospital this afternoon. I think his name is Stuart?"

"Yes, that's my son." Janice smiled. "I hoped you wouldn't mind that I told him about you."

"I appreciate it. He really helped me. He made sure I understood what the other doctors were saying. Plus, I suspect they're all talking to me more freely because of him."

"I'm glad to hear that."

"Is there anything I can do to help?" Jerri asked.

"Not a thing. Have a seat." LuAnn waved at their small table, then removed a pan of garlic bread from the oven and put the buttery slices into a basket.

Jerri dropped into a chair and rested her purse next to her feet.

Tess carried the pan of lasagna to the table, LuAnn added the basket of bread, and Janice grabbed a bowl of salad and some dressing from the refrigerator. Then they joined Jerri at the table.

"We wish you were staying with us," Janice said. "If you come back in the future, you're certainly welcome."

The harsh lines on Jerri's face had softened. "You're all so kind. LuAnn already offered a cot in her suite, and it's tempting, but I feel the need to stay at Michele's right now, especially while she recovers. But staying here in the future would be awesome. The inn is incredible."

LuAnn smiled. "Janice, would you ask the blessing?"

"I will."

When they were done, Jerri lifted her head and inhaled. "I'm starving. All I had to eat today was the breakfast wrap LuAnn bought me and two candy bars from the hospital vending machine. And lots of coffee."

"My goodness." Tess handed her the bread basket. "Candy bars for a meal aren't healthy. Doesn't the hospital have a cafeteria?"

"It does. I didn't bother."

"In that case, please help yourself." Janice pointed at the lasagna. "Take as much as you want. We have plenty."

Jerri ladled a large piece of lasagna onto her plate and grinned. "You guys are exactly as LuAnn described."

"I hope that's a good thing," Tess said.

"Oh, it was. LuAnn called you guys the 'Inn Crowd.'"

"We are that," Janice said.

"It's perfect and a great play on words." Jerri forked a piece of lasagna into her mouth. "Delicious."

"What's the latest on Michele?" Janice asked. "LuAnn said they did some procedure. And she's sedated now?"

"They did. She hit her head hard on the corner of a cement step. It caused her brain to bleed. The doctors called it a closed head injury, and they had to do something called an evacuation of the bleed. And yes, she's sedated at the moment. Like forced rest."

Janice nodded. "But she's going to be okay?"

"Her brain isn't bleeding anymore, but they're waiting to give me more of a prognosis. They're doing what's called neuro checks every few hours. It remains to be seen if there is any permanent brain damage. That could be anything from loss of memory to something longer lasting." Jerri swallowed. "Michele is just lying there so very still. I can't help but think how much more serious this could have been."

"It's difficult to watch a loved one suffer." LuAnn was reminded again of her fiancé, so many years ago.

"It's hard to sit and watch her breathing. And this might be TMI, but I'm beginning to feel guilty for being irritated with her for the last few years." Jerri picked at the crust of her bread.

LuAnn touched her shoulder. "Don't overthink right now. You've had an emotionally trying day. Give yourself a chance to recover before you go excavating your feelings and motivations."

"That's good advice. The good thing is they found no illicit drugs in her system. She's clean."

"That's great," LuAnn said. "Now you can concentrate on that and not a bunch of negative thoughts. You'll need your energy to be there for her when she wakes up. Time then for dredging up the past when you can do something about it."

"That's a good point." Jerri dug into her lasagna with renewed energy.

"Sometimes the three of us reminisce and bring out old school yearbooks," Tess said. "LuAnn has a very large collection. She showed us your picture and spoke about how proud she was of you."

Jerri's eyes grew wide, and she looked at LuAnn. "You did?"

"Of course I did."

LuAnn, Tess, and Janice chitchatted about their day while Jerri finished off two pieces of lasagna and three pieces of bread.

When she'd finished, she patted her stomach. "That was so good."

"Granny's recipe never fails to satisfy," Tess said.

"So, tell us about your dissertation," Janice said. "LuAnn said it has something to do with the Underground Railroad."

"That's a part of it. I'd always heard stories growing up about a relative of ours who was raised by a single young woman. Rumor had it that that young woman rescued my relative from a plantation and escaped via the Underground

Railroad. I have a copy of a poem supposedly written by her. And to top it off, in some papers I found in my grandmother's attic, I discovered what I think might be a note from Charles Finney. I don't know how it all fits in, but if the note is from him, it adds some intrigue to the story."

"Charles Finney the revivalist?" Tess asked.

"Yes. He was quite the abolitionist. He lived in Oberlin, Ohio. From 1851 to 1866, he was president of Oberlin College."

"I had no idea," Janice said. "We've discovered that many Christians during that time were abolitionists, including Prudence, who was a Quaker."

"She's the woman whose journal you found here?"

"Yes," Tess said. "And now that we know you might have some information, we'll get out Prudence's journal and see if there's any mention of this."

"I'll give you a personalized tour of the basement and the tunnel when you're ready," LuAnn added. "And when you've caught up on your rest, you should also visit the Underground Railroad museum. That's where Prudence's original journal is. The curator, Maybelline Rector, is the local expert, and she might be able to fill in some details for you. Tell her we sent you."

"Awesome. Hopefully I can concentrate soon. I need to put my time in Marietta to good use." Jerri leaned back in her chair. "Did LuAnn tell you guys that she saved my life in a manner of speaking when I was young? Like a superhero?"

LuAnn felt her cheeks grow warm. "That's an exaggeration, isn't it? I'm not a superhero."

"Oh, I beg to differ. Teachers are often the unsung superheroes of childhood. And you did save my life in a manner of speaking." Jerri explained to Tess and Janice how LuAnn allowed her to study in the classroom after school. "I didn't know how to study to begin with. And things were so chaotic in my grandmother's home that I couldn't concentrate, so Miss Sherrill—LuAnn—taught me and then suggested I could use earplugs at home. And for the rest of my time in the school where she taught, she made sure I had a supply of them. Those little foam roll ones. I still use them to this day."

Janice smiled with a sidelong glance at LuAnn. "She never told us about that."

"And now you're working on your dissertation," Tess said. "It's fantastic."

LuAnn felt tears coming to her eyes again.

"You're crying," Jerri said.

"They're happy tears." She dabbed the corners of her eyes with her napkin.

"Do you mind telling us more about Michele?" Tess asked. "Our cook said that Michele attends her church."

"That's an interesting connection. Michele talked about her church and the people. In fact, several of them stopped by the hospital to see her. They were really touchy-feely, wanting to hug me all the time." She smiled wryly.

LuAnn and her friends laughed.

"Michele has had a lot of visitors?" LuAnn asked.

"More than I expected. Along with the church people, there were a couple friends from school and a couple of clients." Jerri frowned. "This guy came through the ICU and looked at her for a little while, but he didn't say anything and just left. I don't know who that was. I almost went after him, but I was too tired."

"Where does she work?" Tess asked. "And what is she studying?"

"She works for a cleaning service, so her clients are from all over Marietta. I think she also had some clients she got on her own. And she was going to school at the local community college to learn to be an accountant."

Janice raised her brows. "A busy young woman."

"She is. Even busier than I realized. Sometimes, in passing, she'd tell me that she was saving money to buy a house. The one she's in now is a rental. She wanted something brand-new and shiny." Sadness made Jerri's face droop. "I've realized that part of the reason she didn't really talk about anything deep with me is because I was so standoffish. I used to do that when she was little. Just dismiss her excitement because I thought it was beneath me."

"Realizations like that are a step toward fixing things, when the time is right," Janice said.

Jerri's gaze snapped back to LuAnn and then to Tess and Janice. "I'm worried. Something is wrong. Michele has never asked me to come and see her. And then there was that frantic call this morning, when she checked to make sure I was on my way. Why else would she ask me to come now if something wasn't wrong? And then today I found this weird page in her planner."

Jerri reached into her purse and pulled out a spiral-bound journal. "I hope she won't be mad at me for sharing this, but I want someone else to see it. This is how she keeps track of her life. If nothing else, you'll understand how my sister thinks. She's visually oriented and artistic, and she expresses herself through pictures. I'm a more literal word person." She flipped the pages, found the one she wanted, and handed the journal to LuAnn.

Lots of geometric designs filled the page, along with a bullet-pointed list of initials, times, and then a list of words written in jagged font.

"That is odd." LuAnn held it out so Tess and Janice could see it. "Content aside, Michele is a skilled artist."

"My goodness!" Janice said. "It's like those bullet-journaling pages I've seen on Pinterest, only this one is on steroids."

"She is talented," Tess agreed. "Look at this little picture of a dog."

"Now, look at this page." Jerri pointed.

LuAnn ran her fingers over the words, which were hard to see within all the geometric shapes. "'Something is wrong. Laun'…does that say laundry?"

She handed the journal to Tess.

Janice leaned over to look.

"See?" Jerri pointed.

"I can't read all the words, but it looks to me like the word is *laundering*," Tess said.

The three friends exchanged glances, then handed the journal back to Jerri.

"That's what I thought." Jerri held it to her chest for a moment before tucking it back into her bag. "Wouldn't that confirm that something is going on? Maybe like laundering, as in crime?"

"What if this simply means she was doing some laundry for a client?" Tess said hesitantly. "Like extra work for more money?"

"But she called me and begged me to come, and it had something to do with her work. Isn't it possible she discovered something? Something illegal?"

"If I recall, Michele tended to be dramatic," LuAnn said. "I remember as a youngster you describing her overreactions to things. Could this be more of the same?"

Jerri shrugged and slowly shook her head. "You make good points. Logical points. I thought about all those things already, and I was annoyed when she first asked me to come. Really annoyed because of the time of year and my own schedule. But when she called again this morning, she sounded so scared. Why? She's getting her life together—working and going to school. She has friends and her church. Besides, she's been avoiding me for such a long time. Why would she suddenly desperately want me to come and visit her?"

Tess's brow was wrinkled. "What exactly did she say when she asked you to come?"

"She said she had questions for me. It had something to do with her work. She said I was the most logical person she knew. But she refused to answer any other questions over the phone."

Thoughts in the back of LuAnn's mind began to whirl.

"Have your parents been told about the accident?" Janice asked.

Jerri's gaze flitted toward LuAnn.

"I didn't tell them about your parents," LuAnn said. "It wasn't my business to tell."

"Thank you for respecting me, but I don't mind them knowing." Jerri crossed her arms. "Our father died a long time ago. Our mother is in jail in West Virginia. She has been for a long time. And, no, I haven't talked to her yet."

"So you have no family to call to help you, then?" Tess asked.

Jerri shook her head. "No. Michele and I are it as far as I know."

Janice touched Jerri's arm. "Your mother will still want to know, won't she?"

"Maybe. I don't know. We don't talk much anymore." Jerri stabbed at a lone piece of noodle on her plate. "Still, you're right. I should let her know. Maybe I'll just call the prison and let them tell her."

Silence fell on the group, then Tess jumped up. "Would anybody like coffee? Cake?"

Jerri groaned. "The thought of more coffee today makes my stomach hurt. And I'm stuffed. I can't eat another thing."

"I'm done in myself," LuAnn said.

"And we already ate cake once today," Janice said. "It's best if we don't eat more. Otherwise I'll need to shop those sales after Christmas—for new clothes."

Jerri glanced at her watch. "I'd better get back to the hospital to check in. Then I'm going back to Michele's house to get some sleep. I'll probably end up sleeping with Diesel, since she seems to think she owns everything, including me."

Janice laughed. "Diesel? What kind of dog is it? A bulldog?"

"A scrawny little terrier mix," LuAnn said. "She's about the size of a large cat."

Janice raised her brows.

"That's a really funny name." Tess giggled. "Not normal for a dog that size or gender."

"Personality-wise, Diesel lives up to her name," Jerri said. "She's pushy and a little bit demanding and always going. I'm on a crash course to learn about dogs. I haven't been around a lot of them."

"We have a dog and cat that came unexpectedly into our lives last Christmas." LuAnn told Jerri the story of Huck and Tom, including Tess's original reactions to their little dog.

"I suspect I'll end up liking my sister's pesky little pet."

Tess grinned. "It can happen easily."

Janice stood and took dishes to the sink. "This week we'll look through our copy of Prudence's journal to see if we can find anything about your relative for you."

"I would be grateful. That would be a fabulous addition to my dissertation. Can I help you clean up?"

"No." LuAnn carried the half-empty pan of lasagna to the counter. "You need to scoot. Let me get your coat and walk you to the door."

Jerri waved at Tess, then Janice. "It's so good to meet you both."

"We feel the same," Janice said. "We'll be praying for you and Michele. And about all the questions you have."

Tess nodded in agreement. "I'm sure LuAnn will keep us updated." She looked at LuAnn. "And we'll join you downstairs as soon as we're done here."

LuAnn rode down the elevator with Jerri and walked her to the inn's front door. "Give me a call or text me when you get back to Michele's house later on tonight, please, so I know you're safe?"

"Yes, ma'am." Jerri grinned.

LuAnn held out her arms and Jerri stepped into them.

"It is seriously so good to see you," Jerri said. "I had no idea how much I needed this."

"I think I needed it too. It's like an early Christmas present. And if you're hungry tomorrow morning, you're welcome to stop by here and eat breakfast—my treat."

"That sounds like a good idea. I haven't had time to shop, so I might do that."

Jerri left the inn. LuAnn watched her walk to her car, fighting more tears.

December 15, 1857

The man Jason had found on their front porch was alive. He lay pale and unconscious in their spare room. He'd hit his head, probably on the corner of their porch. Prudence surmised he'd slipped on the ice. She and Jason had wrestled the man's limp body into the bed. Jason loosened the man's clothing while she prepared a hot water bottle.

When Prudence returned, Jason sat on a chair near the bed with two papers in his hands. She nestled the cloth-covered tin bottle next to the man, then tucked quilts over him, up to his chin.

"Thee has been through his pockets?" Prudence asked.

"Yes. To find out who he is."

"What has thee found?"

"These, among other things." Jason handed her two notes. The first was a scrawled couple of sentences.

God is waiting for you. "But God, who is rich in mercy, for his great love wherewith he loved us, even when we were dead in sins, hath quickened us together with Christ, (by grace ye are saved)..." Ephesians 2:4-5. Charles F.

"Is that his name then?" Prudence asked. "Charles?"

Jason shrugged. "I do not know."

"Does thee think he is a traveling revivalist?"

"He has no Bible."

Prudence turned to the second piece of paper. It was a verse written in a beautiful, feminine script. She read the poem out loud.

> Mercy's Song
> Mercy, thou art a babe born
> Mercy, thou art a savior dying
> Mercy, thou art blood freely shed
> Mercy, thou art sins blotted out
> Mercy, thou art Almighty God
> Mercy, thou art freedom.

"Lovely words of truth," Prudence said.

"From a wife, perhaps?" Jason suggested.

Prudence studied the man. Even in pale unconsciousness, his face was lined with weariness. He didn't look like someone who would carry verse to read for leisure, although looks could be deceiving.

"I will sit here tonight," Jason said. "To watch him."

"Does thee think that is necessary?"

Jason stared across the room at the dresser where the man's coat lay. Then he looked back at her. "We do not know who he is."

Prudence felt Jason's unspoken urgency. The fear that always lay between them. Jason's anxiety that someone would discover the packages that Prudence delivered—the men and women she'd aided on their trips to freedom. She and Jason were in agreement about the cause of abolition. But she did the work Jason couldn't do because of his leg injury. That lay between them, always.

Jason's eyes turned again to the dresser, fear lining his forehead. Prudence followed his gaze and gasped. Two revolvers sat there, in plain view. A man wouldn't carry two revolvers for hunting.

Jason's fear fell on her. "I agree, husband."

"Good," Jason said softly. "Go to bed now. And Prudence, please bar the door."

CHAPTER FIVE

When LuAnn joined Janice and Tess in the café kitchen a few moments later, Janice grabbed a box of tissues from the top of the refrigerator and handed them to LuAnn. "Looks like you need these."

"An emotional visit for you," Tess added.

LuAnn wiped her nose. "Thanks. It is emotional, for several reasons. My nose might just remain red this whole Christmas season. You can call me Rudolph." She tossed the tissue into the trash. "Emotions aside, we'd better get the refreshments ready for the committee meeting tonight."

"Right." Janice went to the pantry and pulled out big plastic containers that contained cookies.

Tess pulled out the big silver coffee urn.

LuAnn washed her hands and began plating cookies. She stopped and stared at a chocolate chip cookie in her hand, thinking about Michele's planner. The whole situation was odd. And though LuAnn had expressed some reservations, she had this feeling that something was, indeed, very wrong.

She suddenly felt twitchy, like she was being watched. She turned. Janice and Tess stood in the middle of the kitchen with crossed arms.

"I can feel your eyeballs burning a hole in my head. Why?"

"You've been holding that one cookie for at least a minute."

LuAnn glanced at it. A few of the chips had begun to melt on her fingers. "So I have."

"You should go ahead and eat it," Tess suggested.

"And you've got that look on your face." Janice finished filling the plate that LuAnn had started.

"It's the look that says you're thinking hard." Tess leaned against the counter.

"I'm always thinking. That's why I make lists. To get the thoughts out of my head so I don't overload my brain."

Tess and Janice exchanged glances.

"What?" LuAnn pressed her lips together.

Janice closed the plastic cookie container. "This seems like more than just random thoughts. In fact, this is more like your 'there could be a mystery to solve' look."

Tess chuckled. "I think we're thinking that *you're* thinking about Michele and her cryptic planner. Right, Janice?"

"You're right. That's definitely what *I* was thinking that she was thinking." Janice laughed.

LuAnn waved a hand in the air. "Okay, you guys, laugh at my expense. And maybe I am, but I'm going to stop right now. There's way too much going on at the moment to even consider a mystery, especially since we don't know if it really is a mystery. Perhaps Michele has realized the importance of making things right with people. Maybe she called Jerri to simply make amends and perhaps get some advice about her future. Anyway, I'm not going to give it another thought tonight." Even as she said the words, she knew her brain wouldn't obey.

"Okay, then." Tess snickered as she picked up the coffee urn and headed for the kitchen door.

"Mm-hmm," Janice murmured. "Like it's so easy for any of us brush off a mystery."

"Funny," LuAnn said. "But right now we need to batten down the hatches for the committee meeting. Storm Fern is blowing in tonight, and we really don't know what kind of weather to expect from her."

Gusts of cold air accompanied the arrival of the committee members. LuAnn, Janice, and Tess took turns greeting them at the door. As they arrived, they shed their thick coats and hats and headed for the hot drinks and cookies.

Boomer Aldrich, owner of a local Laundromat, huffed and puffed as he handed LuAnn his bulgy winter coat. His elfish looks belied his personality. "Patsy couldn't make it," he said. "Says it's too cold. She's not feeling well, and her throat is scratchy. She's having trouble talking. Might be laryngitis." Living up to his nickname, his voice boomed through the large room. He moseyed over to fill a plate with cookies.

Brad arrived, as promised. He greeted LuAnn with a broad smile, and she felt lighter and happier. After all, with good friends supporting her, she could deal with anything.

He gave her a brief hug. "Aunt Thelma and Aunt Irene aren't coming. They said it's too cold for old folks to be out. I'm here to represent them and their Victorian decor, as well as to represent myself as a plain old committee member."

"I can't argue with their reasoning. I also appreciate every member of the committee, including the 'plain old' ones."

"This committee member wouldn't miss the last meeting for the world."

Behind them, Boomer's commentary continued to reverberate through the room like a bass drum. "...can't believe how bossy some people are."

Brad glanced over everyone in the room and chuckled. "Boomer is in attendance, I hear."

"Yes, he is." LuAnn smiled. "Patsy stayed home tonight. She has a touch of laryngitis."

"Too bad it isn't contagious." Brad's eyes twinkled. "Sorry. That could be interpreted as a mean comment. I'd better go get some cookies to sweeten myself up." He patted her arm and headed for the snack table.

LuAnn was still chuckling when the Paglinos arrived. She welcomed them and reached for their coats.

"Thank you." Rosemary shrugged off her faux fur wrap. Although she bore a striking resemblance to her mother, their personalities appeared as different as night was from day. Carleen's smile was open and sunny. Rosemary's forehead seemed permanently wrinkled with worry. Her husband, Frank, gave LuAnn a tight smile as he handed her his black wool pea coat, and then he took his wife's elbow and went to greet everyone else.

Fern hadn't arrived yet. Neither had her son Melvin, who often accompanied his mother when she went out at night.

LuAnn was beginning to think Fern wouldn't be in attendance when she burst through the front door. LuAnn greeted her and offered to take her coat.

Fern handed it to her with narrowed eyes. "Took me longer to get here than I thought it would. Hard to see in the cold."

LuAnn thought the comment odd. "Cold or not, I'm glad you're here."

Fern stared at LuAnn with a pinched face. "Surely not after our discussion this morning." Her loud, querulous voice carried across the room. Everyone turned to stare.

Before LuAnn could think of a reply, Brad appeared at her elbow. "Fern, I've missed seeing you the past few meetings. Good to see you tonight. Where is Melvin?"

If it were possible for Fern's face to get any more pinched, it did. "My son is off with his girlfriend doing who knows what." Her angry, bitter emphasis on the word *girlfriend* came across like the gong of a bell.

Brad nodded sympathetically. "Sounds like you could use a cup of coffee. May I get it for you? And perhaps a cookie? I think there're chocolate chip as well as gingersnaps, and I have it on good authority they're freshly made."

Fern's face relaxed, and she looked toward the table. "I love chocolate chip cookies. The more chocolate chips, the better."

"Good. Let's go."

LuAnn ducked her head so no one would see her grin. Brad could charm the prickles off a cactus if he had a mind to.

For several minutes, LuAnn watched the group interact—or not. The Paglonis sipped coffee and observed everyone over their mugs. Boomer slurped his drink and mostly just glared in Fern's direction. LuAnn wondered why. Other members who weren't hosts but contributing in other ways, like a local librarian and some members of the historical society, chatted in small groups. Several of the historical society members would be speaking during the various house tours.

Brad kept Fern distracted. LuAnn felt a surge of sympathy for her. Perhaps Fern felt replaced by her son's girlfriend, and she was taking her resentment out on any handy target.

LuAnn finally walked to the head of the table, called the meeting to order, and then opened her notebook to check her list of things to do for the tour. At the same time, Fern noisily pulled her leather notebook from her purse, almost knocking over her full plate of cookies. She set the notebook down hard on the table, distracting everyone.

LuAnn cleared her throat. "Tomorrow I'll be picking up the tour books from the printer. As discussed, I've arranged for them to be bound, spiral-style. The participants will receive their books here at Wayfarers Inn, since this is the first stop."

"What's in these books?" Fern snapped.

Everyone looked at each other then back at Fern.

"As we've already discussed, they contain the history of Marietta during the time periods each host represents. The book will explain how people would have celebrated Christmas at that point in history, as well as an explanation of the décor and the dessert served."

"I wasn't aware those had been ordered," Fern said.

"We ironed out all the details two weeks ago. Last week everyone approved the copy."

Fern inhaled as if to speak again, but Brad interrupted her.

"They will be beautiful. Even better than we could have hoped. I guarantee it."

LuAnn smiled gratefully at him and continued. "I've already made appointments to come by your houses to give you your copy. Tomorrow I'll visit the Bickerton sisters and Boomer and Patsy. Wednesday, I'll drop by Rosemary and Frank's." She mentioned the times she'd be arriving, and everyone nodded. "We'll confirm then that you have everything you need for Saturday. Does anybody have any questions?"

A few of the attendees asked questions about food, as well as the schedule and the number of participants. LuAnn answered them, then continued.

"As you probably already know, we've met our financial goal. All the tickets have been sold, which means we'll have the money to give to the Reach the Lost Homeless Shelter in time for Christmas. Because of that, they've been able to add a Christmas Eve meal to their outreach."

"That's fantastic news." Brad smiled at LuAnn, and she felt warmth again in her stomach.

"I want to see a breakdown of funds," Boomer demanded.

"The spreadsheet isn't updated yet," LuAnn said. "I have items to add to it."

"I want to see it tonight."

"All right. See me after the meeting." She glanced over the rest of the attendees. "If anybody else would like a copy, I'd be glad to give it to you; however, the final tallies of funds spent and received will be emailed when the tour is complete."

Fern stood and banged the spine of her leather notebook on the table.

"I'm not happy with the decision to allow unticketed participants to view the houses, even if it is on Sunday. Isn't part of the attraction of a tour like this the exclusivity? Won't the people who pay for tickets be less willing to pay next year?"

"As far as I can see, the decision isn't yours to make." Boomer glowered at Fern.

"It was a group decision," LuAnn interjected, trying to keep the two from arguing, although she was probably just as irritated as Boomer. "Ticketed participants get desserts and personalized attention, a lecture about the time period, and the in-depth book. The people who come on Sunday will simply be viewing the decor. They'll be able to purchase a copy of the book if they wish, and there will be a donation box, so there's also the potential of raising more money."

"It's not fair," Fern said.

"We voted on this two weeks ago," Tess said. "It was unanimous."

"I wasn't there," Fern pressed on. "Furthermore, *I* went to check on a couple of people's decor. I wasn't allowed in the houses."

"One of those houses was mine," Boomer roared. "It was way too early. My wife wasn't even up. And then you tried to push your way in."

Fern's nostrils flared.

That must explain why Boomer was so angry with Fern. LuAnn's earlier concern about Fern affecting the hosts was accurate. She had to get this under control. LuAnn placed her hands flat on the table and felt herself morph back into a schoolteacher taking charge of a classroom interrupted by an unruly student. "Fern, you and I should finish this discussion after the meeting. Right now, we need to complete our business so people can get home."

Fern stubbornly remained standing.

Brad gently touched her arm.

Fern blinked as though she'd finally realized that everyone was staring at her. "I suppose." She sat on the edge of her chair and gazed suspiciously from person to person.

LuAnn nodded surreptitiously at Brad with relief. He winked, barely, eyes twinkling.

LuAnn ran over the tour schedule, discussed the brief lectures that would be held at each home, and answered a few more questions. She asked the lecturers to email her with any last-minute changes to their presentations, if they made them. Finally, she closed her notebook.

"As eleventh-hour chairwoman of this committee, I appreciate everyone. You've all been extraordinarily helpful. Fern, I appreciate how much you care about this tour. I know you, like everyone else here, want this to be successful so it can become a yearly tradition." LuAnn smiled at everyone. "Thank you for coming out tonight, and I look forward to seeing all of you on Saturday."

CHAPTER SIX

After the meeting, Boomer followed LuAnn to the office where she made a copy of the committee financial spreadsheet for him. Then he questioned her about each item. By the time they left the office, Fern was gone and the Paglinos were just walking out the door. Boomer grabbed his coat and headed out. Everyone else followed shortly thereafter except for Brad who had wandered to the fireplace to watch the remains of what had earlier been a lively fire.

When LuAnn joined him, he smiled. "Nothing better than a nice warm fire, or embers as the case may be. In fact, these would be the perfect coals for roasting marshmallows."

"They would." She grinned at him. "We should do that sometime."

His smile died. "How are Jerri and Michele? I've been praying about the situation."

LuAnn briefly filled Brad in with the latest, including Michele's journal and Jerri's concerns and suspicions.

"Sounds like you have another mystery on your hands."

"It does, doesn't it? But I don't want to admit it yet." Dishes clinked behind them. LuAnn turned to see Tess and Janice straightening things up. "I need to help clean up."

"I'll join you." Brad followed her to the table where they helped Tess and Janice make quick work of carrying everything to the kitchen.

"Thank you for your efforts in keeping the peace with Fern tonight," LuAnn said to Brad once they were all in the kitchen. Then she looked at Tess and Janice. "All of you."

Brad quirked his brow. "I caught on pretty quickly that Fern had her sights set on you—of course that might have had something to do with the fact that both Tess and Janice asked me to watch out for you."

Tess began pouring out what was left in the coffee urn. "You said Fern was acting strange, LuAnn, but I've never seen her like this."

"I can't imagine what's gotten into her. She's always been bossy, but this is over the top." Janice put away unused tea bags. "Thank you, Brad, for calming her down a little bit."

"Cookies helped," he said, "but she's wound up about something."

LuAnn picked up a sponge and began to wipe the kitchen table. "I'm not convinced it's this committee. She did mention that her son has a girlfriend. Fern seems none too pleased about that."

"Perhaps that could explain her behavior." Janice closed the bag of trash she'd gathered and set it near the back door. "Fern and Melvin have been close. The introduction of a girlfriend could easily lead to resentment on Fern's part."

"Too bad we couldn't just ask her what's wrong," Tess said.

LuAnn stopped mid-swipe and faced her friends. "Well, why not? We could try…or at least I could. Perhaps tomorrow, after I visit Thelma and Irene, I'll pay Fern a visit at her office and see if I can get her to open up."

"I think that's an excellent idea." Janice wiped off a tray and put it away. "Although it might be like walking into the lion's den."

"Maybe she's not feeling well," Brad suggested.

Janice whirled around to face him. "Oh, I hope that's not the case."

"Well, I'll try to find out." LuAnn finished wiping the table. "Meantime, we can all pray for her."

Tess finished cleaning the coffee urn and wiped it with a dish towel. "On a different note, did you see that beautiful leather notebook Fern had? I thought of you, LuAnn."

Janice laughed. "You couldn't help but notice it the way Fern was banging it on the table like a hammer."

LuAnn shook her head. "Don't even start with that notebook. I already had to ask for forgiveness for coveting. It's one of the most beautiful things I've ever seen."

"It is nice," Tess said. "It's the kind you can buy inserts for and change them out as needed."

"There's something appealing about that," LuAnn said. "I can imagine a little pile of unused inserts and then a little pile of used dated inserts, all stacked neatly on a shelf."

Janice grinned. "I can see that making you very happy."

"I can too." Brad stood silently for a moment, then he snitched a cookie from the plastic container before Tess put the lid on. "I'm taking one for the road. I'll pass along all the pertinent information from the meeting to the aunts early tomorrow morning."

"Would you please remind them I'm coming by tomorrow?" LuAnn asked.

"I will do that." He smiled at everyone and disappeared through the swinging door, and shortly they heard the front door shut.

"I'm tuckered out." Tess put the urn away. "And I imagine LuAnn is the weariest of us all."

"You guys have covered for me today, so I'm pretty sure we're equally tired."

Janice waved her arms around the kitchen. "Everything is done. The kitchen will meet Winnie's approval. The guests are quiet, the inn is quiet, and the fire is almost out."

"Time to relax and change into our jammies," Tess said.

"And probably fall asleep where we sit," LuAnn added.

In their common room, Tess got her tablet and settled on the couch with Huck next to her. Tom sat next to LuAnn, wedged again between her leg and the arm of the chair. LuAnn had her copy of Prudence's journal in her lap.

"Hey!" Tess piped up. "I found out that Charles Finney wasn't only an outspoken abolitionist and the president of Oberlin College. I've also discovered a letter he wrote objecting to segregation in the church." She looked over her reading glasses at them.

Janice glanced up from her embroidery hoop. "I'd heard about his revivals, but I didn't know any of this about him."

"I didn't either." LuAnn kept rereading the same page of Prudence's journal over and over. Her mind insisted on wandering to thoughts of Jerri and Michele. Despite her protestations about not wanting to solve a mystery, she realized she wouldn't be able to sleep until she made some notes. She put the copy of the journal down, reached for her notebook and a pen, and began to jot down a few thoughts.

Tess eyed her. "Are you taking notes about the mystery of Michele?"

LuAnn chuckled. "Can't get away with a thing around you guys."

"We know you well," Janice piped up.

LuAnn tapped her pen on the few facts she'd jotted down. "There's not much to write down at the moment, but seeing things in a list always helps me think more clearly."

Janice yawned. "Girls, I think I need to go to bed."

"I won't be long behind you," Tess said.

"Me neither." LuAnn was startled by the sudden ringing of her cell phone in her pocket.

"It's Jerri. I asked her to call me when she got home."

She pushed the button to answer. "Hello. Are you home from the hospital?"

"Yes," Jerri said, breathlessly, "but I think I was followed."

CHAPTER SEVEN

W hat?" LuAnn pressed the phone closer to her ear. "Did I hear you right? You were followed home?"

"I know I sound paranoid, but I'm pretty sure this car followed me from the hospital to here."

LuAnn's heart began to pound. "Is it still there?"

"No."

"Are you inside? Is the door locked?"

"Yes. Whoever it was stopped for a minute, then left."

"Did you call the police?"

Janice and Tess both watched her with questioning frowns.

"I thought about it, but what would I tell them? That a car followed me from the hospital, stopped, and then left? The police would probably think I was a paranoid person looking for attention."

"Well, it would depend on who the police officer was, but I guess you might sound a little paranoid."

"LuAnn, I have to let Diesel out. The backyard is fenced, so I just have to open the door and let her go, but will you stay on the phone with me until I get her back inside?"

"Of course I will." Concern gripped LuAnn's stomach. "But I can come over, if you'd like."

"No need. The car is long gone now. I just checked again. Besides, it doesn't take Diesel long to relieve herself."

Through the speaker, LuAnn heard Jerri opening the door and talking to the dog. She caught herself several times holding her breath until Jerri got back inside.

"All right. My front door is shut and locked. I already checked the back door. We're safe, but I just noticed that Michele's car trunk was open."

"Was it open earlier?" LuAnn asked.

"I have no idea. I don't remember, but it's been a really hectic day. I might not have noticed."

LuAnn took a deep breath. "Are you sure you don't want to come here to stay? You're very welcome. You can bring Diesel."

"I'm sure. I'll be fine. Maybe I'm just overreacting from total exhaustion. Like maybe they were just headed further down the street. But…"

Her words hung in the air. Tess and Janice watched LuAnn with concern.

"If you're sure, then. I leave my phone on at night, so you call me at any time, even in the middle of the night."

"Okay, thank you, LuAnn."

"And please come to breakfast tomorrow morning. I want to see you to make sure you're okay."

"I will. Good night."

"Good night." LuAnn ended the call and told her friends what had happened.

"Stubborn young woman," Tess murmured.

"You don't know the half of it," LuAnn said.

"Do you think it was her imagination?" Janice asked.

LuAnn shook her head. "I don't. Jerri was never subject to flights of fancy. She was hard-pressed to write her fiction assignments for English class. Her forte was nonfiction."

"Just the facts," Tess said.

"Exactly."

"So when she says something is wrong, something is wrong." Tess closed her iPad. "Do you think this has something to do with the mystery of Michele?"

"I have no idea." LuAnn put the phone in her pocket. "It could have just been some creepy person following her."

"Which is disturbing enough all by itself." Tess shivered.

"Yes, it is," LuAnn agreed. "Then again, it might possibly have something to do with Michele's troubles. Perhaps there really is something to look into."

"Maybe, but Michele could wake up at any moment and explain everything," Janice reminded them.

"She might. Or she might not remember anything. The doctor said there could be some memory loss. And even if she does remember, something frightened her." LuAnn tapped her pen on her notebook. "Since she wrote down the word *laundering*, maybe she really did discover someone laundering money."

Tess stroked Huck's head. "Perhaps we should keep our eyes and ears open."

On Tuesday morning LuAnn woke after a fitful night. Her bathroom mirror revealed her lack of sleep. She attempted to cover the circles under her eyes but gave up. She didn't want to look like a clown.

After a quick text to Jerri to confirm she was coming to breakfast, LuAnn grabbed her notebook and rode the elevator downstairs, pondering the questions they'd posed the night before in the light of a new day. Why had Michele asked Jerri to come to begin with? She was already planning a trip to Marietta in the spring to do some research. What was so important that it couldn't wait? The urgency could be chalked up to drama, but that didn't explain why Michele would call her sister. It was totally out of character in their relationship. Especially since Michele seemed to have many friends here in town. And did the car that followed Jerri home the night before have anything to do with Michele? Or was it just a disturbing coincidence?

When LuAnn finally lurched through the elevator doors onto the main floor, the Boycrafts, who were early birds, were already seated in the café, drinking coffee and waiting for breakfast to be served. Robin, one of their regular staff, was away for Christmas, but Taylor was at work, preparing for the breakfast rush. LuAnn was grateful for his help.

She walked into the kitchen where Tess and Janice were helping Winnie with last-minute breakfast preparations.

"Good morning." LuAnn stowed her notebook away in a closet and reached for her apron.

"Morning," Tess said.

"You look kind of done in," Janice said with concern.

"Don't remind me. I saw myself in the mirror." LuAnn eyed the counter. "Winnie, are those biscuits and gravy?"

"Yes," Winnie said. "And eggs and sausage too, if you want them. A cold day deserves a good old farmer's breakfast. It'll get everyone moving."

"One can only hope," LuAnn said, trying not to yawn.

"I guess we don't need to ask you if you texted Jerri this morning to make sure she's okay?" Tess washed a bowl in the sink.

"I did."

"Is she still coming to breakfast?" Janice waited for the coffeepot to fill.

"She'll be here a bit later, probably at the end of the breakfast rush. She wants to stop by the hospital first."

"I'll make sure I save breakfast for her," Winnie said. "You gonna eat with her?"

"Yes, I will."

"Good." Winnie took a pan of biscuits out of the oven.

"That way you can see how she's really doing and perhaps ask her more questions." Janice removed a full pot of coffee from the coffeemaker and put another one on to drip.

"Exactly."

"It's not often one of your students comes to visit," Tess said. "We'll cover for you if the café is still full then."

"You guys have been covering for me all week."

"That's what friends are for." Janice patted LuAnn's arm and disappeared with a hot pot of coffee.

Taylor whirled into the kitchen with the first order of the morning, and Winnie began frying eggs.

"Are you still visiting Fern today?" Tess asked over her shoulder.

LuAnn's stomach tightened. "Yes. I'll probably just drop by her office to catch her off guard. I hope she'll be more likely to tell me what's going on if I do that."

A couple of hours later, when the breakfast rush was nearly over, LuAnn grabbed a cup of coffee and her notebook and sat at a table, waiting for Jerri's arrival. Tess and Janice joined her, dropping onto chairs with their own cups.

"We had a cancellation this morning," Tess said. "That means Jerri could stay here, if she wanted to."

"I doubt she'll come," LuAnn said. "She wants to stay at Michele's and be there when Michele gets home."

"Jerri is quite a young woman," Tess said. "So accomplished, but she's got a hard edge. She seemed uncomfortable when we prayed."

"Yes. She's always been a bit of a skeptic."

"Nothing God can't intervene in and fix," Janice said.

"In a heartbeat," Tess added.

LuAnn opened her notebook. "She has no family nearby, and her friends are in another state. I want to be available to help her with whatever she needs."

"We do too," Janice said.

Tess nodded. "Definitely."

"Last night concerned me," LuAnn said. "And the more I think about it, the less inclined I am to think it was her imagination. She said the car followed her all the way from the hospital and stopped in front of the house. And then there's Michele's trunk being open, which might not mean anything. But all of this would be hard to imagine."

"It would be," Tess said.

LuAnn glanced at the front door and then at her watch. "Maybe Jerri isn't coming to breakfast. What if something happened? I should call her."

"Settle down, mother hen," Tess said. "There's still time for her to get here."

Janice laughed. "I think we all have mother hen tendencies at times."

LuAnn smiled at her friends, grateful for their gentle and concerned hearts. "At the very least, we can offer her advice."

Tess nodded. "We're pretty good at advice."

"We are, if I do say so myself." Janice chuckled.

"And humble," LuAnn said.

The bell over the front door jingled as someone entered the inn.

"Hey, it's Jerri." LuAnn waved her over to their table with relief.

"Hi, you guys," she said in a loud voice as she crossed the room with jaunty steps. When she reached the table, she draped her coat on the back of the empty chair, put her purse on the floor, and sat down. "Sorry I'm late. I ran by the hospital first thing."

Tess eyed her with a wry grin. "I must say, you look fabulous for someone who has been through everything you've been through in the last twenty-four hours."

"After the first hour of tossing and turning, I fell asleep pretty hard." Jerri smiled at them.

"Well that makes one of us." LuAnn laughed. "I worried incessantly about you last night. I think all three of us were concerned."

"Really? You were worried about me enough to lose sleep?" Jerri gazed at all three of them. "All of you were worried?"

"Pretty much," Tess said. "Although I didn't lose sleep like LuAnn."

"Wow. That's really nice. And now I feel guilty for sleeping so well. But I had company to keep me warm, and when I'm warm, I always sleep soundly. For a small dog, Diesel can heat up a bed."

"You needed it," Janice said.

"I'm feeling more normal, that's for sure. Hopefully now that you know I'm doing better, you'll be able to rest tonight."

"I hope so." LuAnn stifled a yawn. "Except that you don't know what's going on with Michele."

"And someone followed you home," Janice said.

"The more I think about it, the madder I get." Jerri jutted her jaw. "The nerve of someone following a lone woman like that."

"You're still sure that's what happened?"

"In hindsight, I'm positive. The car that slowed down in front of Michele's house was the same car that pulled out behind me at the hospital and followed me home. I saw it in my rearview mirror."

LuAnn saw her own concern mirrored on her friends' faces but said nothing.

Jerri eyed the room. "I know I'm a little late, but is there still breakfast left? I'm starving."

"Yes, there is," LuAnn said. "And I waited to eat with you."

Janice glanced around the café and stood. "Not to be rude, but I need to go get the coffee carafe and make some final rounds. Gotta keep our guests happy."

Tess jumped up as well. "I need to get to work too, so I'll take your orders to the kitchen. What would you like? Today we're offering biscuits, gravy, bacon, and eggs your way, in any combo you wish."

"Wow, thank you," Jerri said. "I'll take all of the above with scrambled eggs."

"And I'll take the same," LuAnn said.

"Okay," Tess said. "By the way, when do you want to take a tour of the basement?"

Jerri bit her lip. "I need to have my dissertation in my mind when I do that, and right now all I can think about is Michele, so I'd better wait a few days. How about Thursday midmorning?"

"That sounds like a plan," Tess said. "Now, if you'll excuse me, I'll go to the kitchen and give your orders to Winnie."

As Tess headed for the kitchen, Jerri settled back into her chair and looked around. "I feel pretty special around you guys."

"You are special, hon."

Jerri blinked and avoided LuAnn's eyes. Instead she looked around again. "It's just as pretty here in the daylight."

"I feel blessed to own a third of this place. It's amazing."

"It is. And you're lucky to have friends like Janice and Tess."

"Not luck," LuAnn said gently. "God's blessing. And I am very blessed to have them. Just like I'm blessed to have you. All of you have filled holes inside me that I didn't know needed filling."

"Because you didn't have kids or a husband?"

"Yes, that's partially it."

"So I'm kinda like your kid? And you're kinda like my mom?"

"More like a favorite aunt. You still have your mother."

Jerri's face shuttered, and she looked away, but Winnie saved them from an awkward silence when she waltzed out of the kitchen with a tray that contained their breakfast orders, as well as coffee and glasses of ice water. She put their food down on the table, then tucked the tray under her arm. "So, you're Jerri."

"I am. Who are you?" Winnie intimidated many people, but Jerri met her gaze straight on.

Two peas in a pod, LuAnn thought.

"I'm Winnie Washington. I'm in charge of the kitchen and food here. Your sister goes to my church, so I wanted to check you out."

LuAnn smiled at Winnie's comment about being in charge.

"I've met a number of her church friends at the hospital. Do you know Michele well?"

"Not as well as some of the others in my church, but I do know that she's come a long way. She's one hardworking young woman."

"That's the impression I'm getting. She has a lot of friends. So many people are coming by the hospital, it's disconcerting."

"Our church people like to reach out." Winnie rested her fist on her hip. "Now I have a question for you. Was Miss Lu here as great a teacher as she is an innkeeper?"

Jerri smiled. "I can't accurately compare the two, because I haven't seen her in action as an innkeeper, but she was the best of teachers. And speaking of the very best, this food looks amazing."

"It is amazing. Now I need to get back to making more of it. I'm glad to meet you, Jerri." She twirled around and headed back to the kitchen.

Jerri took a bite of biscuit smothered in gravy. "This is fantastic. Winnie wasn't exaggerating about her talents."

"Winnie is good, and she knows it."

The front bell rang. Brad walked through the door, cheeks red from the cold, carrying a cardboard box. LuAnn hadn't expected him this morning. He saw her and hurried across the room.

CHAPTER EIGHT

"Good morning!" Brad said when he reached LuAnn's table. He set the box on the table and faced Jerri. "You must be the famous Jerri Carrington, who was one of LuAnn's very favorite students, not to mention the smartest."

"Not so famous where I'm from, but here, apparently, I'm front-page news. And the smartest? I might like that title, but I don't think it's true." Jerri giggled, and the freedom of the sound thrilled LuAnn. Jerri was coming alive. Of course, Brad had that effect on people.

"LuAnn was excited about you coming, that's for sure, although we're all sorry about the accident."

"Thank you."

"Jerri, this is Brad Grimes." LuAnn motioned toward a chair. "Would you like to sit and have a cup of coffee?"

He pulled up his sleeve and looked at his watch. "I wish I could, but I have a house to show. Can you believe it? Someone wanting to buy a house this close to Christmas?"

"With a Realtor like you, I can believe it." LuAnn smiled.

Jerri's gaze flew from LuAnn to Brad. "How do you fit in with everything here?" she asked him.

"Well, I was the person who sold these ladies this famous landmark. And now we're all friends."

"I see." She ate more of her breakfast and kept her eyes on them.

Brad slid the box in front of LuAnn. "I saw my aunts this morning. They asked me to pick this up for you from a local gift shop. They'd been trying to find some of these things for you."

"What are they?"

He chuckled. "You know better. I'm not going to tell you and spoil the surprise. You need to open it."

LuAnn pulled the top off the box, peeled back some tissue paper, and smiled in delight. "Acorn dolls!"

"I didn't know what they were, but you must have heard of them already."

"I have, and Jerri mentioned dolls made from nuts as well. People made them at Christmas during the Civil War period. I had hoped to make a couple but didn't have the time."

"Aunt Thelma and Aunt Irene said they should be hung on the tree."

"We'll do it." LuAnn held one out for Jerri to see.

She put her fork down and took it from LuAnn. "I've read about these, but I've never seen any in person." She ran her finger over the doll's tiny dress. "They're so cute. Look at the detail work that went into those clothes."

She handed it back to LuAnn who carefully put it back into the box. "They're precious. I'll be visiting your aunts later this morning, so I'll thank them properly in person."

"You never know what those two will come up with." Brad turned to Jerri. "Well, it's been my pleasure to meet you. I assume I'll see you again. I hope to learn more about your dissertation studies. LuAnn tells me that you have a letter that could be from Charles Finney. That sounds fascinating."

"I'll be glad to tell you more."

"I'm sure these three ladies will have some suggestions for you as well. They're becoming experts in the Underground Railroad."

"I wouldn't go that far," LuAnn said, "but we do have certain resources, like Prudence's journal."

Brad's face grew serious. "I'm praying about the situation with your sister. I know LuAnn is concerned. Don't be surprised if she pulls out her notebook and asks you questions. If there's a mystery to be solved, these ladies can solve it."

"Really?"

Before Brad could say anything else, Tess came out of the kitchen carrying the coffeepot and made a beeline for their table. "Brad, we didn't expect to see you here this morning. Do you want some coffee?" She refilled Jerri's cup.

"No, thank you. I was just making a Christmas-decor delivery from the aunts. I have an errand to run this morning, so I need to get going. I'll talk to you all later."

He waved as he crossed the room. Jerri's eyes followed him until he disappeared through the front door.

"What did he bring us?" Tess asked.

"Thelma and Irene sent little acorn dolls for us to hang on the tree as part of our Civil War Christmas decor." LuAnn showed her the box.

"How sweet of them." Tess began refilling LuAnn's coffee.

"Is Brad your boyfriend?" Jerri asked, her narrowed gaze on LuAnn.

LuAnn choked on a sip of coffee. "What?" The word came out more like a gurgle.

"Are you and Brad an item? Together?" Jerri put her hand on her heart. "Going steady, as you probably would have said back in the day?"

"Jerri, don't ask." Tess finished filling LuAnn's cup. She chuckled and walked to another table to refill coffee cups.

LuAnn stared at her friend's back, then looked at Jerri.

"Really?" Jerri asked. "Is she serious? I shouldn't say anything?"

LuAnn shifted uncomfortably. "Yes, really."

"For real? I mean it's pretty obvious there's a connection between you two."

"He's a good friend—to all of us."

"Right. And that's why when he looked at you his eyes were sort of melty?"

"That's your imagination."

"I don't think so. His eyes didn't seem that way when he was talking to Tess."

Jerri's words hit LuAnn in a way she wouldn't have expected, right smack in the middle of her midsection. She tapped her fingers on the table, raised her brow, and pursed her lips.

Jerri put her fork down. "You have that teacher-finger-brow-lip-thing going on. I used to see it at school. It means, 'you're pushing me and you're about to be shut down, no matter what it takes.'" She giggled.

"That is exactly what my expression means." LuAnn grinned despite herself.

Jerri laughed out loud. "I'll drop it for now, although laughing did me good."

"I'm glad I could provide some relief for you despite being the object of your humor." LuAnn chewed on a mouthful of biscuits and gravy.

Jerri took another bite of eggs, then held up her finger as if she had a question and hurried to finish her mouthful.

"Yes?" LuAnn asked.

"Is what Brad said about you guys solving mysteries true?"

"Yes, I'd say it is."

"Can you help me figure out what's going on with Michele?"

"Maybe. I've been making some notes."

"From what the doctors are saying, Michele might not remember everything, but even if she does, something was wrong, and she'll need help. I even wonder if she might be in danger." Jerri wiped her mouth with her napkin. "The thing is, last night I looked some more in her journal, and I found the word *laundering* in a couple of other places."

"So, it's likely it didn't refer to her doing laundry."

"Right. Cleaning buildings would give her access to seeing or hearing things that most people wouldn't notice. Like papers. And conversations. One thing Michele has always been is observant. That's what makes her a good artist."

"We're going to do what we can to help both of you," LuAnn said. "But we hope and pray that she wakes up and remembers everything so she can explain it herself."

The relief on Jerri's face made LuAnn realize how much their support meant to her.

"What do you have written down so far?" Jerri asked.

"Not a lot. The fact that Michele called you in desperation. That she was frightened of something that possibly had to do with her job. Possibly money laundering. That someone followed you home last night. And the fact that Michele's car trunk was open."

"That's not a lot of information, but it's a start." Jerri's jaw was set in determination.

The two of them finished their breakfast in silence.

"What are your plans today?" LuAnn finally asked. "I'd like to stop by the hospital to see Michele, even if she is sedated."

Jerri reached for her cell phone. "You want to meet me there around two? I'm going to go by the hospital this morning to check on her again and talk to her doctors, then I'm going to poke around town. But I should be back at the hospital by then."

"Two works well for me. I'll meet you in the ICU. And that gives me time for a few other stops that I need to make." LuAnn paused. "I do have one concern. If Michele is in some sort of danger, you might be as well."

Jerri shrugged. "Maybe."

She still had her fearless nature.

"What is it?" Jerri put her elbows on the table. "I can tell you're trying really hard not to make any faces. You don't approve of me looking around?"

"I didn't say that. I'm as intrigued as you are. I don't want to discourage you from checking into things, but I am concerned for your safety."

"It'll be okay." Jerri shrugged, obviously oblivious to her own mortality.

There wasn't much LuAnn could do to convince Jerri otherwise, at least at this point. She certainly couldn't stop her from doing what she wanted to do. LuAnn was pretty sure she'd do the exact same thing in Jerri's position.

LuAnn looked around the café, which was just about empty. "I enjoy talking with you so much, but I need to get some chores done around here."

"And I need to get back to the hospital and check on Michele."

"When I visit this afternoon, I'd like to pray for Michele."

"All right. If you think it will do any good."

"Yes, I do."

Jerri was silent for a moment and then sighed. "You're so much like my grandmother that way. You always have been. I wish I had that kind of faith."

LuAnn leaned toward her. "You can. The first step is realizing how much God loves you."

"That's where it's hard for me. Even believing that God could love me."

"I know," LuAnn said.

Jerri pointed at her empty plate. "Should I take this to the kitchen before I leave?"

"No. I'll get it. I'll see you at two?"

"You will."

Jerri said her goodbyes then put on her coat. Before she stepped out of the inn, she grabbed LuAnn and hugged her. LuAnn watched her leave with a smile.

LuAnn took their plates and headed for the kitchen. Winnie was putting finishing touches on the soups of the day. LuAnn peered over her shoulder at the pot. "That one smells good. You said it was Tuscan sausage soup?"

"Yes. Rich and filling. Perfect for a cold winter day."

"Mmmm. It looks delicious."

"It is delicious." Winnie dug a tablespoon out of the drawer, dipped it into the soup, and handed the filled spoon to LuAnn.

As she took the spoon from Winnie, a memory of her mother came so clearly to LuAnn's mind, she was taken aback. She paused, holding the spoon in front of her lips.

"Are you okay?" Winnie asked. "I don't think it's that hot."

LuAnn smiled. "Yes. Sorry. I was just hit with a memory of my mom."

"Oh?" Winnie looked at her curiously.

"I remembered when she handed me a spoonful of spaghetti sauce from a pot on the stove. We were celebrating my birthday. I was fifteen. That day is one of my favorite memories."

Winnie crossed her arms. "Is that a good thing? Last Christmas you were kinda torn up about her death."

"I was. But I think I'm getting past the terrible raw emotion of grief. I'm beginning to have memories of my mother that don't hurt. Instead they make me happy. I was blessed to have her as my mom." LuAnn blew on the soup spoon, then put it in her mouth. "That is truly delicious."

"I thought so, myself. And I'm glad you're better, Miss Lu. I hated seeing you hurting so much." Winnie turned back to the stove. "I'd best get all this ready to serve for lunch."

"Thank you." LuAnn smiled at Winnie's back. Despite her often brusque behavior, she had a heart of gold.

LuAnn left the kitchen to go upstairs, but on the way, she saw a tall, muscle-bound man at the front desk signing in. His plaid flannel shirt stretched tightly over his shoulders, and his jeans clung to his legs. He was so muscular, she wondered how he even found clothes to fit. He must work out for hours. She hovered in the background and listened as Tess finished signing him in. She handed him a key and explained to him what floor his suite was on.

"How did you hear of us?" Tess asked him as he picked up his duffel bag.

"I, uh, wasn't satisfied with the hotel I stayed in last night. I looked around and found this place."

"Well, I'm glad we had a cancellation." Tess smiled brightly. "We serve breakfast in the morning. You can buy lunch at our soup café."

"Thank you. I'll remember that."

As he turned to go to the elevator, Tess pointed at LuAnn. "That's another one of your hosts, LuAnn Sherrill."

LuAnn walked over and extended her hand. "Welcome to Wayfarers Inn."

He shook her hand, his grip as strong as she expected. "Atley Bradford."

"It's good to meet you. I'm sure you'll be meeting your third host, Janice Eastman, soon."

"I'm sure I will." He shifted restlessly, as if he wanted to get moving, so LuAnn didn't keep him waiting.

He slung his bag over his broad shoulder and headed for the elevator. When he'd disappeared inside, LuAnn walked over to the counter.

"He called an hour ago requesting a room," Tess said. "Since Jerri didn't need it, I figured he could use it."

"Well, that's good. A full inn again."

"Yes." Tess glanced over at the elevator door with a thoughtful frown.

"What's up?" LuAnn asked.

"I'm not sure. I just feel strange about him."

"Why?"

Tess shrugged and looked at LuAnn. "I guess because his eyes are so intense."

LuAnn smiled. "That's better than shifty eyes. Where is he from?"

"His license says West Virginia, but I know nothing else. Usually I can draw people out and they'll talk about themselves and explain why they're in town. Not him. He barely spoke a word–just stared at me. Not that he has to tell me his life's story, of course. It's none of our business, really."

"True, but we love knowing about our guests. It helps us serve them better."

"There seem to be lots of mysteries popping up. Jerri and Michele, Fern, and now our latest guest."

"If he is a mystery."

Tess shrugged.

"I'm going upstairs to change. This morning I have to go by Marty's Print Shop to pick up the tour books. I'll also be visiting the Bickertons. After the lunch rush, I'm visiting Fern and the Aldriches then I'll stop by the hospital."

"Busy day," Tess said. "We'll cover for you here. Janice and I will probably drop by the hospital later in the week if Michele is still there, after things have calmed down."

"Good idea."

"Dropping in on Fern could be interesting," Tess said. "Surprise visits sometimes bring more of a reaction than you expect. But it's always fun to see the Bickerton sisters."

"It will be. And I'll be prepared for whatever happens when I see Fern."

CHAPTER NINE

LuAnn stepped into Marty's Print Shop where Marty, wearing his customary baseball cap, worked behind the counter.

He looked up with a grin. "A wayfarer from Wayfarers come to see me again."

She smiled. He said that every time he saw her. "Hello, Marty."

"You all ready for the Christmas tour? The missus asked me to get tickets. They were sold out by the time I got around to it. She was mad. She waved a finger in my face and threatened to take away my Christmas cookies." Marty leaned across the counter. "She's been dying to see inside some of those big old houses you guys are featuring."

"Then I have good news for you. We've opened the houses for people to look at on Sunday afternoon." She dug into her purse for a copy of the flier she'd hung around town two weeks ago. "We'll have donation boxes out, but people won't have to pay. If you and your wife are available, she can look at the houses to her heart's content." LuAnn handed him the flier. "And here's a thought. You could also surprise her with dinner out afterward to make up for missing out on tickets."

Marty's eyes lit up. "Well now, that's a plan. Maybe I'll get more cookies out of the deal. She's fallen in love with that big Edwardian house that's on the list. Makes me drive by it sometimes."

"That would be Boomer and Patsy Aldrich's house."

"Oh." His grin faded. "I didn't realize that. That might be why she wants to see it."

LuAnn cocked her head. "You say that as if there's something wrong."

Marty shrugged. "Patsy and my wife are friends from way back. Not so close now that Patsy's remarried, but my missus knew Patsy's first husband. Boomer is a recent arrival."

"Really? I don't know them that well, and I hadn't realized their marriage was new."

"Yep, it is. First guy passed away. Several years later, Patsy went on some cruise somewhere, and next thing you know, here she comes with a new husband. They bought that mansion. No one quite knows what to make of him, including my wife. He's apparently much different than the first one. Kinda loud."

"I see." LuAnn waited for a moment to see if Marty would say anything else, but he didn't, so she pointed at the flier in Marty's hand. "That contains everything you need to know."

"Tell you what, I'm going to print some of these and hand them out to everyone I see, maybe get more people to come on Sunday, even at this late date. Could mean more donations."

Mentally, LuAnn went over the tour budget thinking about the cost of printing additional fliers.

Marty laughed. "I see that expression. No worries. I run a print shop, and I'll print them for free. It's for a good cause. Plus, you gave me a way to get back into my wife's good graces, and that might mean she'll make those snickerdoodles I love so much." He put an elbow on the counter. "Besides, I had a cousin who was homeless for a while. He stayed at a shelter like the one you're raising money for, and he was able to get his life back together. I want to contribute."

LuAnn was taken aback by Marty's kindness. "Thank you."

"And now I have what you've come to get." He reached under the counter and pulled out several boxes. "The grand unveiling."

"I appreciate the work you did. That cover and binding was a last-minute committee idea."

"You mean that spiral cover? Easy peasy. And glad to do it for you. In fact, I'm giving you a discount for a good cause." He opened the top on one of the boxes, pulled out a spiral-bound book, and handed it to her.

LuAnn gasped. "They're stunning! Marty, thank you." She flipped through the pages. "They turned out even better than I had hoped."

"They turned out real nice, for sure. I used the best paper I have. I see a lot of things come over this counter, and this design is top-notch. You must have some design skills."

"Actually, Brad Grimes helped me design them, along with Tess and Janice. But Brad is the real talent."

"That Brad is a good man. Does a lot of good things for this community. The other day we saw Brad with some woman in town, and the missus wondered if maybe it was a girlfriend. She's convinced someone will snatch him up before long."

LuAnn wanted to ask about who Brad had been with, but she refrained. The woman was undoubtedly Brad's latest client. LuAnn paid for the spiral tour guide books, and Marty helped her carry them to her car, chatting all the while. But for some reason, she no longer heard what he was saying.

LuAnn tugged her coat closer around her neck against the cold and trudged to the grand veranda of the Bickerton mansion. The wind blew at her hair, and she tried to shove it out of her face. She loved visiting the Bickerton sisters, although her anticipation was diminished by Marty's comments about Brad.

The front door opened even as LuAnn stepped up on the porch. Irene Bickerton Marten planted a fist on her hip and gave LuAnn a once-over through blue-framed glasses. "My lands. You'd best come in fast. You look a fright." The elderly woman stepped aside and urged LuAnn to hurry with a wave.

"Thank you." She walked inside to welcome warmth and leaned down to greet Irene with a quick kiss on her cheek. Then she tried to straighten her hair the best she could.

"Chillier than normal for us." Irene shook her head. "First ice. Now this wind. Reminds me of January 1985. Doesn't bode well for the coming winter. Mark my words, we'll be getting snow soon." The tiny woman motioned for LuAnn to follow her. "Thelma is waiting for us in the library."

LuAnn followed Irene down the long hallway where family portraits hung on the walls. Ropes of Christmas greens and red berries topped the gilded frames.

When LuAnn stepped into the library, she skidded to a stop. A massive Christmas tree, decked with Victorian-style decorations and electric lights that looked like small candles, stood in the front window. On the fireplace mantel, battery-operated candles glowed through greens and red berries. The scent of balsam and wood burning in the fireplace made LuAnn want to curl up in a chair and spend the day reading.

"I think she's gawking," Thelma said from the couch.

"That was the reaction we were hoping to get from people, wasn't it?" Irene asked.

Thelma nodded.

"I am gawking. The tree is magnificent. And the mantel…just outstanding. So very Victorian." She glanced around the rest of the room, noting decorations on every available surface. Then she walked over to the couch and kissed Thelma's wrinkled cheek. When she saw Thelma, LuAnn was reminded of her own mother, but this time, like this morning in the kitchen at the inn, the memory didn't hurt so much. Instead she felt grateful to have a living reminder of her dear mother.

"Won't you take off your coat and sit down?" Thelma's gray ringlets sparkled in the light of the fire.

"I think I'll leave it on for a little while, if you don't mind. It will help me warm up faster. Besides, I won't be here long. I have your copy of the Christmas tour book." LuAnn handed the spiral-bound book to the sisters before she dropped onto a vintage velvet chair as gracefully as she possibly could with cold, stiff muscles and the bulk of her coat wrapped around her. Heat from the fireplace warmed her face.

"This is nice," Thelma said, flipping through the pages.

"Very well done," Irene agreed.

"Thank you for the acorn dolls," LuAnn said. "They're precious and the perfect addition to our Civil War decor. We hung them this morning."

"We thought of you when we saw them a couple of weeks ago," Irene said. "We ordered them on the spot. We're glad to contribute to a good cause."

"That was thoughtful of you. How are you both doing?"

"I've been awake since dawn," Thelma said. "My *arthur-itis* is acting up."

"And her 'arthur-itis' acting up makes me want to act up too," Irene grumbled next to her sister on the couch. "She woke me up squawking at her pill bottle in the bathroom."

Thelma snorted. "It was a new bottle, and the pharmacy forgot that I need an easy-to-open lid. I'm going to call them today and let them know what I think. They should know better." She turned her attention to LuAnn. "So how are Tess and Janice? I'm sure the three of you are busy at the inn right now."

"We are. The inn is full. Two of our visitors have come specifically for the Marietta Christmas in History House Tour."

"We're certainly excited about it," Irene said. "It's a chance to show off this place."

"So, our Victorian decor is what you'd hoped?" Thelma asked.

"It's exactly as I'd envisioned. I came by to ask if you needed any help with preparing for the tour, but it appears you've got everything under control."

Irene chuckled. "We do. Brad is helping."

"He is very helpful." LuAnn felt a hitch in her heartbeat when they mentioned his name. She'd grown to depend on him being there for her, almost taking him for granted. But what if one day he wasn't?

Irene rested her hands on her knees. "We appreciate *helpful* people."

"Unlike the visitor we had yesterday," Thelma said. "Fern McPherson dropped by."

LuAnn sighed. "I know. She told me."

Irene chuckled. "We didn't invite her inside. She was far too pushy."

Thelma nodded. "Like some kind of door-to-door salesman. The kind who keeps pushing, trying to convince you to buy something. That's how she acted. We politely told her, in so many words, that we had everything under control."

"She was mad," Irene said.

"I'm sorry that happened. You could have called me."

"Believe it or not, though we're old, we can take care of ourselves when people are pushy." Thelma grinned.

"Oh, I believe it." LuAnn glanced at her watch.

"Do you have other appointments?" Irene asked.

"I'm sorry. I have to get back to the inn to help with lunch, then I'll be checking in at the Aldriches'."

"Edwardian house?" Thelma asked.

"Yes."

"Now that's one loud young man," Irene said, "even for people hard of hearing."

"He's aptly nicknamed," Thelma added.

LuAnn was amused that Irene called Boomer young when he was probably around LuAnn's age, but then she was probably young to them too. She shifted on the chair. "To return to the original reason I came by, I assume, based on what you've said and how lovely your house looks, that you have everything you need for the tour this weekend."

"We do." The sisters spoke in unison.

"We've hired someone to make the Victorian sponge cakes," Irene said.

"It will be nice to have a house full of people," Thelma added.

They chit chatted about the tour and the weather.

LuAnn finally stood. "Please let me know if there's anything I can help with."

Both sisters began to stand, but LuAnn waved them back down. "I'll see myself out. Be sure to tell me if you need anything."

"We will," Thelma promised. "And watch your eardrums today at the Aldriches'."

LuAnn laughed as she headed for her car.

December 16, 1857

When the first morning light broke the sky, Prudence got out of bed. She had not slept. She joined Jason where he still sat, beside the man they had found the night before.

"Has he awakened?"

"No."

"I have been praying," she said. "I wish to read to him. Even now, he can hear, I am sure."

Jason nodded.

Prudence stood next to the bed, Bible in her hands. "'Seeing then that we have a great high priest, that is passed into the heavens, Jesus the Son of God, let us hold fast our profession. For we have not an high priest which cannot be touched with the feeling of our infirmities; but was in all points tempted like as we are, yet without sin. Let us therefore come boldly unto the throne of grace, that we may obtain mercy, and find grace to help in time of need.'"

"Thee has made an interesting choice," Jason said.

"It seemed right."

The man suddenly moved. "Sabina." He opened his eyes, but they were glazed and unseeing. His arm snaked out from under the covers and reached for Prudence.

She gasped and backed up, but he had grabbed hold of her skirt.

Jason rose from the chair.

The man blinked, and his eyes cleared. "Who are you? Where am I?"

Prudence clutched the Bible to her chest. "Let my skirt go. Then I will answer thy questions."

The man frowned at the fabric in his fist. He dropped his hand. "You…are those Quaker people. I've seen you."

"We are Quakers," Prudence said. "My husband and I. Has thee been watching us?"

He didn't answer.

Jason moved in front of Prudence. "Why is thee here?"

"I mean you no harm." The man glanced around the room and saw his revolvers, as well as the rest of the contents of his pockets on the dresser. "Although I can understand why you might think so."

"We found thee in the storm last night," Prudence said. "Thee had hit thy head on our porch. We tended to thy wound. My husband cleaned thee up. He searched thy pockets thinking to notify thy family." She waited for him to react.

"Thank you for caring for me."

"Thee is welcome," Prudence said.

"We care for all people." Jason's body was stiff.

"I've recently come to know that." The man shifted under the covers and nodded at the book still in Prudence's arms. "You were reading the Bible to me."

"Yes."

"This faith you have…" He looked at Jason. "This is not just a woman's faith."

Prudence frowned at his odd statement.

"What is thy name, sir?" Jason demanded.

"Herman Douglas."

"Prudence, please prepare Mr. Douglas breakfast." Jason looked down at the bed. "We will leave thee now to care for thyself. There is water in the basin on the dresser and a chamber pot under the bed. If thee needs help, call."

Jason walked to the dresser and picked up the revolvers. Then he and Prudence left the room.

CHAPTER TEN

After finishing the lunch rush at the inn, LuAnn said goodbye to Tess and Janice and headed across town to visit Boomer and Patsy. Their large Edwardian home had been built by a wealthy family just previous to World War I, and it was the perfect setting for the time period they represented for the tour.

Boomer answered the door. Five small, white, poodle-looking dogs bounced at his feet. He motioned for LuAnn to come in with a sideways nod of his head while the little dogs jumped at her legs. "Patsy, it's LuAnn," he bellowed down the hall, and then he turned back to LuAnn. "Come on in. Patsy made coffee."

"Thanks." In the grand foyer, LuAnn's attention was immediately drawn to decorated rooms on the right and left. "Wow."

"You approve?" Boomer yelled.

"I do." She refrained from yelling back.

She wanted to go into each room and explore the decorations, but Boomer was already halfway down the hall. She hurried to follow him, trying not to trip over the dogs. They finally rounded a corner into a very large, brick-floored kitchen. Patsy, a petite, bird-like woman, stood at the counter, operating a percolator. She turned and smiled at LuAnn. "Hello, dear."

"Sit! Sit!" Boomer pointed at the table while he took cups and saucers from the counter and spread them on the table. "Patsy's almost ready."

Patsy nodded, attention on the coffee.

"You don't need to go through this trouble for me," LuAnn said. "I'm only here to check—"

"Nonsense!" Boomer hollered as he brought a baking dish to the table. "Apple brown Betty. We're serving it on the night of the tour. Thought you might try it." He deposited three pieces on plates and slid one in front of LuAnn. Then he proceeded to take small pieces from his plate and feed the dogs.

"Thank you." LuAnn wasn't hungry but didn't have the energy to argue. Besides, it looked delicious.

Patsy brought the percolator to the table and smiled down at the poodles.

"Go ahead and pour her some," Boomer ordered. Patsy gave Boomer a sideways glance, then looked at LuAnn. "Cream? Sugar?"

"Just cream," LuAnn said. "How are you feeling?"

Patsy settled at the table and invited one of the pups to sit on her lap with a sigh. "I'm a bit worn out—"

"Patsy's better today. Got her voice back, but she just lost her help this week, at least for the time being." Boomer poured himself a cup of coffee. "Bad timing."

"Oh dear," LuAnn said. "I'm sorry." She took a bite of the dessert. It was as good as it looked.

"She's a lovely girl," Patsy said. "Recommended to me by my daughter, who is a professor at the community college."

Boomer grumbled something under his breath, which surprised LuAnn. Apparently, he could be quiet when he wanted to be.

"Boomer developed some issues with her," Patsy continued, "but I loved her, and she kept this place spotless. She has fantastic attention to detail. I will hire her back if I can."

Is it possible? No, it can't be...

"Attention to detail, nuthin'," Boomer grumbled. "She was nosy."

"You just got mad because she dusted your desk."

"I told you I didn't want her in my office."

They glared at each other.

LuAnn redirected the conversation to find out more information. "Boomer, what do you do that you can work from home?"

"Laundromats," he said. "And my office is here at home, and I don't like anyone in there."

Patsy straightened her shoulders. "I'm sorry, LuAnn. We have an ongoing disagreement about Boomer's office. I can't stand clutter."

"I don't want people in my business." He slurped his coffee. "And it's my room to clutter as I wish."

Patsy rolled her eyes. "At any rate, I miss my girl, and I'll have to find someone to help me until she's recovered." She delicately sipped her coffee.

"What happened to her?" LuAnn asked.

"Klutz," Boomer said.

Patsy's eyes glinted. "She fell."

What were the odds? LuAnn set her coffee cup on the saucer. "Her name wouldn't happen to be Michele, would it?"

"Now, how would you know that? Mind reader?" Boomer raised a bushy eyebrow.

"No. She's the sister of one of my old students who is in town, and I knew she was hospitalized."

"You don't say." Boomer eyed LuAnn. "Sister, eh? Didn't know she had a sister. She from around here?"

"No. She's in town visiting, and now she's caring for Michele."

Patsy smiled. "How nice that she's here for her sister. Is she staying at the inn?"

"No. She's staying at Michele's house while Michele is in the hospital."

"I'm glad she has someone. I was worried about her." Patsy's forehead wrinkled. "She was distracted about something recently, but she wouldn't talk to me when I asked. I wondered if her concerns distracted her, and perhaps that's why she fell."

Boomer grunted. "Probably boyfriend troubles or something. Or bad grades in school."

Patsy straightened her spine. "She was doing well in school."

"Humph." Boomer finished his apple brown Betty and stood up. "I'm going to go to work."

"That's fine. I'll finish up here with LuAnn."

LuAnn watched him leave. Her first impression had been wrong. Patsy was more intrepid than she appeared. And Boomer was definitely bossy. In a confrontation between him and Fern, she didn't know who would win.

"I apologize for that. Boomer has been a little moody lately. I'm not sure what's going on with him." Patsy sighed again.

"I hope the tour hasn't been too much of a strain on either of you."

"It's not. In fact, it's a good distraction for me." She smiled eagerly. "Do you approve of what we've done?"

"Yes, absolutely, and I'd love to see it up close before I leave. And by the way, this dessert is outstanding."

Patsy's face brightened, and after they'd finished their coffee and food, she walked LuAnn through the two decorated rooms, followed by the five bouncing dogs. LuAnn admired every detail. Like the Bickertons, Patsy had gone above and beyond what LuAnn had expected, although she was concerned that the dogs might be a problem in a crowd. After she'd admired everything and expressed her delight, Patsy walked her to the front door.

"And don't worry about my babies," Patsy said, as if she'd read LuAnn's mind. "We'll be shutting them in our bedroom for the tour."

LuAnn smiled. "Since you no longer have Michele here, will you need any extra help getting ready?"

"I have a few feelers out for temporary help. But I appreciate you asking. I'll let you know if that changes."

LuAnn had never before visited Fern's place of work, a small house off Main Street that held the offices for McPherson

Salons, a string of hair and nail salons owned by her and her son. From a distance, the white siding and blue shutters looked pristine. But as LuAnn got closer to the building, she noticed paint chipping off the shutters and places where the white siding was dirty. It didn't seem logical that a building owned by Fern, who was so detail oriented, would be neglected.

She'd decided to give Fern a copy of the spiral-bound tour book as her excuse for coming by. She walked into the office, and a tiny receptionist, whose name plate said TISHIA, looked up and greeted her with a squeaky-voiced hello.

"Is Fern in?" LuAnn asked.

"Um. Do you have an appointment?"

"No. I was in town and thought I'd stop by. I work on a committee with Fern. I'd like to speak with her for just a moment."

"I'm not sure this is a good time." The girl nervously glanced from LuAnn to a closed office door, and LuAnn suddenly realized why.

Raised voices emanated from behind it. LuAnn thought she heard a man say, "...fire her." Fern said, "...up to something." The male voice began yelling louder, but LuAnn couldn't discern all of his words, just, "...maybe it's time." Fern's voice began to sound pleading, and then the door blew open and Fern's son Melvin, a youngish man whose pinched face very much resembled hers, stormed down the hallway, past LuAnn. Tishia ducked her head as though waiting for things to fly through the air. He glowered at LuAnn, then grabbed his coat from a coat tree and left, slamming the door.

"He was in a hurry," LuAnn mumbled.

"He's been mean lately," Tishia whispered without looking up from her computer monitor.

Fern appeared in the doorway of her office, red spots on her cheeks. "Tishia, have you ordered that light I asked for? I need—" She stopped when she realized LuAnn stood there. For just a moment, her face went slack. "LuAnn? Did you..."

"We can't hear much out here," Tishia squeaked, "so no worries."

Fern straightened her back. "What do you want, LuAnn?"

"I brought a copy of the tour book for you, and I thought we could discuss a few things. If this isn't a good time, I can come back later."

"I hope you haven't made more changes that I don't know about," Fern growled.

That did it! LuAnn decided to take the bull by the horns. "The committee, of which you are a part, has not made any more changes. If they had, you would know because we all would have discussed them last night at the meeting, which you attended. I do not arbitrarily make decisions on my own. I simply stopped by here today, out of courtesy, to deliver this book and to give you a chance to discuss any additional concerns you might have." LuAnn even surprised herself, but she was tired of Fern acting like a bully without giving LuAnn or anyone else a reason why.

Tishia blinked in the background, hands poised over her keyboard.

Fern lifted her chin, meeting LuAnn's gaze with what might have been respect. "Well, I suppose we could go to my office. Do you want coffee?"

"No thank you." LuAnn didn't want to risk the acid backlash from drinking coffee in this environment.

Fern turned to Tishia. "Would you please bring me a cup? Lots of sugar."

LuAnn followed Fern down the short hallway, passing another office, probably Melvin's. She glanced inside as she passed, noting the papers strewn over his desk. Several framed photos of Melvin and his mother, Melvin and a woman, as well as Melvin in group shots, sat on the credenza along the wall, but LuAnn didn't have time to study them.

Once they were in Fern's office, Fern motioned toward a chair and plopped into her chair behind her desk. LuAnn sat down slowly. Fern had some of the same pictures of her and Melvin on her desk that he had in his office.

The receptionist crept in with coffee in a mug that advertised the business.

"Don't spill, and please turn my light on," Fern ordered, but her voice was kinder than LuAnn was used to hearing. "And would you please run up the street and get me some of those chocolate drops?"

Tishia nodded, turned on the light, and scampered out, shutting the door behind her.

"What do you want to discuss?" Fern took a sip of coffee and squinted at LuAnn over the top of her cup.

LuAnn pulled the spiral book from her purse and handed it to Fern, who brought it close to her face, then flipped through it.

"Do you approve?" LuAnn asked after a few moments of silence.

"Nice paper."

LuAnn wanted to cheer in victory. A positive comment. Maybe the only one she'd get, but she'd take it. "Marty's gave us a discount because he wanted to support our cause, so we were able to get excellent quality for a lower price."

Fern nodded, stared at it a moment longer, then put it down on the desk.

"Fern, if I've personally offended you in any way, I want to discuss it."

Fern shrugged but didn't reply.

LuAnn pressed forward. "If there's a particular reason you have a problem with me, I'd like to work it out."

Fern blinked, and tension creased her whole face. "I just don't like the idea of people viewing the historical houses for free. Where did you get such an idea?"

"That wasn't my idea, although I thought it was a good one. Two other committee members suggested it—at the same time, I might add. We'll have donation boxes at each house, and they will be obvious, as well as information about the charity. I hope people will donate."

"People don't usually give money if they can get something for free."

"If it doesn't work out, the committee most likely won't do it again next year, if there is a next year."

Fern grunted.

"Is that the only problem you have?"

"I guess." Fern pinched her lips tight.

LuAnn suspected there was more going on, but she didn't know what, and Fern obviously wasn't going to open up to her. Fern's complaints had to be an outlet for frustration in another area.

"I might have been asked to temporarily lead this committee, but I do not want to seem like the grand pooh-bah. And I'm sorry if I've somehow come across that way to you." She picked up her purse and stood. "You're welcome to call me anytime if you have something you want to talk about. Anything at all. And I'll see you during the tour."

Fern looked up at LuAnn. She opened her mouth, then shut it, and for a moment, LuAnn thought maybe she'd say something else, but she didn't.

As LuAnn walked toward reception, Tishia crept down the hall with a small bag.

"Goodbye," LuAnn said to her.

The receptionist waved nervously and went to deliver the candy.

LuAnn went to her car not quite sure if she'd scored a victory or not.

CHAPTER ELEVEN

After visiting Fern, LuAnn drove to the hospital. Jerri was waiting for her in the ICU.

"Hey," LuAnn said. "How are things?"

"They're going well. Michele is heavily sedated and not aware of stuff yet, but the doctors are optimistic they'll be able to bring her out of sedation soon."

"Are the visitors continuing to pour in?"

"Yes. Today there was this guy who said she cleaned for him. Plus her church people, who like I said, are way too touchy-feely."

LuAnn chuckled. "I guess that means they hug you a lot."

Jerri rolled her eyes. "All of them. When they arrive and when they leave. It's a wonder they don't spread the flu or colds wherever they go." Her lips twitched at the corners of her mouth, and she wiggled her eyebrows. "Even lice."

LuAnn laughed out loud. "You and bugs. You've always hated them. But you know full well cold and flu are spread through direct contact with the germs in the air. You're probably breathing in more of them as you walk around here than you are hugging people."

Jerri harrumphed but there was a twinkle in her eyes. "I'm sure germs can be on the shoulders of coats from all the hugging and carrying on. And lice—they're spread from hair to hair contact, you know. Hugging equals hair contact."

Jerri's sardonic humor, accompanied by a tiny grin, was so reminiscent of the young girl she'd been years ago, LuAnn felt like crying and laughing at the same time. "Yes, I suppose that's possible. I could always buy you a lice comb for Christmas. Then you can check every night to see if you've acquired any hitchhikers."

Jerri giggled.

"May I go pray for her now?" LuAnn asked, still smiling.

"Sure."

"Two of us can go in the room at one time. Do you want to join me?"

Jerri planted her feet. "No. It's best that I'm not there. I'll just put negative vibes in the air."

"I don't believe in vibes, and even if I did, they wouldn't be more powerful than God. However, I'll do as you ask and go in alone. And I'm praying for you too."

"I wouldn't expect anything less, and thank you for not pushing me." Jerri headed down the hall to sit and wait.

LuAnn walked into Michele's room. The young woman was hooked up to an IV and all sorts of monitors. LuAnn rested her hand on Michele's arm, closed her eyes, and prayed. When she was done, Michele shifted on the bed.

"God loves you so," LuAnn whispered to her and walked out of the room.

Jerri jumped to her feet. "She looks good, doesn't she?"

"A lot better than yesterday when they put her into the ambulance. And she appears to be well taken care of."

"She is. I make sure of it. I like her doctor. And Stuart came by again to check in on me."

"I'm glad you're being taken care of as well. Are you going to be here for a while today?"

"Yes. I think today is crucial in her recovery."

"Would you like to come with me to the cafeteria for a few minutes, maybe get a drink and a snack? I have a couple of things to tell you."

"Okay. And I have something to give to you."

As they walked down the hall, a woman, whose curled blond hair reached below her shoulders, strode toward them. She looked familiar, but LuAnn couldn't place her.

"You must be LuAnn Sherrill," she said.

"I am. How do you know me?"

"You're one of the owners of that lovely inn along the river. I've been there for lunch." She turned to Jerri. "And you must be Michele's sister, Jerri."

"Yes…"

"I'm Doria Sanders." She held out her well-manicured hand.

Jerri took it, slowly. "I'm sorry, but I don't know who you are. Am I supposed to?"

Doria laughed. "My apologies. I own the cleaning service where Michele works. Sanders' Spotless Cleaning Service. I just assumed you'd know that."

Jerri nodded. "I knew Michele was employed by a service, but I didn't know the name."

"When Michele didn't report to work, I made some calls. That's how I found out she'd fallen." Doria glanced down the hall and pulled up her purse strap, her fingers covered with rings, including a large diamond on her left hand. "Is Michele in a coma?"

"Sedated," Jerri said.

Doria frowned. "Is she in danger?"

"No danger of death, if that's what you mean."

"Brain damage?" Doria asked. "Like amnesia?"

LuAnn felt Jerri bristle.

"They don't know."

"Do you mind if I go visit her for a minute?"

LuAnn could tell that Jerri wanted to say no, but finally she acquiesced. "Go on. There aren't any rules saying you can't."

"Thank you." Doria headed for Michele's room.

"Let's go." Jerri whirled around and stalked toward the elevator, where she pressed the button several times.

"It won't come any faster," LuAnn murmured.

Jerri gave her a sidelong look. "I know. But it makes me feel better."

LuAnn decided this wasn't the best time for a lecture about patience, especially since there were more pressing issues. Like Jerri's reaction to Doria. "You were rather abrupt with her."

"I was, I guess."

"Why?"

"I'm...not sure. I need to figure that out."

The elevator door opened. LuAnn left the topic alone as they rode the elevator down to the floor where the cafeteria was.

Once they reached the cafeteria, LuAnn told Jerri to go sit. "I'll cover this."

"You don't have to buy stuff for me," Jerri said. "You already fed me breakfast."

"You're right, I don't have to, but I want to."

Jerri looked about to protest, but after a moment agreed. "Okay. Just a power bar or something. I'll go get us a seat."

LuAnn bought two bottles of water and a granola bar, then sat in the chair opposite Jerri. She slid the bar and a water across the table.

"Thank you. You're not eating?"

"No. I've had way too much food already today."

Jerri rested her frowning face in her hands.

"Crabby much?" LuAnn asked.

Jerri smiled. "I remember you saying that to me when I was in high school."

"I did." LuAnn sipped some water.

"I'm acting crabby, aren't I?"

"Yes, but I understand that you have a lot on your plate right now." LuAnn studied Jerri while she stared at the wall. "It seems like a lot of people care about Michele."

Jerri's eyes met LuAnn's. "Most of them, yes."

"But you don't think Doria is one of them?"

Jerri drank some water and wiped her lips on a napkin. "I don't like her."

"You decided that pretty quickly. Why? You don't know her."

Jerri shrugged. "I'm not sure. I've been watching everyone who comes to visit Michele. Most of them are very open and seem like good people, but Doria didn't settle well with me."

"I respect your ability to read people, but is it possible that your emotions are skewing things?"

"I suppose that's possible. In fact, I'm probably looking at everyone with suspicion because of whatever reason is behind why Michele asked me to come." Jerri opened her granola bar. "She was afraid because of something to do with work. And that woman was her employer. Plus, she was a little snooty."

"Perhaps she was, just a little bit. But remember, Michele's clients were all over the place."

Jerri's face sagged. "That's true. And I sound like a bitter, judgmental person, don't I?'

"Not bitter." LuAnn reached across the table. "More than anything, you sound like someone who is trying to watch out for her sister. And I agree, Doria did not come across well. But maybe she felt defensive. Or maybe she was worried about her employee. But even when I have a negative gut feeling about someone, I try not to let it impact how I treat them. Being gracious is never a waste of time."

"That's a good point. You can learn more about them when you're nice to them. And if someone else ends up being a jerk, it only makes you look better."

That wasn't the point LuAnn had been trying to make, but she let it go.

Jerri nibbled on the granola bar, then put it down. "Doria was the exact opposite of the people from Michele's church, but they make me uncomfortable too, just in a different way. They grab me right there in the hall and insist on praying for me. In front of everyone. What am I going to say or do? Object and look like a bully while I hurt their feelings?" Jerri shook her head. "So I have to let them do it."

LuAnn laughed. "You're trying your hardest to run from God, and it seems like He's following you everywhere you go in the form of His people."

"It does seem that way." Jerri took another swig of water.

"I have some information for you. I don't know if we should be encouraging you in your investigation, but I doubt you're going to stop."

"We? You mean you, Tess, and Janice?"

"Yes."

"You're really going to help me?"

"We're keeping our eyes open and ears to the ground, so to speak."

"That's awesome. What did you find out?"

"Michele was cleaning for a couple who are part of the Christmas tour. Boomer and Patsy Aldrich. I visited them before I came here."

"Really?" Jerri leaned forward, intensity on her face. "Where do they live? Could they have been the people she was worried about?"

LuAnn told her the street the Aldriches lived on. "And I have no idea if they're the people Michele was worried about. I do know that Patsy is mother-in-law to one of Michele's professors at the community college, and she's the one who recommended Michele to them. Since they didn't hire Michele through her employer, I would imagine she made a little more money from the job. I found out that Boomer didn't want Michele cleaning his office. And Patsy mentioned that Michele had recently become withdrawn, like something was bothering her."

"Now that you mention that, one of her church people mentioned she'd been distracted lately." Jerri popped the last of her granola bar in her mouth and chewed it slowly while she crumpled the wrapper. "That means that whatever was bothering her was big enough that other people noticed."

"Looks that way." LuAnn sipped more of her water.

After a couple of minutes of silence, Jerri said, "That was kind of her professor to get her that job. It seems like Michele was surrounded by a lot of people who really cared for her. For all my comments about her church people, I see that getting involved with that church helped Michele more than I thought. I'm glad she found them. They take care of her."

"Having people to lean on is nice. I think it's the way God made us to be with each other. Sometimes it's easy, when you're a strong person, to think you have to handle everything alone."

"I have friends, but I don't think many of them would even come and see me if I were hospitalized. They'd be too uncomfortable and wouldn't know what to do. And they certainly wouldn't pray for me, not that I'd want them to. Still, it's a weird and awful realization."

"Perhaps it's time to make some changes. Find people to be around who really care. Church is a good place to start."

Jerri twisted her lips. "I've been thinking about that a lot lately, especially seeing how much Michele has changed."

"If you need to talk, I'm here for you." LuAnn looked at her watch. "I need to head out of here. I have some chores to do. An innkeeper's job is never done, you know."

"Oh!" Jerri reached for her purse. "That reminds me. This is a copy of that letter from my grandmother's attic that I think is from Charles Finney, as well as that poem." She pulled out two folded pieces of paper.

"That's great. It will help us research Prudence's journal to see if your family did come this way." LuAnn took the papers, reached into her purse for her notebook, and stuck them inside.

"You still make lists." Jerri pointed to LuAnn's notebook. "I remembered you always did that. That's why I do the same."

LuAnn smiled. "I do. Sometimes I feel like it's the only way I can remember everything I have to remember, including mystery clues."

"I'd think you of all people would have one of those leathered-covered journal things I've seen on the internet."

Images of Fern's notebook flashed through LuAnn's mind as she put her notebook back in her purse. "I've considered it. Seems extravagant."

"Maybe, but really nice." Jerri stretched. "I stopped by that Underground Railroad museum you told me about. I'll go back there when I can concentrate a little better. Maybelline is a hoot, by the way."

"That's one way to describe her." LuAnn smiled. "And we have you scheduled for your tour of the basement on Thursday."

"I'm looking forward to it."

CHAPTER TWELVE

That evening, LuAnn and Tess ate burgers for dinner while Janice visited with her daughter and grandson. She'd made them promise not to discuss the mystery of Michele or the situation with Fern until she returned. But when Janice got home and got settled, Tess's daughter had called with a minor emergency, and now she was tied up on the phone while LuAnn and Janice waited for her in their common room.

LuAnn sat in one of the comfy chairs, slipped off her shoes, and tucked her sock-clad feet under her. She'd texted Brad earlier to tell him how things were going. He'd taken a while to get back to her. Her thoughts immediately went back to the conversation with Marty. *Stop it, LuAnn. All of your friends deserve to be happy, whatever that means.*

She pulled her notebook into her lap and began jotting notes about Michele and her mystery.

"I wish Tess would hurry," Janice said, her cross-stitch in her lap and Tom snuggled next to her. "I really want to hear about your day. I assume you gathered some clues."

"Just a couple. And remember, we're not sure yet we have a real mystery."

"It's enough of a mystery."

Tess appeared in the doorway in her pajamas and robe, Huck at her heels.

"How is Lizzie?" LuAnn asked.

"Lizzie is in a tizzy." Tess laughed. "The Christmas holidays plus three four-year-olds equals chaos."

"So true," Janice said. "Sometimes I miss having little kids around. But then I sit here and think about how nice it is to be able to eat when I want to and relax at night instead of getting kids ready for bed. Besides, I get my fill of kid stuff with Larry."

Tess stretched, then sat on the couch on the opposite side of Janice and plumped a pillow behind her back. "It does feel good to relax."

"Now can we please talk about today and the possible mystery?" Janice asked.

"I don't know. I'm kind of tired." LuAnn teased her and looked at the ceiling. "I might just want to call it a day."

Janice grabbed a pillow and threw it at her.

LuAnn pretended to scowl. "You'd best behave, young lady, or I'll send you to bed early!"

"You'd have to carry me, and I doubt you could do that." Janice made a face at her.

LuAnn shook her finger. "Don't make me take away all your cookies for a week."

"Uh-oh," Tess said. "She's pulling out the big guns now. I'd shape up right now if I were you, Janice."

Everyone laughed.

"Okay, LuAnn, please spill whatever it is you have to say so Janice doesn't get in any further trouble. Besides, I'm itching to hear it all myself."

First LuAnn updated her friends about Michele's condition. Then she got up and gave Tess the copy of Jerri's letter that might have been from Charles Finney and the poem.

Janice scooted over to look at them with Tess.

God is waiting for you. "But God, who is rich in mercy, for his great love wherewith he loved us, even when we were dead in sins, hath quickened us together with Christ, (by grace ye are saved) ... " Ephesians 2:4–5. Charles F.

"Wow. It could be," Tess said.

"And check out this poem," Janice said. "Or maybe it's a song."

Mercy's Song
Mercy, thou art a babe born
Mercy, thou art a savior dying
Mercy, thou art blood freely shed
Mercy, thou art sins blotted out
Mercy, thou art Almighty God
Mercy, thou art freedom.

"That's beautiful," Tess said.

"It really is," Janice agreed.

LuAnn took the papers. "Tomorrow we can start searching Prudence's journal."

Janice returned to her original position. "Okay, tell us about Fern. Were you able to get things straightened out with her?"

"Not exactly, but she did like the spiral tour book."

"You're kidding!" Tess exclaimed.

"I'm not. Well, she didn't exactly say she liked it, but she did say the paper was nice. And she didn't criticize it."

"After the hostility I witnessed the other night, I'm shocked," Janice said. "But it's good. Maybe she's coming around."

LuAnn filled them in on the rest of the conversation in Fern's office. "But it was the argument she was having with her son when I got there that bothered me the most." She related what she'd heard and observed. "And for just a moment, Fern acted as if she was afraid I'd overheard them."

"I don't know her son well," Tess said. "I've seen him at the meetings in the past, but he's never said much."

"Perhaps they're having differences on the job, and that's the reason she's so grumpy," Janice suggested. "Sometimes children get impatient with their parents. She can be bull-headed, and they do work together."

"Possibly." LuAnn put her finger on a page in her note-book. "Now, about the mystery of Michele, I have some interesting pieces of information. I found out that Michele cleaned for Boomer and Patsy Aldrich."

"No kidding," Tess said.

"When I went to Marty's to pick up the books for the tour, he told me that Boomer and Patsy haven't been married very long. No one seems to know a lot about him."

"They're an interesting couple," Tess said.

"They are," LuAnn agreed. "They seem to be opposites. He can be loud and overbearing. She's quiet, and at first glance, it appears a lot of things go over her head. But today I realized that's not the case. She's aware of everything, and she knows exactly what her husband is like. She's more in control than I thought. I've totally underestimated her."

"You gotta watch the quiet ones," Janice said.

"But that's not the most important piece of information." LuAnn relayed Patsy's concern for Michele. "And Boomer was mad because Michele cleaned his office at the house."

They stared at each other when LuAnn was done.

"What does he do?"

"He owns a Laundromat and works from home."

"I'd say you've gathered a lot of information," Janice said.

After a moment of silence, Tess leaned forward. "So what are your guts saying?"

LuAnn and Janice exchanged glances.

"I think something is going on," LuAnn said.

"I do too," Janice agreed.

LuAnn's cell phone rang in her sweater pocket. She pulled it out and smiled. "It's Jerri, probably reporting in that she's home from the hospital." LuAnn pushed the button. "Jerri? Are you home?"

"Yes, I've made it, but someone broke into the house. I'm sitting in my car."

"What?" LuAnn sat up straight, and her notebook fell to the floor. "Are you okay?"

Janice and Tess stared at LuAnn, eyes wide.

"I'm okay. Just really, really mad that someone would do this."

"Is Diesel okay?"

"She was with Mrs. Brewster when it happened. I picked her up before I discovered the break-in."

"Did you call the police?"

"I did. I'm waiting for them."

"Okay, I'll be there shortly."

"You don't have to come—"

"I most certainly do. You sit right there and wait."

LuAnn ended the call and jumped to her feet. "Michele's house has been broken into."

"Oh no," Tess said. "Was Jerri inside when it happened?"

"No. She only discovered it when she got home from the hospital."

"Hopefully whoever it is has long gone," Janice said.

"I'm going over there." LuAnn picked up her notebook and put it in the chair.

"Not alone, you're not." Tess firmed her lips.

Janice put her cross-stitch on the couch. "I'll go with you since Tess is already in her pajamas."

Tess nodded. "As hard as it will be not to know what's going on, I'll stay here and man the inn in case anyone needs anything."

"Thank you. Janice, I'll let you drive, if you don't mind." LuAnn pulled on her shoes. "I think our guts were right."

The cold nighttime air bit at LuAnn's face as she climbed from the car at Michele's house. A police car was parked out front.

"Thank God," she murmured. "Jerri didn't have to sit here alone very long."

"Yes, that's a good thing," Janice said.

As they hurried up the cracked cement sidewalk, LuAnn noticed a curtain next door at Mrs. Brewster's house twitch. But before she could think about it, Janice knocked on the door and they heard muffled, high-pitched yapping.

Jerri opened the door, and Diesel bounced at her feet. She scooped her up in her arms. Her cheeks were drawn.

Behind her stood a police officer. "Hello, Janice and LuAnn."

"Randy!" Janice said. "This is a pleasant surprise."

LuAnn was relieved. Janice knew Randy Lewis from years ago, when he was just a child and attended the church her husband pastored. Now, as an adult, he'd proven himself to be a wonderful police officer. LuAnn could trust him to do a good job.

Jerri turned to Randy. "Can they come in?"

"Certainly. I'm about done here."

Jerri stepped aside and waved them in with her free arm. "Thanks for coming, you guys."

LuAnn looked around. Clean but worn furniture filled a main living area. A short hallway led down to what appeared to be a kitchen.

She faced Jerri and Randy, who hovered in the hallway. "So, what's going on? What happened?"

"The door was cracked open when I got here. I know for a fact that I locked it. I'm careful about things like that. After Officer Lewis got here, he looked around with me. A lot of Michele's stuff was shuffled like someone had pawed through it. It appears that even the things in Michele's drawers were messed up. The clothes were all jumbled."

"Couldn't that be normal?" Janice asked.

Jerri shook her head. "No. She's obsessive about keeping her clothes folded. Has been since she was a kid."

"Was anything taken?" LuAnn asked.

Jerri sighed. "Nothing obvious. The TV is still here. I can't find her laptop, just the cord, but I couldn't find that when I first arrived, so I can't say for sure that anyone took it. If there was anything else missing, I wouldn't know."

Randy sidled over to a small table in the hallway that held pictures and picked one of them up. "Is this Michele?" he asked.

"Yes," Jerri said.

"Did you tell Randy about being followed last night?" LuAnn asked.

Randy looked up from the picture with raised brows. "Followed?"

"No, I didn't." Jerri explained to Randy what had happened the night before. "Maybe someone was casing the house?"

"Doesn't sound like it." Randy said. "If someone was trying to determine when a house was empty, they would be watching the house, not following you."

"That's true." Jerri sighed. "Well, there's this one big guy who walks through the ICU, but he never hangs around. He just looks at me, then Michele, then leaves. It's weird."

"I don't mean to sound dismissive, but a lot of people come through the ICU," Randy said.

LuAnn felt frustrated. "What can be done?"

"About someone possibly following Jerri home? Not much officially, but I suggest caution. Be aware of your surroundings. Watch for the same vehicle. Get a license plate number."

"What about the break-in?" LuAnn asked.

He shrugged, glancing at the picture in his hands with a lowered brow. "I'll write a report, however there's nothing else I have to go on."

"Fingerprints?" Janice asked.

Randy shook his head. "How do you eliminate one finger-print from another in a house, especially a rental like this? This kind of crime is hard to solve, especially since nothing has been taken. However, I'll do my best."

"I understand." Jerri put Diesel back on the floor. The little dog ran from person to person, sniffing shoes.

Randy put the picture down, forehead still creased in a frown. "I don't know if this means anything, or if I should even tell you." He let out a long stream of breath. "I guess I will. I didn't put two and two together about whose house this was until I saw this picture." He pointed at the framed photo he'd just been staring at. "A couple of weeks ago this woman came to the police department. She approached another officer and said something to him. I couldn't hear the conversation, but she got insistent. He rolled his eyes and finally disappeared, I assume to get someone for her to talk to.

"She waited a little while, fidgeting. She looked scared and avoided looking at me. Then she suddenly turned and left. When he came back, he asked me where she was. I told him she'd left. He rolled his eyes again and said, 'That one is a waste of time.' When I asked him why, he said something about how he'd caught her with some people who were doing drugs at one point, years ago. Then he shrugged and said, 'I suppose I could be wrong, but people don't usually change.'"

"That's a shame," LuAnn said.

"He's a cynical man—that can happen in law enforcement officers. He's one who never forgets when someone does something wrong. Sort of judgmental."

"Could you ask him what it was about?" Jerri asked.

"I did at the time, but he just shrugged and said she never told him what it was about. Just wanted to talk to someone in authority." Randy put on his hat. "At any rate, I need to head out and get this report written." He grabbed the doorknob, then turned to Jerri. "Please be cautious. Lock your doors even though you have a good alarm system there." He smiled at Diesel who wagged her stubby little tail and danced at his feet. He petted her and left.

Jerri shut the door behind him a little harder than necessary and locked it. Then she whirled around. "Some people still remember Michele for what she was. It's hard to catch a break when you've done anything wrong. Judgmental is right." Her eyes flashed. "I was a little angry before. Now I'm just plain mad."

"At what, exactly?" LuAnn asked.

Jerri paced the room. "I don't know. I guess I'm mad that someone broke in. Mad that Michele fell to begin with. Mad that I don't know what's really going on. Mad that people just assume other people can't change. Most of all I guess I'm mad because I feel so helpless."

"I don't blame you," Janice said. "But I'm surprised you aren't frightened too, after a break-in."

Jerri stopped pacing and snorted. "Frightened is like before I went to live with my grandparents, walking the streets by myself in the dark looking for my mom because we were out of food and my little sister was hungry. This is nothing. Besides, it wasn't as if someone was actually here when I was inside the house."

Janice gasped. "Your mom left you alone as a child?"

LuAnn swallowed. "You never told me you had to do that."

"That was before I met you, so by that time, it didn't matter. It just seemed normal. I had to take care of Michele. She was so little."

"My goodness, honey," Janice said. "You were a helpless child yourself back then and there you were, caring for your sister."

"Someone had to do it." Jerri shrugged, and then her eyes filled with tears. "Being here, in her house, has reminded me that she is my sister. I don't know if that makes sense, but I need to make things right with her, if I can. I also need to help her with whatever was scaring her." Jerri squared her shoulders and pounded her fist in her other hand. "I'm going to get to the bottom of this. If Michele wakes up and remembers, good.

If she doesn't, well I'll figure it out. Besides, this break-in helps me."

Janice's mouth fell open. "How does it help you? I'm horrified."

"As am I," LuAnn said.

"This means I'm right that something happened to scare Michele. That's why she wanted me here. That's why her journal was all jagged and scary. And doesn't what that police officer said confirm all of this?"

"You can't be sure this break-in had anything to do with Michele's fears," LuAnn said.

"But we can't be sure it didn't."

LuAnn recognized the spark in Jerri's eyes. She'd been a spitfire when she was young, and she still was. LuAnn also knew no one would convince the young woman otherwise once she'd set her mind on doing something. The best thing LuAnn and her friends could do was help.

Janice had a deer-in-the-headlights look on her face. LuAnn hopped onto a different topic. "Would you feel safer at the inn? The offer to stay on a cot in my suite still stands."

"That's awfully nice of you," Jerri said, "but no. I'm going to stay right here. Like Officer Randy said, Diesel will bark her head off if anyone comes into the house." She smiled at the dog.

"I'm glad to see that the relationship between you two is headed in a good direction," LuAnn said.

"Apparently dogs have their uses." Jerri leaned down and scratched Diesel's head.

LuAnn noticed that Janice put her hand to her mouth to stifle a yawn.

"We're going to call it a night. Please call me as soon as you wake up tomorrow morning."

"Okay, I will. Thank you both so much for coming. Knowing you're all there for me, supporting me, is wonderful. I would be feeling pretty alone right now if it weren't for you."

"Keep your phone next to your bed. Don't answer the door unless you know who it is. And don't hesitate to call me at any time if you need me. Those are orders."

"Yes, ma'am." Jerri leaned over to whisper in LuAnn's ear. "Thank you so much. This means more than I can say."

As Janice and LuAnn left the house, she glanced again at Mrs. Brewster's house. Sure enough, a curtain twitched. LuAnn wondered how much the woman really saw. Perhaps Randy should have checked next door before he left.

CHAPTER THIRTEEN

LuAnn woke very early on Wednesday morning and couldn't get back to sleep, so she got dressed and headed for the kitchen with her notebook in hand. She, Tess, and Janice had been up too late the night before discussing the break-in. She hoped her friends would get enough sleep, unlike her.

When she entered the café, she was surprised by the scent of baking cookies. She hurried to the kitchen.

Winnie was at the counter, scooping cookie dough onto a baking tray. She whirled around. "What are you doing down here so early?" She narrowed her eyes. "You need sleep. You've got circles under your eyes. Not to mention I thought I'd have a little bit of peace and quiet."

LuAnn felt like crying at Winnie's tart tone but ignored the urge, passing the emotion off as weariness. Instead, she filled Winnie in on the break-in at Michele's.

Winnie's eyes softened. "That poor child. And it's no wonder you look peaked." She grabbed a bowl from the cupboard and pulled out a canister of her very own pancake mix. "Make yourself some coffee. I'll whip up some pancakes. That's what I'm serving this morning, anyway."

LuAnn followed her directions, and shortly Winnie handed her a plate piled high with a stack of pancakes that LuAnn couldn't possibly finish. However, she accepted it gladly, knowing it was Winnie's way of loving her.

"I'll be lettin' the prayer line at church know what happened. Now put a lot of butter on those pancakes and a big dollop of that real maple syrup. It'll stick to your ribs and get you going."

"Yes, ma'am." LuAnn obeyed.

"Go on, now!" Winnie waved toward the door. "Go sit out in the café and let me finish my cookies in peace. You need some quiet of your own to think about this mystery."

LuAnn did what Winnie ordered. She sat at a table at the front of the café where she could see the river, but the view didn't soothe her like it normally did. She put her notebook next to her coffee mug and poked holes in her pancakes with her fork. Winnie made the perfect classic pancakes, at least in LuAnn's opinion. Fluffy with just the tiniest bit of chew. Unfortunately, today LuAnn had no appetite. She had too much on her mind, uppermost of which was Jerri. They'd spoken briefly before LuAnn came downstairs. Jerri was up early and doing well but still mad because of the break-in, and she was ready to take on the world.

Although LuAnn was glad Jerri was okay, she was concerned by Jerri's desire to fight whatever there was to fight, which at this point was akin to shadowboxing. None of them had enough information to know what was really going on.

Jerri had declined to join LuAnn for breakfast, saying she had some things to do. But that didn't relieve LuAnn's mind. Michele had been scared of something that was all too real.

And Randy's comments confirmed that. But did the break-in have anything to do with anything?

LuAnn thought she'd better notify Brad about what happened, since she'd kept him in the loop up until now. She texted him. He replied a few minutes later with a "wow" emoji and promised to talk to her later because he wanted an update.

LuAnn was slightly miffed that he didn't offer to call her or come by the inn, but it was still early. She stuffed a fork full of pancake in her mouth and chewed slowly. Then Janice and Tess walked down the stairs together. They were up early too. They waved and disappeared into the kitchen.

A few minutes later, Tess came swinging out of the kitchen carrying a full plate and marched toward LuAnn.

She was followed shortly by Janice. "We went to wake you up, but you were already down here."

"Really? Why would you wake me?"

"We think it's time to officially declare that we're solving this mystery," Tess said as she pulled out a chair and sat next to LuAnn. "We're going to meet in the kitchen after the breakfast rush so we can include Winnie since she knows Michele."

Janice sat down across from them and looked down at her plate. "Wow, these pancakes look amazing."

"They are, but I can't eat," LuAnn said.

"You must really be upset. Who can resist these?" Tess lifted a fork full, dripping with syrup and butter. "I can't believe Winnie is making cookies before breakfast. But she was amazingly accommodating despite grumbling about never being left alone for a minute around here. You must have really buttered her up, no pun intended."

LuAnn laughed. "She's worried about my health. She says I look peaked. Her solution? Eating."

"You do look tired, but I understand why," Janice said.

LuAnn stabbed another piece of pancake. "Winnie also ordered me to solve Michele's mystery."

"She said the same to us." Janice was making quick work of her pancakes. "And she's agreed to join us after breakfast."

Tess eyed LuAnn with concern. "You've got a lot on your plate, another pun not intended. On top of the mystery of Michele, there's the Christmas tour and Fern. And I have this feeling there's more going on with you than what we know."

LuAnn ignored the unspoken question behind Tess's concern. She didn't want to say anything about the comments Marty had made about Brad, which still vexed her.

"I guess I do have a lot on my mind, but it shouldn't be impacting me as much as it does. I can't do any more about Fern than I already have. I've tried to clear things up, but she doesn't want to talk. In regard to the tour, I have a few last-minute things to get done. For instance, I'll be stopping by the Paglinos this afternoon before I visit Michele again, to give them their copy of the book and to make sure they have everything under control. I also need to corral all my thoughts for my small lecture points during the tour on Saturday."

"We'd like to visit Michele too," Tess said. "I could join you there today, and Janice could go with you tomorrow."

Janice nodded in agreement, chewing a big mouthful of pancakes.

"That would be great. I'm sure Jerri would love it." LuAnn sighed. "Until I saw Jerri walk off that bus, I'd forgotten just how maternal she made me feel. I guess I didn't expect this depth of emotion."

Janice nodded. "It's funny how we can think we're so aware of how we feel about things, but then we can be dumbstruck when God reveals something we didn't realize was there."

The comment made LuAnn squirm.

"So." Tess tapped the table with her hand. "We have an official mystery to solve."

"And if Michele wakes up and remembers everything?" Janice asked.

"Then we can use whatever we know to help her," Tess replied.

LuAnn put her fork down. "Bottom line is, Michele discovered something that made her scared. Randy mentioned that she had been at the police station, which confirms what all of us think. Right now, Michele is relatively safe at the hospital, but at some point, she could be in danger, and by association, so could Jerri. And to make it worse, Jerri is running around, thumbing her nose at danger."

"That girl," Tess said. "Was she this much of a handful when she was a teenager?"

"And then some. But back then, there wasn't a crime involved—at least that I knew of. But apparently I didn't know everything."

"Michele's fine at the hospital—unless you watch mysteries on television where the bad guys sneak past all the nurses and cause all sorts of havoc." Janice stopped when she realized LuAnn and Tess were staring at her with open mouths.

"That's not helping," LuAnn said, but she smiled.

"Not in the least." Tess chuckled.

Then LuAnn's smile died. "But danger isn't out of the question. Are you guys sure you want to do this?"

"Goodness gracious goat, don't be silly," Janice said. "We've been in danger before. Besides, we're the Inn Crowd. All for one and one for all, right Tess?"

"Absolutely. How could we not do this with you?"

"Thank you both."

Janice finished her pancakes and looked at her watch. "We'd better start getting ready for the day. Winnie's tolerance won't extend to us shirking our duties."

Tess nodded. "She's right. We'll talk further after breakfast in the kitchen. Maybe Winnie will have some thoughts as well." She finished her pancakes and began to prepare the café for breakfast.

LuAnn had eaten as much as she was going to. She balled up her napkin and put her silverware on her plate. They'd solve this mystery, just like they'd solved so many others. She wasn't alone.

December 16, 1857

Prudence went to the barn to feed her chickens. She'd left Jason and Herman Douglas eating eggs and fried slabs of bacon. She had no appetite. She was not scheduled to work at the inn today or tomorrow. That was good. Her concern was that she'd gotten news of a package delivery coming the next day. Herman's presence made for bad timing. She dreaded telling Jason.

Patience pecked Prudence's leg.

"What troubles thee now, bird?" Prudence asked as she flung feed for the chickens.

Suddenly, over the clucks and squawks of the birds, she heard the soft nicker of Charity, their draft horse, then she heard another horse nickering in answer.

"Is that what thee wants me to know?" Prudence murmured to Patience.

Prudence stepped from the pen and walked around the shed. There stood a tall chestnut mare, fully saddled. Prudence held out her hand, and the horse came willingly.

"Thee must be Herman's horse and very hungry." She stroked the animal's soft muzzle, then she led her to the barn, removed the tack, and tended to her.

When Prudence was done, she hurried back to the house. When she walked inside and removed her cloak and scarf, the men looked up at her, plates cleaned. They did not appear to be talking.

"I believe thy horse has found thee," she said. "A chestnut mare?"

For the first time, Herman's face brightened. "I'm relieved. I raised her from a filly. I'm fond of her." He began to stand.

Prudence put out her hand. "I've cared for thy horse. She's in the barn, eating."

"Thank you." He sat again.

"What business does thee have here in Marietta, Herman?" Jason asked.

Prudence stood behind Jason, a hand on his shoulder.

"Family matters," he answered.

After a moment of silence, Jason said, "Surely thy matters are peaceful if family is involved, yet thee carries weapons of violence."

Prudence was surprised by the intensity of Jason's voice, but she understood why. Herman Douglas wasn't telling them the whole truth.

"'Tis an evil world," Herman finally said. "Wild animals lurk, waiting to pounce. Man as well, sometimes the worst of the wild animals."

"Man is the crown of God's creation even though the world lies in the power of the evil one," Jason said. "And God is merciful."

"My husband speaks truth." Prudence felt her spirit rise. "God *is* merciful. Instead of giving man what he deserves, God sent His son to show His mercy. Those who turn to God, who give Him their hearts, are converted. There are many of us." She wondered why she felt so moved to tell Herman Douglas the Gospel message.

"So I've seen." Herman sat quietly, eyeing both of them. "You sound much like my recent acquaintance, Mr. Charles Finney. A man of great conviction. He spoke to me at length one whole day about sin and God's love. And the next day, he spoke to me again and then gave me that note."

"Is that the first thee heard of God and His mercy?" Jason asked

Herman shrugged. "The men in my family thought religion a crutch for women and children. But my sister spoke of God as if He were real. She was like a saint..." His voice cracked. "I've recently been reminded of that fact." He stood. "I'm sorry. I'm grateful for your hospitality, but I must leave."

"So soon? Thee has barely recovered." Prudence had mixed feelings. Concern for his welfare. Relief that he would be gone by the time she picked up her package.

"I have an appointment to keep." Herman waited.

Jason retrieved the revolvers. "Thy property. We will pray for thee."

"I expected nothing less."

CHAPTER FOURTEEN

The breakfast crowd had finally dispersed. LuAnn finished tidying the café, then grabbed her notebook and headed for the kitchen. Winnie bustled in the background, working on soup for lunch. Janice was helping her cut vegetables. Tess sat at the table and tapped the screen of her iPad, a filled coffee mug next to her arm.

LuAnn put her cleaning supplies away and washed her hands.

Tess lifted her coffee mug. "Here's to solving another mystery."

"Another mystery," LuAnn and Janice echoed.

"About time," Winnie said. "LuAnn, you sit with Tess and work on it. Me and Janice'll finish the prep work. I got most of it done earlier."

"All right." LuAnn sat at the table. "And we are now assuming the break-in had something to with Michele's fear, correct?"

Everyone nodded.

"Which means it has something to do with one of her jobs."

Tess sipped her coffee. "To that end, I thought we should start with money laundering, since that's what Jerri thinks Michele discovered."

"Since Michele's planner indicated that, I agree with you." LuAnn flipped open her notebook. "We'll be able to build a suspect list, if nothing else."

"I've already looked up ways to launder money," Tess said.

"Tell us."

"It's basically the process of making dirty money look legal. Money gotten from sales of illegal things like drug trafficking, illegal gambling, medical fraud, extortion, or from insider trading. The easiest way to do it is to place the money in businesses that have a lot of cash flow, like restaurants. Once the money looks legal, it can be used."

"Wow. Easier than one would think. And it could be anything from small amounts to large amounts."

Tess nodded.

Janice turned, holding an onion in her plastic-gloved hand. "So how do you think Michele would even know that someone was laundering money? She was a house cleaner, not an accountant."

LuAnn looked up from her notebook. "Good point, but she was taking accounting classes, so finances would interest her, wouldn't they?"

Tess closed the iPad. "She could have observed something, like spreadsheets on someone's desk. Then studied them and realized something didn't make sense."

"Or she might have seen suspicious people or overheard a suspicious conversation," LuAnn added.

"And most people ignore the help," Tess said. "Meaning, they talk in front of them. Live in front of them. Leave stuff out on desks and tables. Especially after someone has been working for them for a while."

"True. We talk about stuff in front of our employees all the time." Janice grinned at Winnie.

Winnie grunted. "I'm not really an employee anymore. More like family."

"I won't argue with that," LuAnn said.

"And we're not guilty of a crime, so we don't have to watch what we say." Tess paused. "Unless we're talking about clues and don't want our guests to hear us."

"But wouldn't a criminal be more careful than that?" Janice asked. "You'd think they'd watch out for who's around them."

Tess shrugged. "Perhaps whoever it was just assumed that Michele wouldn't know anything about finances. Or perhaps she overheard a conversation no one knew she could hear. Or saw an exchange between people she shouldn't have seen. There are any number of possibilities."

"True," LuAnn said. "And then maybe she realized they suspected her of discovering something, and she got scared, so she called the one person who had always defended her and protected her, no matter what."

"Jerri." Janice turned to Tess. "You should have heard the story Jerri told us last night about how when she was little, she would sometimes have to wander the streets at night, looking for her mom because Michele was hungry."

Winnie gasped.

Tess blinked like she'd been struck. "I can't even imagine a life like that. No wonder she's so tough."

"Even after she and Michele moved in with her grandmother and grandfather, it wasn't easy," LuAnn said. "Neither of her grandparents was in good health. Jerri was always the caretaker."

"That means she needs us," Janice said.

"Yes, it does." LuAnn tapped her finger on the table. "So...if the break-in had to do with money laundering, what were they looking for?"

"Evidence?" Janice suggested.

"Michele's laptop is missing," Tess said. "Maybe that has something to do with it all."

"That could be. Why don't we start building a list of people who have had contact with Michele and who have access to or who own businesses that could be used to launder money?" LuAnn sat with her pen poised over her notebook.

Tess nodded. "And then we can check them out and see if they make viable suspects."

"Agreed," Janice said.

"I'd say Boomer Aldrich should go to the top of the list," LuAnn said. "He has a chain of Laundromats. Lots of cash flow there. And I know from talking to him when I visited yesterday that he didn't care for Michele. He said she was nosy. In fact, he banned her from cleaning his office, much to Patsy's dismay."

Janice nodded slowly. "If he banned her from his office, he could very well have been covering up some kind of nefarious activity."

"Nefarious?" Tess laughed. "Have you been watching *Sherlock Holmes* in your room at night?"

Janice's eyes twinkled. "I'm not going to admit anything. But Boomer does seem like a viable suspect. He didn't want Michele around, and he has a business that lends itself to money laundering."

"Do you think that the housekeeping service Michele worked for is a possibility?" LuAnn asked.

"I suppose it's a possibility, although I don't think they deal with a lot of cash," Tess said.

"I met her boss yesterday. Her name is Doria Sanders, and the business is called Sanders' Spotless Cleaning Service. Jerri had a very negative reaction to Doria, who is just this side of snooty, but that doesn't mean she's guilty of a crime." LuAnn paused. "Jerri has good instincts. But they could be clouded right now by her emotions."

"What did you think about Doria?" Tess asked.

LuAnn shrugged. "To tell you the truth, I wasn't really looking for suspects at the time. I was more concerned about Jerri, so I didn't stop to study Doria. She did look familiar though, and she recognized me. She said she's been here for lunch."

Tess tipped her head to one side. "I wouldn't write Jerri's instincts off. She seems like a savvy young woman."

"That's true. I'll add Doria to the list, just in case." LuAnn wrote the name in her notebook.

"Hey, maybe Winnie could keep her ears open at church."

Winnie, who had been listening to everything they said, turned. "I can do that. Michele is a good egg. She deserves a break. So does Jerri."

Janice finished chopping veggies and pulled off her gloves. "What about somebody coming into town to stake things out? Somebody involved on the other end of things, like maybe a drug ring or a gambling ring? Someone who would break into Michele's house because they know she knows something?"

"You mean like a scary bad guy who's a stranger in town?" LuAnn asked.

Janice smiled. "Some muscled enforcer who goes around collecting people's debts?"

"Like Atley Hamilton, maybe?" Tess suggested.

LuAnn and Janice stared at her.

"Are you serious?" Janice asked. "He's nice enough."

"Maybe. But I hate to say this because I wasn't trying to listen, but I heard him talking on his cell phone yesterday, and he said something like, 'what else do you want to know?'"

"Hmm. Could be suspicious," LuAnn said.

"Or not." Tess shrugged. "I just get this feeling he's hiding something. Not to mention that I feel like he's scrutinizing me."

"You mean like this?" Janice put her head in her hands and fixed a wide-eyed gaze on Tess.

Tess laughed.

"Well? Do I look guilty?"

"It's not the same, and you know it."

Janice chuckled. "I'm sorry. I couldn't help it. But if he's guilty of anything, why would he stay here?"

"Because he knows we know Jerri, who is Michele's sister? And he could find things out?"

"It's a stretch," LuAnn said.

"A big stretch," Janice added.

Tess shrugged again. "I've been right before."

"That's true." Janice pointed to LuAnn's notebook. "We should write him down."

"All right. I'll add him to the list because he stares and he's really, really big. Just to satisfy Tess." LuAnn flashed her friend a big grin.

Tess gave her a thumbs-up.

"What about Michele's neighbors?" Janice asked. "Maybe one of them saw something the night of the break-in."

"That's a good point. I did meet Michele's neighbors the day of the accident. They both watch Diesel sometimes. And I happened to see one of them watching out of her front window the night Michele's house was broken into."

"According to the mysteries I've watched," Janice said, "many older women look out their windows a lot because they don't have a life and they're nosy."

"Older women like us?" Tess asked. "I look out the window, but it's only to check the weather. And to look at the cars in the parking lot."

"We don't count." Janice snickered. "We have a life."

"That we do," LuAnn said. "But we can be nosy when the circumstances call for it."

Everyone laughed.

"Still, I wouldn't mind dropping by to talk to Michele's neighbor since I've already met her. The problem is, I need to come up with a reason. I don't want to just knock on the door and start asking questions."

"Cookies," Winnie said over her shoulder. "Take her some of my cookies to thank her for looking out for the dog. We've got plenty."

"Great idea," LuAnn said. "Mrs. Brewster has been very helpful to Jerri, especially with Diesel. She deserves your cookies." LuAnn wrote it down and then wrote, *talk to her.* "I'll tell Jerri before I do it, so she knows."

"Her last name is Brewster?" Janice asked. "Like Mortimer Brewster in *Arsenic and Old Lace*?"

This time LuAnn and Tess both stared at Janice with open mouths.

She put her hands in the air. "Okay, yes! I've been binging on old movies and detective shows."

"You could have told us," LuAnn said. "We'd have watched them with you. Maybe they would help us solve this mystery."

"What about the Boycrafts' daughter and her husband?" Winnie suddenly said. "The Paglinos?"

"Why would you have the least amount of suspicion of them?" LuAnn asked.

"Well," Winnie said. "I know them from church, and a month ago or so Michele volunteered to help them clean out their basement or something like that. I think they own a dry cleaning business."

"Really? That's one of the kinds of businesses that could be used for laundering money." LuAnn made a note in her notebook.

"That's what I'm saying." Winnie nodded.

Janice snapped her fingers. "You know what? I overheard the Boycrafts talking about how their daughter had some financial problems."

"This is all good, and it gives us another suspect, but they seem as big a stretch as Atley."

Janice looked at Winnie who put veggies into a big pot on the stove. "Winnie, do you know anything else about them?"

Winnie turned and crossed her arms. "I do recall they were struggling for a while. Someone said something about them losing their house, maybe? I don't know how things are going now. They aren't the friendliest people."

Janice scratched her head. "They could possibly be open to a way out of immediate money issues."

"I hope they're not guilty," Tess said. "I love the Boycrafts, and I know it would hurt them if their daughter did something like this."

"It would," LuAnn agreed. "But we're checking into every-thing, so it's worth looking into. I'm scheduled to go by their house to check on the decor and give them their brochures. I'll see what I can find out."

"Following any clue is valuable at this point," Janice said. "Maybe if we gather enough information, Jerri will feel as though we're accomplishing something to solve the mystery, and it'll keep her from putting herself in a dangerous situation."

"Or not," Tess murmured.

LuAnn read off her list. "Boomer Aldrich, Atley Hamilton, Rosemary and Frank Paglino, and Doria Sanders." She tapped her pen on her lip. "It's a start."

"Shall we divide up the work?" Tess suggested. "I'll have another go at Atley Hamilton."

"Should we research him online?" LuAnn asked. "I always feel a little funny about doing that—at least until I know that someone is a bona fide suspect."

"There is a matter of privacy," Janice said, "but social media is just that, social. I could just put in his name and see what comes up. And while I'm at it, I'll look into Doria and the cleaning service. And maybe I can somehow find out the names of some of the people Michele cleaned for."

"We have a plan," LuAnn said. "We all know how much I like that."

Winnie cleared her throat. "Speaking of plans, the clock is ticking. Lunch will be served soon. Lots to do before then."

LuAnn laughed. "I guess we'd all better get to work before Winnie fires us."

CHAPTER FIFTEEN

Midmorning, LuAnn and Tess were in the basement folding laundry—a never-ending job, especially with a full inn. LuAnn's cell phone rang in her pocket.

"Hello," she answered.

"Are you busy right now?" Jerri asked without saying hello.

LuAnn smiled at Jerri's intensity. "I am, but I can be interrupted. Are you all right?"

"I am. I went to see that very loud man, Boomer, and his wife, Patsy. I think maybe he's louder than I am, if that's possible."

LuAnn's stomach clenched. "I didn't know you were going to go see the Aldriches."

Tess raised a brow as she put a folded white towel on a stack.

"I didn't either until you told me that Michele cleaned for them. I realized it was the perfect opportunity to find out more about Michele. I'm going to pick up some of Michele's hours to help Patsy prepare for Christmas."

"Wait...you got a job? With the Aldriches?"

Tess stopped folding the towel in her hand and stared at LuAnn.

"In a manner of speaking."

"On top of watching out for Michele? What about your dissertation?"

"The cleaning job is for this Friday to help Patsy get ready for the tour and then for the following Monday to help her get things cleaned up afterward, so it's not for long."

"Are you sure that's a good idea?"

"Well, I hope I'm keeping Michele's job open for her. And I think it could be a good place to find some answers to why Michele was scared. That man Boomer is hostile towards her, if you ask me."

"He might be, but I'm concerned about your time, not to mention your safety."

"No biggie. I'll be fine."

LuAnn could almost see Jerri's dismissive shrug.

"But the bigger thing is," Jerri rushed on, "I got the name of Michele's accounting professor. Her name is Katie Mironoff. I've made an appointment to go see her. I'd like you to go with me, if you can."

"Her accounting professor?" LuAnn was beginning to feel like her head was in a wind tunnel.

"Patsy Aldrich's daughter-in-law. She's the one who got Michele the cleaning job with Patsy and Boomer."

"Yes, I learned that," LuAnn said. "But why do you want to talk to Michele's professor?"

Tess put the towel down and crossed her arms.

"Patsy said that Michele sometimes helped Katie with things. According to her, they were closer than just student and teacher. I'm hoping she can give me insight into my sister's life. I also want to ask her if Michele seemed afraid, and if so, did she say anything about why."

"You're going to ask her that point-blank?"

"I don't know what else to do. I've searched Michele's house again. I still can't find her laptop. I searched her phone. Her text messages are mostly about work and church. I also checked the phone's photo gallery. The weird thing is there are no pictures there. For people our age, that's really weird."

"Searching someone's phone is getting kind of personal."

"You have that tone in your voice," Jerri said. "I recognize it. You don't think any of this is a good idea."

"I didn't say that."

"You didn't have to. But will you come anyway? Please? Because if there is any laundering going on, an accounting professor might at the very least be able to help us."

"Unless she's involved, or her family is involved."

"That could be true. I'll just have to play it by ear. I can't find out information without looking for it. I promise I'm being careful."

LuAnn sighed. "I'm not sure you understand the meaning of being careful. At least not like normal people."

"I have to do this, LuAnn!" Jerri's raised voice sounded desperate. "I'm worried. I think it has something to do with drugs or gambling. I mean, what do bad people do with money gotten from either of those? They have to launder it."

"Yes, but—"

"I intend to find out. With or without you. But it would be easier with you."

LuAnn looked at Tess, then up at the ceiling. Finally, she asked, "When are you going?"

"Right before lunch. Can you do it then?"

"Lunch is so busy here—"

Tess tapped her arm and mouthed, *It's okay.*

"All right. I can meet you at the school at eleven thirty."

"Okay, good. I'll see you then."

LuAnn ended the call and related the whole conversation to Tess.

"That girl!" Tess repeated what she'd said earlier.

"Tell me about it. And I thought she was a challenge when she was young. This is a whole new level."

"If Boomer is guilty, he could get suspicious."

"I know." LuAnn stacked folded sheets. "Maybe going to see this professor today will cool Jerri's jets. Keep her from doing something stupid."

"I have my doubts." Tess picked up the towel again and finished folding it. "But on a positive note, the two of you might gather some clues."

LuAnn sighed. "Jerri has always reminded me of a squirrel, skittering around. Fearless. Curious. Climbing around on things she has no business being on. Slightly arrogant in a naive sort of way. Unfortunately, like a squirrel, Jerri could get in a jam and hurt herself if she doesn't watch her step."

"That's a great analogy. And frightening."

"Tell me about it. When she was in high school, I had the illusion of control, like I knew what was going on in her life. Now I've realized she only told me what she thought I should know." LuAnn grabbed a pile of sheets. "I'm going to take these upstairs, clean some guest rooms, and then I'll head out to meet her at the college."

LuAnn stepped into the café area from the basement, balancing the stack of sheets. The large room was empty except for Atley Bradford, who was seated on a sofa near the fireplace, his neatly folded coat on the cushion next to him. He'd helped himself to one of Winnie's freshly made cookies while he drank coffee and poked at his cell phone with his index finger.

Janice was at the desk in the office. When she saw LuAnn, she leaned out the door and waved LuAnn over.

She lowered her voice to a whisper once LuAnn was inside. "I couldn't find much about Atley. Just a private Facebook page, which I can't access. But I did find a website for Sanders' Spotless Cleaning Service. They only handle commercial customers, so any residential jobs Michele had were ones she got herself. Doria is relatively new in town. She bought the business from her brother. I'll send you the link so you can see it. I think I might go visit the office right after lunch, if Tess is free to stay here and take care of things. Then I'll report in."

LuAnn put the folded sheets on the desk. "You're going to just walk in and start asking questions?"

"No. I'm not sure what I'll say, but I'll think of something. I was a pastor's wife, remember? I know how to make small talk." She paused and glanced over at Atley. "Except with muscle-bound men who are very tall and stare a lot."

LuAnn grinned at her friend's comment, then filled Janice in on Jerri's call.

"That girl!" Janice said.

"Exactly what Tess said, twice now." LuAnn picked up the iPad and studied the Sanders' Spotless Cleaning Service website. "Good picture of Doria. Looks the same as she did at the hospital. Perfectly coiffed. It is interesting that she's relatively new in town."

"I thought so."

Tess came through the basement door with a stack of towels. She stopped when she noticed Atley in front of the fireplace, then hurried toward the kitchen.

"What is she doing?" LuAnn wondered out loud.

"I have no idea."

A moment later she came back out into the big room, minus the towels but carrying a coffeepot.

"She's not going to talk to him right now, is she?" Janice whispered.

"I think she is," LuAnn whispered back.

They tiptoed out of the office and pretended to look busy at the counter while Tess headed for Atley with purpose in her step.

"Would you like fresh coffee?" she asked when she reached him.

"What I have here is fine." He glanced at his watch. "Besides, I have someplace to be."

"We have plenty. And I might be able to scrounge up some different kinds of cookies for you."

He looked up at her. "As tempting as that is, I have some errands to run. Besides, with all these sweets lying around, I could gain weight fast."

"Very true." Tess laughed. "Do you have family around here?"

He frowned. "Why do you ask?"

"Because, uh, some of our guests are here for the holiday to see family."

"I won't be staying through Christmas," he said.

LuAnn and Janice exchanged glances.

Tess shifted nervously. "Well, is there anything we can do for you? Is your room to your satisfaction?"

That earned her a slight smile. "Everything is just fine. The bed is comfortable. The place is spotless. I have no complaints whatsoever."

Tess hovered over him.

"Did you need something else?" he asked. "I'm very happy with the accommodations. I hope I haven't given the impression otherwise."

"Um, do you need the name of a gym?"

LuAnn slapped her hand over her mouth to keep from laughing,

Atley just stared up at her. "No. Are you a regular gym-goer?"

"Oh no. I mean, I work out, but not at a gym. We do stretches and things here. However, I could ask around if you need one. Do you belong to a gym at home?"

"I do. I'm sure that's pretty obvious." He flexed his bicep with a lifted brow, then he unfolded his large frame from the chair and stood, towering over Tess.

She backed up. Once again, LuAnn was impressed by the sheer size of him.

He picked up his coat. "I appreciate all the, uh, helpfulness." One side of his mouth twitched as he slipped a massive arm into his coat sleeve.

"Well, let us know if you need anything else."

"I certainly will."

"And I'll take care of your plate and cup."

"Thank you." He nodded at her, walked across the lobby, and left the inn.

As soon as the door shut, LuAnn started laughing. "'Do you need a gym? Do you belong to a gym at home?' Seriously, Tess! You were kind of clutching at straws there."

Tess blushed. "I was caught off guard. I couldn't think of anything else to say."

Janice giggled. "You'd think you'd have learned some subtlety after all these mysteries we've solved."

"He's a little intimidating. All that muscle mass up close. But there's something about him." Tess's forehead wrinkled.

"I have to agree with you," Janice said. "I'm not sure it's bad, but I'm not sure it's good either."

"Exactly. He's sort of fierce underneath that calm voice."

"He totally avoided the question about family," LuAnn reminded them.

"That's true. I was so nervous by that point that I hadn't even noticed that."

"Well, we'll figure it out, I have no doubt," Janice said. "Tess, if you don't mind, I'm going to run over to Sanders' Spotless Cleaning Service after I'm done with chores to see what I can discover." She snickered. "I sure hope I do a better job asking questions than you just did."

"I hope you do too," Tess said and turned to LuAnn. "What time are you visiting Michele this afternoon? I'd like to meet you there."

LuAnn told her and grabbed the stack of sheets. "I'm going upstairs to clean some guest rooms. Then I'll add this information to my notebook and head off to the college. It'll be interesting to see what I learn."

CHAPTER SIXTEEN

LuAnn and Jerri met in the foyer of the building where Professor Mironoff had her office on the grounds of Washington State Community College.

Jerri greeted LuAnn, determination on her face. "Are you ready?"

"In a minute. First, we should discuss how you're going to approach the professor. We should have a plan before you go walking into her office. Perhaps some subtlety is in order?" LuAnn thought of Tess's conversation with Atley earlier and almost started laughing again.

"Good point." Jerri creased her brow. "Problem is, I'm not subtle on a good day, and I don't know how to be subtle about this. How can I ask if Michele was afraid without being blunt? Besides, I can't imagine the professor would be guilty of money laundering."

"I tend to agree, but we should still be cautious. How about some chitchat first? Let's get a feel for who she is. And even if all seems well, I'd suggest you leave the term 'money laundering' out. Just ask if Michele seemed nervous about something."

"Okay. Good idea." Jerri's nostril's flared. "Especially since the professor is related by marriage to Boomer. He's a suspect in my book."

"Tess, Janice, and I agree with that, but you must tread carefully. If he is guilty of something, he could be dangerous. If he isn't, we don't want to impact his reputation or ours, or perhaps make matters worse between him and Michele."

"I agree. And I'll try to be subtle." Jerri rolled her eyes. "Which takes a lot of effort for me."

LuAnn laughed. As they walked, LuAnn filled Jerri in on everything she had in her notebook. By the time they reached Professor Mironoff's office, Jerri was fully updated.

She knocked on the door.

"Come on in." A pleasant voice greeted them.

Jerri opened the door, and they walked inside.

The space was neat and exact. A woman with black hair framing her round face stood behind her desk and smiled. "Hello. I'm Katie Mironoff. I assume you are Jerri and LuAnn."

"We are," Jerri said.

"Please, have a seat." Katie waved at a couple of green chairs in front of her desk.

Once they were seated, she sat down and smiled at LuAnn. "It's good to meet you. My mother-in-law has spoken highly of you in relation to the Marietta Christmas in History House Tour. I have tickets, and I'm looking forward to it. Patsy is most excited about showing off her house. She's put a lot of work into the place."

"She's done an amazing job—with the house and the decorating."

"I helped with that." Katie grinned.

"Well, you, your mother-in-law, and father-in-law did a great job," LuAnn said.

"*Step*father-in-law," Katie corrected. She shook her head and sighed. "I hope this doesn't sound disparaging, but Boomer likes to be in charge. Not only that, he gets too wound up in the details. Sometimes it's just easier to get things done when he's not there. It's quieter too."

LuAnn could see how those things might be an issue.

"Can I get either of you something to drink? Coffee? Soda?"

"No, thank you." Jerri seemed tense.

"I'm fine," LuAnn said.

Katie smiled at LuAnn then eyed Jerri again as she sat down. "So you're Michele's sister," she said, almost to herself.

"Yes. Is that good or bad?"

Jerri was already on the defensive. LuAnn gently shoved Jerri's foot with the toe of her shoe.

Jerri took a deep breath.

"Neither. More a curious thing than anything else. It's always fascinating to meet my students' family members. It fleshes them out. Gives them more dimension. You're working on your dissertation, I hear."

"I'm just beginning my research."

"Before her accident, Michele mentioned that you had plans to come to Marietta this spring to do some local research about the Underground Railroad. Tell me about it."

Jerri briefly explained her topic and research. She relaxed as she talked.

"Marietta is a great place to find information, and it would be fantastic if you can actually place a relative here. The information about Finney is fascinating. I'd heard he was an abolitionist, but I'd love to know more. And it's helpful that you have a friend at Wayfarers Inn. That gives you access to a building that was part of the Underground Railroad." Katie took a sip of her bottled water. "Please tell me, how is Michele? Can you fill me in with some details about what's going on, like what happened and the prognosis?"

Jerri told Katie about the accident. "At this point, she's making progress. They've said a few things about brain damage, like some memory loss, but that remains to be seen. They think they'll be lessening the sedation levels soon. Depending on how things go, she might be going home by early next week."

"Wow! That's fast."

"It is. I'll be hanging around to take care of her for a couple of weeks."

"I'm glad you'll be here for her. I've spoken with the powers-that-be. Michele will be able to complete her exams when she's recovered enough to do so."

Jerri inhaled. "I hadn't even thought of that."

Katie nodded. "Yes, she's missing a crucial time in the semester."

"Thank you for looking out for her."

"You're welcome. She's a very special student. I want her to succeed."

"I understand that Michele sometimes helped you out around here."

"When she had the time, which wasn't often. She had a lot of cleaning jobs, mostly commercial through Sanders'. When my mother-in-law needed help, I arranged for her to do the work privately. I wanted Michele to make as much money as possible. I sometimes wondered if the person she worked for took advantage because Michele worked so hard." Katie leaned forward. "I understand you'll be helping Patsy by picking up a couple of days while Michele is incapacitated?"

"Yes. Word got out fast about that."

Katie laughed. "Patsy and I talk a lot. My own mother has passed away. Patsy doesn't have a daughter, so we've pretty much filled in those gaps for each other."

LuAnn felt a brief spasm of longing. She did miss talking to her mother.

"Are you doing this to keep her position open?" Katie asked.

"Partially."

"Don't worry about that. Patsy will hire Michele back." Katie crossed her arms on her desk. "Listen, I know you two didn't just come here to simply chat. What's up?"

Jerri looked at LuAnn, who tilted her head. She couldn't make the decision for Jerri, but she was leaning toward trusting Katie.

Apparently, Jerri was too. "I'll just be blunt. Michele called me last week and begged me to come here. She said she had some questions for me and needed my help, but she wouldn't clarify on the phone. It sounded urgent."

Katie raised her brows.

Jerri clasped her hands. "I guess I'd like to know if you were aware of anything going on in her life that she might be afraid of."

"Hmmm." Katie narrowed her eyes. "Funny you would ask that. I hadn't thought about the fact that she might be afraid, but she was acting strange."

"How?" Jerri asked.

"Well, she was normally so friendly. Helping me with papers and schedules when she could. Then one day she dropped in and asked me an odd question that I didn't think anything about at the time. After that I didn't see her so much."

"What question did she ask?"

"How easily books could be cooked."

Jerri inhaled. "What did you tell her?"

"It's a piece of cake. People do it all the time, in big and small ways. You simply have two sets of books. One is the real one and one is the fake. You only show people the fake one. I've even known spouses to do it—one of them keeps two checkbooks and only shows their spouse the fake." Katie glanced at the wall behind their heads, then back at them. "I guess I didn't pay much attention, because Michele is a dreamer. She always asked what-if questions. She was pursuing a degree in accounting, but frankly, I thought she should have been concentrating on something in the creative arts. Perhaps writing or illustration."

"I've seen just a smidgeon of her art work," LuAnn said. "She's exceptionally talented."

"She is. But since you've expressed concern, I'll confess that Patsy and I were concerned too. Michele even missed a scheduled cleaning day at Patsy's. The two of us briefly compared notes because it just wasn't like her. When Patsy tried to find out more information from Michele, she clammed up.

I thought it odd, but I got busy before I could talk to her, and then I heard about her accident."

Jerri sat back hard in her chair and sighed. "That's all she asked?"

"That's it." Katie smiled. "She did tell me how you've always looked out for her, and how if she ever needed help she could count on you."

"She said that?"

"She did. And she said you were the smartest person she knew."

Jerri tapped her fingers on her thigh and shifted in her chair. "Michele had a laptop, right?"

"She did. She was very proud of it too. Top of the line. She saved her money for months so she could have something with the power to zip through complicated spreadsheets like fire on dry wood."

"It's missing."

"Has it been stolen?"

Jerri shrugged. "I don't know. I can't find it."

"Oh dear." Katie clasped her fingers together. "I hope not. She worked hard for that machine."

They chatted a little longer but learned nothing else.

As they were ready to walk out the door, Jerri turned to Katie. "Would you mind not telling anyone we're asking questions?"

"Okay, mum's the word. I won't say a thing."

As LuAnn and Jerri left the building, Jerri sniffled. Then she stopped walking and dug into her purse. "I need a tissue. My eyes are leaking."

"Oh! You're crying. I guess that's one way to describe it." LuAnn reached in her bag and pulled out two. "I've been keeping them on hand lately." She touched Jerri's shoulder. "What's wrong?"

"I feel so guilty." Jerri blew her nose. Tears welled in her eyes. "Michele was bragging about me. And all this time I thought she was saying horrible things about me to everyone."

"Neither of you were being honest with the other. Relationships go both ways. How could you have known how she felt if she never said anything to you? If there's guilt to be had, I suppose you could say it's pretty much fifty/fifty. But guilt isn't productive. You have to concentrate on how to be productive right now. Michele needs you. You're here. Sounds to me like God is having mercy on you and giving you a chance to restore this relationship."

"Thank you." Jerri sniffled. "I'll think about the God part. And mercy reminds me of that song from my grandmother's attic."

"It does, doesn't it?"

"Do you think we can trust Katie?" Jerri asked.

"If we can't, we'll probably know about it soon enough, but her concern for Michele was real. I don't think she has any part in whatever is going on. Hopefully she's as good as her word."

CHAPTER SEVENTEEN

LuAnn headed for the Paglinos' right after leaving the college. As she rounded the circular driveway in front of their house, she thought how perfect their massive French revival home was for the World War II time period they represented for the Christmas tour. At the same time, she wondered if they really were having money problems. The mortgage on a house like this one would be steep.

She exited her car, crossed brick paving blocks to the front door, and tapped the brass knocker.

Frank threw the door open with a smile, which faded when he saw her. "Yes? LuAnn?" He looked over her head. "I wasn't expecting you."

"I stopped by to give you a copy of the Christmas tour book that each participant will be receiving on Saturday." She pulled a copy from her purse and handed it to him.

Frank took it, staring at it like he had no idea what she was talking about. "I didn't remember that." He made no move to let her in.

"I also wanted to check to make sure you have everything you need and that you're confident your decor is complete and prepared for Saturday."

"Oh yeah." He scratched his head. "We're not quite done decorating. Rosemary will be here soon. We're, uh, expecting company."

LuAnn managed to peer over his shoulder and saw a living room on the right filled with boxes. A large, half-decorated tree sat in a corner of the room.

"Don't worry." He'd noticed her expression. "It'll be done by Saturday."

"Is there anything I can do to help? I'd be glad to give you a hand finishing things up."

He lifted his chin. "No. We got it covered. We'll probably finish tonight."

She shifted awkwardly. "All right, then, I'll say goodbye."

"I'll tell Rosemary you were here."

"Please remember that I'm available to help if you need it."

"Sure thing." His smile was closer to a grimace. He shut the door in her face.

LuAnn was so shocked, she didn't move for a minute. Then she turned and walked back to her car. She had no idea how to handle this situation. The thought that one of the tour hosts wouldn't fulfill their commitment hadn't occurred to her. Should she talk to the Boycrafts? Probably not. Although Rosemary was their daughter, the Boycrafts were guests at the inn. LuAnn shouldn't impose on them. She decided to pray and give it to the Lord.

As she turned on her car, another car whipped in beside her, Rosemary behind the wheel. She looked at LuAnn, mouth in an *O*. Then she hopped out of the car, ran around to LuAnn's car, and motioned for her to open her window.

"Sorry. I forgot you were coming," she said breathlessly.

"I gave Frank a copy of the book we'll be handing out at the beginning of the tour."

"Good. Thanks. I guess you noticed we aren't done decorating yet?"

"I did. I offered to help."

"No need. We'll get it done. I promise." She bent lower. "How is Michele? We heard all about her accident at church and how her sister is here caring for her, and she used to be one of your students."

"Oh?" LuAnn was surprised by Rosemary's sudden chattiness, her broad smile, as well as the fact that she knew so much about Michele and Jerri.

Rosemary laughed. "You know how people like to talk."

LuAnn did know. And talk could be used for good, but it could also be used for bad. "As far as I know, Michele is getting better."

"I'm glad to hear it."

A dark blue sedan pulled around them and parked in front of the house. Rosemary looked up and waved.

"I have an appointment with someone, so I'd best get inside and make some coffee."

"All right. I might give you a call tomorrow and make sure you don't need my help."

"I appreciate that, but there's no need. We'll be fine."

Rosemary walked away to greet a man in a suit who had gotten out of the other vehicle. LuAnn started her car and drove around the circle and down the driveway to the street. Then her cell phone rang. It was Brad. She pushed the SPEAKER button and said hello.

"Hey. You sound discouraged or something."

"Probably more like 'or something.'"

"You want to talk about it?" he asked.

She told him what had just happened at the Paglinos'.

"Hmmm. Sounds like a bit of a dilemma." He paused. "I have to be somewhere shortly, but I also want to know more about what's going on with your mystery. I have an idea. How about you guys meet me at Over the Moon for pizza tonight? My treat. You can eat lots of cheesy goodness to soothe your concerns, and while we're there, give me updates."

She laughed. "Cheesy goodness might do the trick. I'll ask Tess and Janice. I think we can all get away from the inn for a little while. What time?"

"How about five thirty? Oh, and bring Jerri, if she can come. I wouldn't mind getting to know her a little better."

"I'll ask her. See you there." As LuAnn pushed the button to hang up, she felt inordinately relieved to hear from Brad, and she looked forward to the evening.

LuAnn arrived at the hospital at the same time as Tess, and they parked near each other.

"Everything still fine at the inn?" LuAnn asked, pulling her coat tight around herself.

Tess pulled her scarf tighter around her neck. "It is."

"Brad wants to know if he can take us all out to Over the Moon for pizza tonight, including Jerri."

"That sounds great. I'm in the mood for some pizza. Did you ask Janice?"

"I texted her. She said yes."

Tess stopped and grabbed LuAnn's arm. "Isn't that Atley?" She pointed at the lone figure of a man across the parking lot opening a car door.

LuAnn squinted in the cold sunlight. "Sure looks like him. And that looks like his car."

The man looked up. Tess waved, but he turned quickly, ignoring them, and ducked into his vehicle.

"I wonder if that was him," Tess said. "If it was, that was rude."

"If it was, maybe he didn't recognize us. He's never seen us outside the inn. And we are wearing heavy coats."

"Maybe, but he acts suspicious, and he avoids conversation."

"Even when we try our hardest to engage him," LuAnn teased.

Tess playfully slapped her arm with a gloved hand. "No fair bringing up my failures."

"Failure on all our parts," LuAnn reminded her. They began walking toward the entrance of the hospital. "Besides, our mysteries are usually solved, one way or another, so perhaps we'll solve the mystery of Atley too."

"Especially if he has something to do with Michele."

"That's true. Meanwhile, let's go see how she's doing. Perhaps she'll wake up and explain everything."

"Which would be good."

Jerri met them at the ICU, smiling, eyes bright. "Hey, I just got here a little while ago."

"How is she?" LuAnn asked.

"She's coming out of sedation. I'm so excited. One of the nurses talked to her earlier. But she's been asleep since I got here. I'm going to hang around the rest of the day if I have to, waiting for her to wake up."

"While she's asleep, do you mind if we go pray for her?" LuAnn asked.

"Not at all. I'll wait here."

LuAnn and Tess went into the room. When they finished praying, Michele opened her eyes. She frowned at them. "Who are you?" She looked at LuAnn. "You look familiar."

"I'm LuAnn, one of Jerri's old teachers. This is Tess, and she's my friend."

"Oh. Were you praying for me just now?"

"Yes."

"Thank you." Her smile was weak but bright. "I'm in the hospital. I guess that's obvious, right? The nurses said I fell and hit my head. I need to talk to Jerri. The nurses say she's here. She worries about everything."

"Jerri is here now." LuAnn pointed through the glass.

"Really?" Michele squinted. "Wow. She is! How did she find out I fell? Did someone call her?"

LuAnn and Tess exchanged glances.

"We'll let her tell you the details," LuAnn said. "We're just glad you're okay."

"All right. Me too." She closed her eyes.

They left her room and went out to the hallway.

Jerri danced for joy. "She opened her eyes! Did she talk to you?"

"She did," Tess said.

"I'll see you guys later, okay?" Jerri turned to go to the room.

"Wait." LuAnn reached out and tugged on her arm.

Jerri whirled around, excitement lighting her eyes.

"She doesn't remember asking you to come. She thinks someone called you when she fell. We didn't tell her anything, so you'll need to fill her in."

"Oh." Jerri's face drooped. "That means she doesn't remember anything."

"We'll pray that it's only temporary, okay?"

Jerri nodded, but skepticism was etched on her face.

"And one more thing," LuAnn added. "We're all meeting Brad at Over the Moon tonight for pizza. You're welcome to join us."

"I might like that. Text me directions and time?"

"I will, and now we'll leave you to spend some time with your sister. Enjoy. And remember God's mercy."

Jerri suddenly hugged LuAnn. "Thank you."

December 17, 1857

Cold weather gripped Marietta like the claws of an eagle and would not let go. Snow fell as Prudence trudged through the snow to pick up her package. Jason had argued with Prudence about leaving, but she refused to shirk her duty.

She shivered, imagining how cold the runaway would be, coming from a warmer climate. She wondered how Herman was faring and hoped he'd reached a warm place.

The boat had arrived when Prudence reached the river. She tried to hurry, then lost her footing, and slipped on the bank. When she landed, her ankle twisted beneath her.

With great effort, she managed to get to her feet and whisper the code word to the pilot of the boat, who then helped a tiny pale woman and a dark-skinned child disembark to stand on the bank with Prudence.

"I must go," the man said. "Before this snow gets worse." He shoved off before Prudence could say anything else to him.

Prudence tried to stand on her twisted ankle but saw stars from pain. "I seem to have hurt myself," she said breathlessly. "But we must get to the tunnel before the weather turns worse."

"I will help you." The woman reached for her. "Give me your hands. You can lean on me." She was surprisingly strong for her size. "Take us where we are to go. We'll ask the Lord. He will strengthen and help us."

The child had taken Prudence's other hand, smiling despite her shivers.

"What is thy name?" Prudence looked down at the little girl.

"Sarah."

Slowly they picked their way to the tunnel entrance. They'd almost reached the door when Prudence heard the rush of footsteps behind her. Her pain and the snowfall had made her careless. She hadn't been listening for anyone's approach.

"Stop! Both of you."

The woman next to her gasped. Prudence recognized Herman Douglas's voice.

"He does not know why thee is with me," Prudence whispered. "I will say thee is a fellow servant in the house."

"He knows me," the woman said. "That's my brother, Herman. And he's the reason I have Sarah. Herman wanted to sell her after her parents died. I refused and ran away."

Herman approached them, leading his horse.

Prudence remembered Herman's revolvers and fought fear along with the pain that threatened to blind her mind and her eyes. She took a breath of freezing air and turned to face the man she'd fed and cared for.

"Herman, thee followed me."

"I did."

"How did thee know to do so?"

"I have connections," Herman said. "Hard to come by, but I found them. And I've been following my sister for a while now."

"What does thee intend to do?"

"I intend to take both of you back to your cabin."

"No. I will not allow thee to bring danger to my husband. He is innocent."

"You can't have Sarah, Herman." The woman picked up the child and wrapped her arms tightly around her. "I will die first."

"The death of my sister is not part of the plan," Herman said.

"You can't carry all of us," Prudence said. "We aren't moving."

"Prudence." Herman's voice was soft, and she finally looked into his eyes. "I already assured you I would bring you no harm."

"This child, then?" his sister asked.

"No, Sabina, not the child, not you, and not Prudence."

Sabina. The name he'd called as he'd come back to consciousness.

"I am not the man I was," Herman said. "You must trust me. And frankly, at this very moment, I want to get all of us out of this confounded cold and snow. I can't feel my fingers or my nose. And obviously Prudence has hurt herself. She can ride the horse. We must go before someone gets frostbite."

Prudence turned to Sabina, the fog of pain making her vision dim.

"We have no choice," Sabina said. "I'm inclined to believe him. I've never heard him talk like this before."

CHAPTER EIGHTEEN

LuAnn, Tess, and Janice walked into Over the Moon, relieved to get out of the cold night air. Brad was already there at a table with Jerri. He had her laughing, which wasn't unusual for him. LuAnn inhaled the warm scent of baking pizza as she followed Tess and Janice across the brick-walled room. They grabbed chairs, and LuAnn was forced to sit next to Brad, something she was pretty sure they all did on purpose, but she didn't mind. She was glad to see him.

After they ordered pizzas and drinks, Tess turned to Brad. "Haven't seen you around much."

"I'm in the process of closing a house deal, and I'm...doing a couple of other things."

Tess and Janice exchanged a glance.

"Well, doing things is good," Tess said quickly. "Especially around Christmas."

"Absolutely," Janice piped in. "We've done a lot of things too."

"And I hope to hear about some of them tonight," Brad added, picking at a paper napkin.

LuAnn thought he was acting odd. So were Tess and Janice, for that matter.

"Jerri told me Michele is awake," Brad said.

"How is she tonight?" Janice asked.

Jerri's smile lit her face. "She's good. Really glad to see me. They might be moving her to a regular room tomorrow since she's recovering so quickly." Her smile faded. "But she doesn't remember anything that helps us. The doctor said her memory might still return, but it's hard to say."

LuAnn stopped thinking about Brad and focused on what Jerri was saying. "Does she remember being afraid?"

"Maybe, just a little bit. I warned her to be quiet about all of that. But right now, her biggest concern is her missing laptop."

LuAnn decided right then and there that if it didn't turn up, she'd buy a new one for Michele herself.

"How much are you telling her about what's happened and what we're doing?" Tess asked.

"Pretty much everything. I figured she should know, and I hope it will shake some of her memories loose, but so far, it hasn't. When I told her about the visit with her professor, she didn't remember talking to her about her concerns."

LuAnn quickly updated the group about the visit she and Jerri had with Michele's professor.

"Well, I have some information for us that might help." Janice grinned. "LuAnn, I hope you brought your clue list."

"I did." LuAnn reached inside her purse for her notebook.

"Out with it," Tess said. "The whole way here, you looked like the cat who ate the canary. Obviously, this is something big."

"Yuck." Janice grimaced. "I've always hated that canary adage. I picture a large cat, covered with scars, standing on top of a pile of feathers, licking his lips."

Tess pressed her hands on her stomach. "Yuck is right. And thanks for that picture at dinner."

Brad and Jerri snickered.

"You started it," Janice said. "But you'll get your appetite back when I tell you what I found out today."

"What?" everyone said at the same time.

Janice grinned and wiggled her eyebrows.

"Out with it, Sherlock."

"As you know, I visited Sanders' Spotless Cleaning Service today and spoke with Doria. They cater especially to commercial clients. You won't believe this, but McPherson Salons—Fern—is one of her clients. And guess who cleaned for them?"

LuAnn inhaled. "Michele."

"No kidding," Brad said.

"Michele not only cleaned their offices but also the salons after hours."

"Who is Fern?" Jerri interrupted.

"Oh boy," Brad murmured.

At that moment, the server came with their pizzas. Brad said a blessing over the food.

Jerri waited while everyone helped themselves before she asked again. "Well? Fern?"

LuAnn explained who Fern was and her position on the committee.

"Right now, she's very, very grumpy," Janice said.

"That's putting it mildly," Brad said between bites.

"Could guilt be making her act that way?" Jerri asked.

"I hope not." LuAnn put a slice of pizza on her plate. "Just the thought of her being involved with something like this upsets me. She might be acting badly right now, and she can be a curmudgeon, but I've always respected her."

"Agreed," Janice said.

"Still, we need to add her and her son to our list." Tess tapped on LuAnn's notebook.

LuAnn jotted down the information Janice had provided, and then she looked up at Janice. "Did you tell Doria about your connection to Michele through Jerri?"

"No. I didn't mention Jerri. I didn't want her to know that. I just told her I'd heard of her by way of Michele. She automatically assumed I wanted to know about cleaning services and gave me references."

"Wow," Tess said. "You're getting really good at collecting information."

"I prayed before I went. I was a little nervous, to tell you the truth."

"What did you think of Doria?" LuAnn asked. "I only saw her once at the hospital, and that was brief."

"And I didn't care for her," Jerri added.

Janice chewed thoughtfully. "Well, she seemed very concerned about Michele, wondering if she would get her memory back."

"An employer would be interested in a valuable employee's health," Tess said.

"True," LuAnn said.

"And I don't see how she could be a part of money laundering," Janice added. "A cleaning service doesn't deal in a lot of cash."

"That's true, but she gave us a link from Michele to the McPhersons." LuAnn chewed on a bite of pizza. "Remember when I told you that I heard Fern and her son arguing?"

"Yes," Tess said.

"I thought it was nothing, but now I wonder what was going on. Fern's receptionist said something about Melvin being mean." LuAnn tapped her pen on her notebook. "That could be because she was forced to take sides in a business spat between Fern and her son, but it could also be because she knows something is going on."

"You know what?" Jerri twirled a piece of her hair with her index finger. "I was thinking of getting some advice about my hair. I could make the rounds of their salons and ask questions. Then maybe see what I can discover. I can also check in with Doria and make sure Michele still has a job."

"How many salons do they have?" Brad asked.

"In Marietta, they have three hair salons, which also include nail salons," LuAnn said. "I think they might have some shops in another town."

"Well, I'm going to check into them," Jerri said. "Friday. I'll see what I can find out."

LuAnn inhaled to say no, but Brad gently rested his hand on her arm. "How about I drive you? A client canceled on me, and I have some free time on Friday."

Jerri's eyes flashed in surprise, then she smiled. "That sounds like a deal."

Tess looked at LuAnn. "An excellent idea."

"I can't argue," LuAnn said. "And it'll give you another chance to practice your subtlety."

"I do need practice with that," Jerri said. "So, what exactly am I trying to find out?"

"Good question." LuAnn rested her head in her hands. "How about asking if they've seen anyone who looks out of place in the salon lately? Overheard conversations. Things that don't feel right."

"In other words, use my instincts," Jerri said.

"Exactly," LuAnn said. "And you, my friend, also need to be thinking about your dissertation, even while we work on this mystery."

"I have been. I've visited Maybelline again at the museum. I'm finalizing some research about Charles Finney. Did you know that he was not only a staunch abolitionist, he also hated church segregation and he let women pray out loud in church during his meetings? That caused quite a stir."

"I had no idea," LuAnn said.

"Speaking of your dissertation, I had some time this afternoon to look at Prudence's journal for signs of your relative," Tess said.

"And?" Jerri asked.

"I think maybe I found her. And Charles Finney."

"Wow! That's awesome."

"I'll make a copy for you and give it to you tomorrow after your tour of the basement."

Jerri beamed. "I'll be there."

"So, tell me more about your dissertation," Brad said.

Jerri's face lit, and for the rest of their meal, she regaled them all with tidbits of her studies. LuAnn watched, so proud of the woman she'd become.

Their server came by and took the mostly empty pizza pans, offering to box up what was left.

"Good idea," Tess said. "Jerri? Brad? Either of you want to take that home?"

Jerri shook her head. "It would go to waste. I haven't been home enough to eat there."

Brad shook his head also. "No. I have to go out of town tomorrow, and I won't be returning until late. I'll pick up dinner on the way home."

"I guess we'll take it home," Janice said. "Perhaps a late-night snack."

Brad paid for their pizza, and then he walked them to their cars. LuAnn watched him head for his. He hadn't offered an explanation of where he was going. Not that he had to, but normally he bordered on chatty. And if that wasn't bad enough, LuAnn wondered why it bothered her so.

CHAPTER NINETEEN

On Thursday morning, while Taylor handled the last of the breakfast crowd, LuAnn and Janice drank a final cup of coffee in the café before getting to work. Tess was upstairs, checking some rooms that had been vacated. LuAnn had her notebook in front of her, looking over her clues.

"Jerri's coming to see the basement today, right?" Janice asked.

"Uh-huh," LuAnn murmured.

"Tess said this is the copy of Prudence's journal page for Jerri." Janice pushed a piece of paper to LuAnn.

"That's good," LuAnn said absentmindedly. "I can give it to her when she gets here for the tour."

"Are you really listening to me?"

LuAnn looked up at her friend. "Of course I am."

"You've been in your own world since dinner last night. You didn't even talk much before bed."

"I have a lot of things on my mind." LuAnn pointed to her notebook with the tip of her pen.

Janice leaned toward her. "If you need to talk, we're here."

"I know that, and I think we've talked ourselves crazy about all this stuff. Now we need more clues."

Before Janice could reply, Atley stepped out of the elevator and headed for an empty table, which happened to be near them. He nodded in their direction as he sat down in his usual position, facing the front door. LuAnn's chair faced him, making it easy to observe what he did, which she did over her coffee mug. She wondered if it had been him at the hospital the day before. He didn't act like anything was out of the ordinary, not that she would know what ordinary was for him.

Taylor swept out of the kitchen, noticed Atley, and took his order. After he was done, Atley glanced at LuAnn and gave her a slight wave. She smiled in return, then averted her eyes. Apparently, she wasn't as surreptitious as she'd hoped. She turned her gaze back to her notebook.

"What's on your to-do list today?" Janice asked.

LuAnn looked up at her. "Chores. Checking a few last items of preparation for the tour on Saturday. Jerri's tour of the basement. And after you and I go to the hospital today, I'm going by to see Michele's next-door neighbor, Mrs. Brewster."

Taylor whipped back through the swinging kitchen doors with a heaping plate for Atley.

Before LuAnn could say anything else, Randy Lewis, dressed in his uniform, walked through the door and headed directly for their table.

"Hi, Randy." Janice smiled at him. "This is a pleasure. Did you stop by for coffee?"

"No, but now that you asked, I'd love a cup to go."

"Certainly. It's on the house." Janice motioned at Taylor, who skidded to a stop on his way back to the kitchen.

"Strong with cream," Randy said.

Taylor smiled and went to get it.

"Have a seat while you wait," LuAnn said.

Randy glanced around the room, then sat on a chair and scooted it up to the table. He had yet to smile.

"What brings you here?" Janice said.

"I wondered how Jerri is faring after the break-in. I stopped by her sister's house, but Jerri had already left."

"How thoughtful," Janice said.

Atley perked up and stared at them. LuAnn met his gaze, and he quickly looked back at his plate.

"It's not really thoughtfulness." Randy leaned toward them. "I'm concerned about Jerri. She seemed pretty determined to find out who broke into Michele's house." Frown wrinkles creased his face, and for a minute, he seemed a million miles away. LuAnn sensed he wasn't telling them the whole story.

"It's nice that you're so concerned," Janice said.

LuAnn hoped he'd say more, but he remained quiet. Then his gaze sharpened and focused on them again. "At times I get concerned when people who aren't law enforcement want to solve crimes."

His words hung in the air. They solved mysteries, and Randy knew it.

"Anyway," he finally said, "if you see Jerri, will you let her know I'm asking? Perhaps if she knows I'm watching, she won't do anything unwise. Sometimes people do unwise things when they get involved in situations they shouldn't get involved in."

Taylor brought Randy his coffee, and he nodded his thanks.

"We'll definitely keep an eye on Jerri," LuAnn said.

"I'm sure you will." He stood.

"We wouldn't want anyone to do anything unwise, would we LuAnn?" Janice smiled.

"Oh no." LuAnn shook her head.

Randy looked at them both, rolled his eyes, and for the first time since he'd gotten there, he smiled. "Please, just be careful. All of you. And it wouldn't be a bad idea to have me on speed dial. You know…just in case you need me."

He turned and left. LuAnn caught Atley's gaze again, but this time she realized he'd been watching them openly. He quickly returned to eating his breakfast. Why was he so interested in their conversation? He hadn't shown that kind of interest in anything any of them had done since he'd arrived.

She turned back to Janice and leaned in close. "That was unexpected."

"And a little scary in more ways than one. If Randy is concerned, we should really be concerned."

"My thoughts exactly."

LuAnn looked up from the reception counter when Jerri walked through the front door for her tour of the basement. Tess was in the office, catching up on some paperwork, and she waved through the open door. Janice was in the basement folding laundry.

"How is Michele?" LuAnn asked when Jerri reached her.

"Recovering quickly now, but she wants her laptop. I still can't find it."

"Did you tell her you'd looked all over for it?"

"Yes. I feel bad about it. All her school work is on it. She's also concerned about passing her exams. She doesn't remember what she doesn't remember about her schoolwork, if that makes sense."

"It does." LuAnn picked up the photocopy of Prudence's journal page from where she'd put it on the counter. "Tess found this for you."

LuAnn stood next to Jerri as she read it.

I have recently been reminded that although all Christians do not agree about certain aspects of Biblical doctrine, it appears that many of us are united in these beliefs: the sanctity of life and the evils of one human believing they have the right to own another. I've seen proof of this from a man who, by an act of Providence, was our guest. In his possession was a note from a preacher who has dedicated his life in service to God and showing mankind God's mercy. This note helped convince our guest that saving a child's life is worth more than what this world has to offer. Mercy's song.

Jerri looked at LuAnn. "Wow. That's amazing."

"It is."

Jerri tucked the copy into a leather portfolio she carried. "And now I'm ready for my tour. I have my cell phone to take pictures and to make audio notes. And paper to write on."

"Good." When they reached the hidden door, LuAnn stopped. "Before I forget, Officer Randy stopped by this morning to check up on you. He actually went by Michele's house first, but you'd already left. He's concerned."

"Concerned about my safety?"

"Yes."

Jerri fidgeted with her phone. "Police officers don't usually do things like that unless there's a good reason. It's not like he knows me or Michele that well. That's just one more confirmation that something is going on."

"He wasn't very forthcoming. He just expressed concern about people who try to solve mysteries who aren't police." LuAnn pointed to the door. "But right now, it's time to think about your dissertation. Are you ready?"

Jerri nodded.

When they reached the basement, Jerri said hello to Janice who was folding towels, then looked around and began snapping pictures. LuAnn showed her the rooms where escaping slaves would have stayed. Jerri stepped inside one of them, speaking notes into her phone. LuAnn waited. When Jerri was done, LuAnn moved the stool that hid the tunnel entrance and she and Jerri crawled through it and entered to where they could stand upright. As the two of them walked the distance to the river exit, then back again, Jerri snapped more pictures and commented into her phone about the tunnel walls and her feelings of claustrophobia.

When she was finally done, LuAnn replaced the cover to the tunnel and moved the stool back into position to hide it. "Have you seen enough?"

Jerri's eyes were watery. "Yes, I think I have."

Back upstairs, she took a picture of the hidden door, then put her phone into her pocket. She stood there, hugging her portfolio to her chest and biting her bottom lip.

"You're awfully quiet. Do you have any questions?"

"Not at the moment. I feel overwhelmed. Being down there makes it easy to imagine the fear the runaways must have felt. It's so stark and closed-in, but it also represented hope. Can you imagine the mix of emotions they all felt? *What is this place? Who runs it? Will I be caught?* And they were so dependent on other people. They must have felt helpless too. *Can I really trust this person? I don't even know them.* To think that I had a relative who passed through here is emotional."

"It is emotional. And it's amazing too. Even more amazing is that there were people who risked their own lives to help them. People they could trust, like Prudence."

Jerri winced. "I guess there's a lesson there for me to learn."

"A lesson for all of us to learn. We all need each other, and I think in this day and age, when we're all so independent, it's easy to forget that. And it's not just us needing other people. It's also being unselfish enough to give of ourselves to others when it really counts."

"Do you mind if I sit down for a couple of minutes and review my notes? I want to make sure I've gotten all the nuances of my observations and feelings."

"I think that's a great idea. There are cookies there on the table, made fresh by Winnie."

LuAnn walked Jerri to a chair next to the fireplace.

Jerri picked up a plastic-wrapped package of cookies and sat on the couch. "Winnie does love to cook."

"That she does."

Jerri stared at the flames and sighed. "It's so peaceful."

"It is," LuAnn said. "I'll leave you to your thinking. I'm going to get some work done."

"Okay." Jerri was already looking through the pictures on her phone.

LuAnn grabbed a sponge from the kitchen and began to disinfect the empty tabletops in the café. She had just finished the last one when the front door opened and Atley walked in.

"Good morning," LuAnn said to him.

He nodded.

Jerri looked up, then she jumped from the couch and pointed at Atley. "That's him! That's the man whose been showing up at the hospital."

CHAPTER TWENTY

Jerri dropped her portfolio on the couch and ran across the room. Atley stood with crossed arms, feet planted, and a deep frown on his face.

A few scattered guests sitting in the café watched, surprise and worry on their faces.

LuAnn smiled at them. "Everything is fine. Just a surprise meeting." But no one looked at her. They all stared at Jerri and Atley.

Jerri halted two feet in front of Atley. "Who are you?

Tess stepped out of the office. "What's going on?"

"I don't know," LuAnn said, "but Jerri, you need to stop yelling, right now."

"But this is the guy I've seen coming and going at the hospital. I've never been able to catch him." Her voice was only slightly quieter as she poked at his wide chest with her index finger. "I want to know why you've been at the hospital and why you ignored me when I tried to catch you."

Tess's mouth hung open.

"I wonder if we could all go sit down and talk about this." LuAnn motioned toward the fireplace area.

She turned and smiled at everyone again. "It's fine, please don't worry." Then she herded Jerri and Atley to the fireplace area.

Atley dropped onto a chair. Jerri sat back down on the couch, perched on the edge of the cushion.

LuAnn sat on a chair next to Jerri. Tess joined them, sitting on the hearth.

"Well?" Jerri demanded. "Who are you, and why have you been at the hospital?"

Atley took a deep breath, then sighed. "The short story? I'm here because of your mother."

Jerri sat back, expression slack.

"Can you explain, please?" LuAnn asked him.

"I met Jerri's mother at the jail in West Virginia during a church service that I regularly hold. I'm an associate pastor, and I hold services for the incarcerated."

Janice came through the basement door with an armful of folded towels. LuAnn crooked her finger at her, inviting her to join them.

"I don't understand," Jerri snapped.

Janice dropped the towels on the bar and approached the group with wide eyes, standing next to LuAnn's chair.

"I got to know your mother at the church service at the penitentiary. She teaches Bible studies for the women."

"My mother teaches Bible studies?"

"She does."

"I can't believe that."

"She's one of the most dependable Bible study teachers we've had at the prison."

Jerri snorted. "If you think she's dependable, you don't know my mother."

"Perhaps you no longer know your mother." Atley's eyes glinted. "When she heard about Michele's fall and she couldn't get any information from the hospital, she asked me to check things out. Coming here was the easiest way to do so."

"Why didn't you just tell us who you are?" LuAnn asked.

Atley raised his brow. "Isn't that obvious? Jerri's mother didn't want to upset her. I knew you had been her teacher, but I didn't know what kind of people any of you were. If you felt about her like Jerri did, you might have asked me to leave. If Michele hadn't improved, I would have said something, but I wanted to check things out first. And since Michele appeared to be getting better so quickly, I decided to remain incognito."

"Why did you stay here at the inn?" Janice asked.

"Probably for the same reason you think I did. To observe and to make sure Jerri was in good hands. Despite Jerri's doubts, her mother is as concerned about her as she is about Michele."

"Spying," Jerri growled.

"Call it what you want to. My priority was to relieve your mother's mind. She has enough to deal with in her situation without the extra worries that her daughters will come to harm."

Jerri shook her head.

"Didn't it occur to you that you'd run into Jerri here?" LuAnn asked.

"I tried to avoid being in a position where she'd see me if she came in."

"You're a little hard to miss," Tess murmured.

He grinned. "That's true. I took my chances. But I wasn't expecting her to be here at this time of day, so I didn't watch closely enough."

"Were you in the hospital parking lot yesterday?" Tess asked.

His face turned red. "I was. I hoped you wouldn't notice me."

"Like Tess said, it's kind of hard to miss you," LuAnn said.

Confusion and anger flitted across Jerri's face. "I find this all hard to believe."

Atley crossed his legs. "I can understand that. Your mother can too, to tell you the truth. Even she can't believe how much she's changed since she met the Lord."

Jerri grunted her incredulity.

"I know many of your memories of your mother aren't good. She knows that too. But Jesus Christ changed her. She's not perfect, but she's changed."

Jerri shook her head. "Hard to believe. I mean, what if it's like those prison remorse things that people do, and it's not real?"

Atley shrugged. "I wouldn't be honest if I said that never happens. It does. I'm cautious, but I also have to give people who say they've repented the benefit of the doubt. Trust me, I've been disappointed. But if a prisoner doesn't give me a reason to think otherwise, I take them at their word. I could cause someone to turn away from God if I didn't take a step of faith myself and believe them. God gives them mercy. I do too." He turned to LuAnn. "I'm sorry if you feel deceived. This was an awkward situation. I overheard your conversation this morning.

My apologies for listening, but it was hard not to hear what that police officer was saying. I already had some concerns based on some things your mother relayed to me. But I had no idea that Michele's house had been broken into. Now I'm definitely concerned. Among other things, it certainly adds stress to an already stressful situation. That can't be good for Jerri or Michele."

Jerri watched him with crossed arms.

A light bulb went on in LuAnn's head. "Are you the one who followed Jerri home from the hospital that first night after the accident?"

"I am. I was concerned because I knew she would be upset and probably tired. I wanted to make sure she was safe. I realized when I got there that I was more obvious than I'd intended because the street was quieter than I thought it would be."

"You scared me," Jerri said, a resentful pout on her lips.

"My apologies. I was tired and wasn't thinking clearly myself."

"How did you know about Michele's accident so quickly?" LuAnn asked.

"Someone from Michele's church called the jail shortly after it happened to notify her mother."

He looked at Jerri. "Your mother knows how you feel about her, and she doesn't blame you. And by the way, you are just as your mother described. Intense and determined."

Jerri grunted and stared at her hands.

"If you don't want me to bother you, I won't, but I want to stay a little longer, if that's okay with you ladies." Atley glanced from Tess to Janice to LuAnn.

"You already have the room booked," LuAnn said.

"I guess we acted weird around you," Tess said.

"You did. Following me around, offering things. Like information about a local gym." Atley chuckled and flexed his right arm. "I do work out. But when I'm traveling, I can do floor exercises."

Tess shook her head. "Sorry about that. We were trying to find out if you were some sort of criminal."

"Because I have muscles?"

"We were looking for strangers in town."

"I don't understand," he said.

"They solve mysteries," Jerri said.

"You mean like Miss Marple? Is that what that police officer was referring to this morning?"

"Yes," LuAnn said.

"They're trying to figure out what's going on with Michele," Jerri said.

Atley's eyes narrowed. "Besides the break-in, why would you have reason to believe something is wrong?"

LuAnn, her friends, and Jerri all exchanged glances.

"You don't trust me," he said.

"We don't know you," Jerri snapped.

Janice eyed him. "My question is, why can't I find very much out about you online? It's like you hardly exist. Just a private Facebook page."

Atley laughed long and hard. "Now that takes the cake. You looked me up. The irony is, you won't find much about Atley Bradford online. That's my normal name. You'd find my name as associate pastor deep in my church's website, if you hunted long enough. That's about it."

"Why wouldn't we find much about Atley Bradford online?" Janice crossed her arms.

"Because I'm better known by my other identity. I'm also D. Wrecker."

Jerri gasped, and her jaw dropped.

"Dee…Wrecker?" LuAnn asked. "Am I missing something?"

"I have no idea who that is," Tess said.

"Me neither." Janice twisted her mouth to the side.

"He's a wrestler," Jerri said. "It's the letter *D*, not the name Dee. A play on words, sort of. 'D' instead of 'the.'" Jerri narrowed her eyes and studied him. "You are the Wrecker, aren't you? I wouldn't have recognized you on the street without your weird hair and outfit, but now I see it."

"A wrestler?" LuAnn asked softly.

"No wonder you have muscles on muscles," Tess said.

Atley laughed. "After I found the Lord, I got tired of smacking people around for a living, even when it was choreographed. God began to lead me in a different direction. I went from wrestling into prison ministry. Now I'm wrestling a different kind of enemy—the enemy of our souls. The inmates love it. My past career has been like a wide-open door to preach the gospel, so that's the name you'll find most of my information under."

"Knock me down with a feather," Tess said.

"Me too," LuAnn agreed.

Janice shook her head. "I can't say I'm a wrestling fan. I don't think any of us are."

"I'm not as big a fan as I used to be, although I still have friends in the business." Atley crossed his arms. "So, why do you think something is going on with Michele?"

LuAnn made a spur-of-the-moment decision to trust him. "Because of the phone call she made to Jerri asking her to come."

Atley fixed his gaze on Jerri. "She asked you to come? You didn't come because of her accident?" For some reason, he didn't sound surprised.

"No. It was more like she begged me to come." Jerri pursed her lips, then reluctantly continued. "She was scared of something."

"Something to do with her job, perhaps?" Atley asked.

Everyone went silent. They could very clearly hear the crackling of the fire, Winnie singing in the kitchen, and the guests talking in the café.

"You know about that?" Jerri finally asked.

"Michele has been in regular contact with your mother. Something happened that frightened her. Though she was very careful about what she said, for a number of reasons, your mother caught the gist of what was going on. She's the one who suggested Michele call you. Michele didn't think you'd come, but your mother insisted you would."

"Michele talks to Mom regularly?"

"She does."

"Seems your mother knows you well," LuAnn said to Jerri, then she turned to Atley. "You already thought there was something wrong?"

He shrugged. "I didn't know. Neither did her mother. Michele could be dramatic. But things have changed now that I know her house has been broken into. Was anything taken?"

"Not that I know of," Jerri said. "Her laptop is missing, but it was missing before the break-in."

"That's odd. Do you think there's imminent danger to Michele or yourself?"

"I don't know," Jerri said. "Nothing else has happened at the house since the break-in."

Atley stretched his back. "I'm sure there's much more to all of this, but I have a couple of things I have to do. Jerri, now that everything is out in the open, I'd like to go to the hospital with you and introduce myself to your sister. She should know how concerned your mother is."

"Perhaps I could go with you?" LuAnn suggested before Jerri could object. "I can get to the hospital around two thirty, after the lunch rush."

Jerri frowned at her but didn't argue.

"That's a good idea, and I can be there then." Atley unfolded his massive body from the chair. "I'm relieved all has been revealed. Makes things a lot easier, and I can walk around here without worrying about being seen—or being questioned." He laughed again as he headed for the front door.

Jerri watched him from the side of her eyes.

As the door shut behind him, Janice crossed her arms. "Well, that's something I didn't see coming."

"Maybe we should have, as big as he is," Tess joked.

"I saw him just fine at the hospital," Jerri said. "And I don't like being kept in the dark."

LuAnn patted Jerri's shoulder. "He did what he thought was best."

"That's what he says."

Tess stood. "It sounds to me like your mother might really care what happens to you and Michele. Maybe she has changed. And it sounds like she was depending on you to help your sister."

"As she always did," Jerri grumbled. "Jerri always picks up the pieces."

"You sound pretty resentful," LuAnn said.

"That's an understatement."

"Whatever your mother's motivations, Atley was doing what she asked, acting as a pastor," Janice said. "My husband would have done the same for one of his members. If what he says is true, Atley's not here for selfish reasons. In fact, he really didn't have to come at all."

Jerri rubbed her legs, and suddenly a tear trickled down her cheek. "I'm sorry, you guys. I don't mean to be rude and bitter, and I know I sound like it a lot. I'm probably a big disappointment to you."

"We aren't disappointed in you," Janice said quickly.

"Concerned is a better way to put it," Tess said. "You're so prickly. You suspect everyone of being against you."

"I know I'm prickly. But you don't know my mother. There were so many times she promised to change, but she never did. If you want to know the truth, I think I'm afraid to try to believe my mom again." Jerri started to cry in earnest. LuAnn's friends looked like they wanted to cry as well.

Janice grabbed a tissue from a box on the table next to the sofa and handed it to Jerri.

She sniffled and wiped her eyes and nose. "And now my eyes are leaking again. I'm not used to that, and I don't like it."

Everyone smiled.

LuAnn stepped back. "Why don't you go back to Michele's house and gather your thoughts? Prepare yourself to allow Atley to do what your mother asked him to do. Keep an eye on Michele. Maybe consider giving your mom another chance. Remember the mercy song? And I'll see you at the hospital in a while. We can talk more then, if you need to."

"Yes, ma'am." She grabbed more tissues and stuffed them in her pocket.

"And make sure you lock the front door on the house."

"I will." She picked up her portfolio, grabbed her coat, and disappeared through the front door.

"That explains my feelings about Atley," Tess said.

"You were right." LuAnn stood. "There was something different about him."

"Very different." Janice picked up her load of towels. "Like 'out of our realm of experience' different."

"I guess we can eliminate him from our list of suspects," Tess said.

"Pretty much," LuAnn replied, "but we should probably verify he is who he says he is."

"I can do that," Janice said. She raised her eyebrows. "This pastor's wife could use a walk on the wild side."

LuAnn laughed. "Now instead of hearing about detectives and old movies, we're going to start hearing about The Crusher and The Destroyer, huh?"

Janice rolled her eyes, and LuAnn, though she was still laughing, sent up a quick prayer that Atley Bradford, aka D. Wrecker, was on the right side of all this, whatever "this" turned out to be.

CHAPTER TWENTY-ONE

Michele had been moved from ICU to a regular room that morning. Atley was sitting in the waiting area when LuAnn and Janice arrived.

He waved at them. "I'm waiting for Jerri. I wouldn't dare go in Michele's room without her and risk making her mad."

"Smart man," LuAnn said. "We're going to go visit Michele and pray for her now before Jerri gets here, just so we don't make Jerri uncomfortable."

"Say." Atley leaned forward. "When you're done, would the two of you mind waiting around for me while I visit Michele? I won't be long. I want to have a word."

LuAnn looked at Janice, who nodded.

"Sure. We'll wait."

"Good. Thank you."

When LuAnn and Janice walked into her room, Michele was awake, with an iPad in her lap. She looked at them and beamed. "Hi. Jerri said you guys were coming. I remember you, LuAnn. And you must be Janice."

"You look great for someone who's been through what you have," Janice observed.

"Even better than yesterday." Michele's head was still bandaged, and she wore the typical ugly hospital gown, but she was so much improved, LuAnn wanted to applaud.

"I think it's all the prayer," Michele confided.

"I'd agree with that," LuAnn said, "and we're going to pray for you again."

"Good. Maybe I'll get better so quickly, I can go home early."

They joined hands, and Janice led the prayer.

When they were done, Michele laid her hands on top of the iPad. "Jerri said you're trying to figure out why I called her— why I was so afraid."

"We are," LuAnn said.

Michele frowned. "It's frustrating not to be able to remember everything."

"I can only imagine," Janice said.

"But Jerri's been doing her best to help me. She even went through my planner and my phone." She grinned. "I pretended to be mad at first, but I couldn't be. She's trying so hard. Just like all of you are. And I appreciate it."

They chatted for a few minutes until they heard Jerri outside the room, and the rumble of Atley's low voice.

Michele snickered. "Jerri said she's bringing someone to meet me. She doesn't know I already know who it is. My mother managed to get word to me and told me about Atley. But I'm just going to let Jerri think she's running the show. She's bossy like that, and if it makes her feel good, I'm for it. I'm just grateful she's here."

LuAnn and Janice laughed and headed for the door.

"LuAnn?" Michele said softly.

LuAnn turned around to face her. "Yes?"

"I'm sorry I didn't contact you all this time after you moved here. I guess because Jerri was so weird, and the two of us were kind of at odds, I figured you wouldn't want to talk to me or something. You were her teacher, after all."

"I'm sorry you felt that way, but I understand. And it's just fine. From now on, we'll talk."

"Good. Thank you." Michele heaved a sigh of relief. "Now send my prickly sister and my mother's friend in here. I can't wait to meet him."

Out in the hallway, Jerri pulled LuAnn and Janice away from Atley. "What if seeing him affects Michele badly?"

LuAnn and Janice exchanged smiles.

"I don't think that will happen. I think she'll be glad your mother was concerned enough to send Atley." LuAnn rested her hand on Jerri's back. "Now, at the risk of sounding bossy, go introduce him to your sister, and be nice."

Jerri rolled her eyes. "I'll try."

"By the way, he's exactly who he says he is," Janice said. "I checked. He has a prison ministry at the penitentiary where your mother is incarcerated. I even talked to the pastor of the church Atley attends, and he verified everything, including how successful Atley's outreach is."

Jerri put her hands on her hips. "You guys are really fast."

"We solve mysteries sometimes, remember?" LuAnn said. "Now, go on."

"Okay. I don't feel very nice, but I can play along."

"Good girl. Feelings often follow actions."

Jerri plastered a fake smile on her face and strode up to Atley. "Are you ready?" She flashed a glance at LuAnn, who nodded encouragement and bit her lip to keep from laughing.

A smile tugged at the corners of Atley's mouth. "I'm ready."

LuAnn and Janice strolled to the waiting area.

Janice giggled as she sat down. "She's a hoot."

LuAnn joined her. "She is spunky. Just wait until God gets a hold of her."

"She'll be a powerhouse," Janice said.

LuAnn smiled and breathed a prayer. *Lord, Your purposes in our lives are sometimes unexpected and surprising. I'm grateful. Thank You for Your mercy. And thank You for allowing me to be a part of Jerri's life as a teacher. But You're the Master Teacher. Thank You for teaching me.*

"I wonder what Atley wants to talk to us about," Janice said a few minutes later as they waited for him.

"Hard to say, but nothing will surprise me today." LuAnn pulled out her phone to check her email when a soft voice said, "Excuse me?"

LuAnn looked up. Fern's receptionist stared down at her.

"Hello. Tishia, right?"

"That's right. Tishia Collins." The woman's face twitched. If she had whiskers, she'd look like a frightened little mouse, but at least she wasn't ducking her head.

"I'm LuAnn Sherrill."

"I know. I remember."

LuAnn pointed at Janice. "This is my friend, Janice Eastman. Janice, this is Fern's receptionist."

Janice's eyes widened, and she extended her hand. "I'm glad to meet you. LuAnn told me about you."

"She did?" Tishia began to wring her hands. "Uh, I came to see how Michele is. Fern wants to know and sent me."

"Michele's sister and a friend are in there with her right now," LuAnn said. "But I'm sure Michele would love to see you. You're welcome to wait with us until they come out."

Tishia nodded but didn't sit. "Jerri is her sister's name, right?"

"Yes." LuAnn wondered how Tishia knew Jerri's name.

"So Michele is awake?"

"She is."

"I know that sometimes people lose their memory when they hit their heads. Did she lose hers?"

LuAnn was surprised by the question. "That's something you should ask her yourself."

"Okay." Tishia looked down at her shoes.

"Are you and Michele friends?" Janice asked her.

Tishia shrugged. "Not so much like going-out-to-eat friends, but she cleaned the office. She kept inviting me to church. I didn't go." Then Tishia clamped her lips shut and kept an eye on the hallway outside of Michele's room.

LuAnn tried a couple of other times to get Tishia to talk, but she wouldn't engage.

Finally, Jerri and Atley came out of Michele's room. Atley was smiling. LuAnn and Janice went to meet them, bringing Tishia along.

"Jerri, this is Tishia. She's a receptionist at McPherson's, one of the places Michele works. She wanted to say hello to Michele."

"Really?" Jerri studied Tishia, who mutely nodded. Jerri then waved in the direction of Michele's room. "Go on in. I'm sure she wants to see you. She wants to see everyone. I'll be there in a minute."

LuAnn rested her hand on Jerri's arm. "I'm planning to go by and see Michele's neighbor Mrs. Brewster to take her some cookies as a thank-you for helping you by watching Diesel."

"That's really nice of you."

"It was Winnie's idea. Mrs. Brewster has been good to you and Michele, and it gives me an opportunity to find out if she's seen anything lately that we could add to our list of clues."

Jerri's eyes widened. "Good ideas—questioning Mrs. Brewster and bribing her with cookies."

LuAnn cringed. "I'm appreciative for everything Mrs. Brewster has done for you. And I do want to ask her a few questions."

"Whatever." Jerri bounced on her heels. "Now I'd better go and check up on this Tishia person."

She scurried back to Michele's room. LuAnn and Janice headed for the elevator, accompanied by Atley.

"How was the visit?" LuAnn asked.

"Excellent. And I think it's possible that Jerri's warming up to me. She didn't snarl at all."

They all laughed as they rode the elevator down.

"I thought Michele was doing well," Janice said when they reached the lobby.

"Spiritually as well as physically," Atley said. "She's happy to have Jerri around, and it appears that she might be going home soon. But she still hasn't recovered her memory."

"That concerns me," LuAnn said, "for a number of reasons."

"It does me too." He opened the outside door for them, and they walked out into the cold air.

When they reached LuAnn's car, he rested a hand on the hood. "I wondered if you would mind filling me in about how you're proceeding in solving what's going on with Michele. Perhaps later on this evening at the inn? That might be easier than me trying to convince Jerri to talk to me. We're making progress in our relationship, but I don't think she's ready yet to personally confide in me."

"We'd be glad to do that, right, Janice?"

"Yes. You might have some ideas for us."

LuAnn unlocked the doors. "How about we meet tonight in our living area, maybe eight-ish? That will give us privacy. The guests have taken to sitting by the fireplace at night. Take the elevator to the fourth floor. We'll be expecting you." What she didn't say is that his size sometimes got people's attention, and she wanted to avoid anyone overhearing them.

Janice nodded. "I'm in. Tess is going shopping with Lizzie, her daughter, tonight, but I'm pretty sure she'll be back by then."

Atley smiled. "Good. I'll see you around eight."

December 17, 1857

At their house, Jason met Prudence, Herman, Sabina, and Sarah at the front door.

"What has happened?"

Prudence saw terror in his eyes.

"Your wife has sprained her ankle," Herman said. "This is my sister, Sabina, and Sarah, the child she ran with from our father's plantation."

"Prudence?" Jason whispered, helping her into the house.

"I believe I have witnessed a miracle tonight. But I must sit. I've sprained my ankle."

Jason removed Prudence's coat and settled her on a chair next to the fire. After retrieving a blanket and placing it over her shoulders, he looked over his shoulder. "Herman, explain thyself."

"Don't fear," Herman said, tending to his sister. "I mean none of you harm. I came to this state to stop my sister from taking this child north. God had other plans."

"The woman—Sabina—and the child, Sarah," Prudence said. "They're wet and cold too. Sabina may wear one of my dresses. The child can wear one of thy shirts."

"Yes." Jason showed Sabina their bedroom and clothes, then he returned to where Herman squatted next to the fire, and Prudence sat motionless in a chair, watching him.

"Herman?" Prudence said, softly.

He turned to Jason and Prudence. "I saw in your eyes the same Spirit I saw in the eyes of Charles Finney. I kept seeing his gaze in my mind while I lay in your bed. I remembered the words he wrote." Herman pulled the piece of paper from his pocket. It shook in his hands. "I don't understand what I'm feeling."

This was a holy moment. God was doing something in Herman's heart.

"Thee doesn't have to understand to surrender to God," Jason said.

"I am a violent man. I've done some violent things."

Prudence's heart stopped. Would she have to report him to the law? "Has thee committed murder?"

"No. But I might as well have, returning slaves to my father. This child is not the first I've hunted." Two tears fell down his cheeks, and he wiped them away with rough, worn fingers. "My heart is stricken with sorrow."

Prudence and Jason exchanged a glance.

"Shall we pray with thee, Herman? For forgiveness?"

"Yes, please."

"And afterward we will read to thee about a man named Saul."

CHAPTER TWENTY-TWO

LuAnn pulled onto Charles Street and parked along the road between Mrs. Brewster's Cape Cod and Michele's house. LuAnn had a soft spot for the New England architecture, with the dormer windows and sloping bedroom ceilings.

As she turned her car off, a curtain twitched in Mrs. Brewster's front room, but when she answered the door, she pretended to be surprised and splayed her hand over her heart.

"My goodness, I wasn't expecting anyone." She narrowed her eyes and got closer to LuAnn. "You're one of Jerri's friends, right?"

"I am. My name is LuAnn Sherrill."

"Have I seen you before?"

"Yes. I was there the morning of Michele's accident."

"That's why you look familiar." Mrs. Brewster stuck her neck out like a turtle and looked around outside as though searching for someone hiding. Then she focused on LuAnn again. "Is everything okay?"

"Yes, it is. I wanted to bring you some cookies as a thank-you for watching Diesel for Jerri." She held up the box Winnie had packed earlier.

"That's nice of you."

"They're fresh out of the oven today. Our cook just finished baking them."

Mrs. Brewster blinked. "You have a cook?"

LuAnn laughed. "Not for me personally. I'm one of the owners of Wayfarers Inn. It's a bed-and-breakfast. Our cook is named Winnie, and she's been baking lots of Christmas cookies."

"I've heard of that place. It's along the river, right?"

"It is."

Mrs. Brewster relaxed. "You want to come in for a minute?"

"Sure." LuAnn's teeth were beginning to chatter, and she was relieved to get out of the cold.

The inside of the house smelled like fried sausage. Mrs. Brewster pointed to a bold floral couch in the small front room.

"Can I get you anything? Coffee?"

"Maybe half a cup?"

Mrs. Brewster went to the kitchen then returned with two mugs and handed one to LuAnn.

She wrapped her hands around the cup, grateful for the warmth. "Thank you."

"You're welcome." Mrs. Brewster sat on a recliner and rocked slowly. "How is Michele doing?"

"Very well. She might be coming home soon."

"Oh, that's a relief. I was upset when she fell. I called one of her church friends as soon as it happened. Michele gave me some emergency phone numbers."

That explained how Michele's mother found out so quickly.

"She resembles her sister a little bit, although Jerri has a tart way of speaking."

LuAnn smiled. The description was apt.

"How do you know Jerri?" Mrs. Brewster asked.

"She was a student of mine years ago. I'm a retired teacher." LuAnn took a sip of the slightly bitter coffee. "How long have you lived here?"

"I moved in right after Michele. I was the one who found that little dog, Diesel. She was wandering along the side of the road." For the first time, Mrs. Brewster's face relaxed into a big grin. "As soon as Michele saw her, she fell in love. I'd kinda wanted to keep the little thing, but dogs are expensive. At the time I couldn't afford it. I could now, but Michele loves her so much. I can't take her away."

"I'm glad it worked out." LuAnn wondered how Mrs. Brewster's income had grown and how to ask her more about it. But she needn't have worried. Mrs. Brewster was eager to talk.

"My son lived here for a while, but he moved out, and suddenly I was without his rent. I wondered how I was going to make it, but then I got this boarder. He's part-time, but he pays well."

"The man I saw the day Michele fell?"

Mrs. Brewster nodded. "He travels for business. Michele overheard that he needed a place to live."

LuAnn's heart beat faster.

"He was at some place where Michele was cleaning and mentioned he was looking for a place to stay when he came into town. She sent him to me."

"That was nice of her."

"She is nice and so industrious. Goes to school to get a degree but isn't above cleaning people's houses. Even for free. She cleaned for me a couple weeks ago when I had the flu."

"That was kind of her." Even while she spoke, LuAnn wondered if Michele had seen something here that scared her.

"She's very kind in an old-fashioned way," Mrs. Brewster said. "She carries that Bible of hers around and can get a little preachy, but she also lives the talk, so I don't mind."

The best witness for God, LuAnn thought.

The older woman sipped her coffee and glanced toward the window.

"This seems like a nice neighborhood," LuAnn said.

Mrs. Brewster wrinkled her nose. "It can be, I guess, but there's also some riff raff."

"Really? Were you aware that someone broke into Michele's house?"

"Yes. And that's what I mean about riff raff. One day my tenant was outside, and this fancy-schmancy dark car pulled up. He was out there talking to whoever was in it. When he got inside, he said someone was lost and asked directions, but I think it was drug dealers, and my boarder just didn't know it."

LuAnn blinked. "Why drug dealers?"

"Who drives cars like that around here?"

Almost anyone could. Still, it could be a clue.

"But I'm not worried anymore," Mrs. Brewster said.

"No?"

"Nope." She leaned forward. "I think my boarder carries a gun."

LuAnn inhaled, but before she could ask any other questions, the front doorknob began to jiggle. Mrs. Brewster glanced at a clock on the table next to her chair. "That will be him. This is one of the evenings he stays here."

The man LuAnn had seen the day Michele fell walked into the house. He wiped his booted feet on the small carpet in front of the door. When he noticed LuAnn, a frown creased his forehead, then disappeared.

"I wondered whose car that was parked along the street." He was a big man, almost as tall as Atley, although not as muscled.

He wore blue jeans and a collared dress shirt under his leather coat. LuAnn wondered if he also wore a holster.

Mrs. Brewster craned her neck to look at him. "This lady is a friend of Michele's sister. She brought me some cookies to thank me for watching the dog. That means we have dessert tonight."

"That's nice." He walked into the small living room. "I'm Kenley Ackerman."

"I'm LuAnn Sherrill." She stood and extended her hand, all the while wondering if he really did carry a gun or if Mrs. Brewster's imagination had just run wild.

He took her hand briefly and looked her over.

Mrs. Brewster pushed herself to her feet. "I got sausage and eggs for dinner."

"Good enough. I'll be down shortly. I'm going to wash up. It was nice to meet you, LuAnn."

"You too." LuAnn faced Mrs. Brewster. "I should head home."

"Much as I like the company, I gotta finish dinner, anyway." Mrs. Brewster took LuAnn's mug and walked her to the door. "I'll be waiting to see if Michele needs any help. One good turn deserves another."

LuAnn left the house, and Mrs. Brewster quickly shut the door behind her. Then she noticed Randy parked in front of Michele's house. She went to the driver's side, and he rolled down the window. "Hey, LuAnn. I didn't expect to see you here. I'm just checking in to make sure all is well. I guess Jerri still isn't home."

"What's going on that you're so concerned about?" LuAnn asked.

He tapped his finger on his thigh and thought for a moment. "Knowing the situation, I guess. From what I've gathered, Michele has really pulled her life together. I want her and Jerri to feel safe."

"That's nice of you." He wasn't telling her the whole story. "Jerri is still at the hospital right now. I told her you'd been asking about her. Michele is out of ICU, and she might be going home soon."

"That's good news." His radio crackled, and he adjusted the volume. "Why were you here?"

"I brought some cookies to Mrs. Brewster to thank her for watching Diesel."

Randy nodded slowly. "I see."

"She's convinced her boarder has a gun."

Randy glanced at Mrs. Brewster's house. "How would she know that?"

"I have no idea, and she could very well be imagining things. She said she saw drug dealers on the street in a black car too." LuAnn waited to see if Randy would confirm or deny that possibility. He did neither.

"Just tell Jerri I've been keeping an eye on the house. Nothing has happened since the break-in, so I doubt there's any immediate danger here." Randy met LuAnn's gaze with furrowed brows. "But please be careful, LuAnn."

"Okay, I will."

Randy waited until LuAnn got back in her car and started the engine, then he drove away. As she pulled out, she noticed the upstairs curtains of Mrs. Brewster's house move. Maybe Mrs. Brewster wasn't the only one twitching the curtains.

CHAPTER TWENTY-THREE

That night, LuAnn headed for the kitchen to grab some cookies for the meeting with Atley. Some of their guests were in the café area with laptops. Three others sat in the fireplace area. LuAnn took a moment to check in with some of them before going to the kitchen. As she chatted, Merrill and Carleen Boycraft walked through the front door, faces wreathed in smiles and cheeks red from the cold, wearing look-alike coats and the same color jeans. Carleen waved and motioned for LuAnn to come and talk to them.

"Hello," LuAnn said when she reached them.

"Good evening." Carleen smiled broadly. "We were hoping to see you."

"Is everything okay?"

"Oh yes," Merrill said. "We just finished helping the kids complete the Christmas decor for the tour. Rosemary mentioned you'd been concerned it wouldn't be done in time."

"I didn't exactly say that, but I have to admit I did think it."

"It's all finished now." Carleen whipped out her cell phone. "I took pictures for you." She fiddled with the screen, then handed the cell to LuAnn.

LuAnn thumbed through the pictures. The décor was perfect, and she was relieved. However, in several of them she noticed a man sitting on a settee, wearing a suit. He looked a lot like the man she'd seen arriving at the Paglinos' the day before. She pointed at him. "Do they have other family members staying with them?"

"Oh no. That's a new business associate of theirs who stopped by while we were there." Carleen leaned toward LuAnn. "The kids hit a rough patch recently, but things have turned around for them."

Merrill tapped Carleen's shoulder. "Honey bun, you don't need to tell people their business. Nothing is for sure yet."

Carleen tapped her lips with her index finger. "You're right, sweetie. I'm just relieved."

LuAnn smiled at them. "Thank you for showing me the pictures. The tour will be perfect."

"Good," Merrill said. "Glad we could relieve your mind. Our minds are relieved too, after spending the whole day with the kids." Merrill took his wife's arm and tugged her toward the elevator.

"Oh, wait! More cookies!" Carleen pointed at a glass-covered plate on a side table in the sitting area. She made a beeline for them. "We're so happy to be staying here. The inn is fabulous, and so is the food. And the cookies are a big plus. We're going to tell all our friends when we get home."

"Thank you," LuAnn said. "And let us know if there's anything else we can do."

They stepped into the elevator, and the door shut. As LuAnn continued to the kitchen, she wondered what kind of business associates the Paglinos had gotten.

Atley arrived on the fourth floor right on time. LuAnn invited him to sit in their most comfortable armchair. After Tess handed out cookies and drinks, she and Janice settled on the sofa. Tom and Huck immediately headed for the newcomer. Tom hopped onto Atley's lap, and Huck was very interested in his shoes.

LuAnn sat in her usual chair, notebook in her lap.

Atley finished an oatmeal raisin cookie and sighed. "I'm going to have to work out extra hard when I get home. I'm pretty sure I'm gaining weight by the hour here. That cook of yours is a master chef."

"She is that," Janice agreed. "We're fortunate to have her."

"Without further ado, what do you ladies believe is really going on?" Atley asked.

"We're leaning toward some sort of money laundering scheme," Tess said.

"Why?" Atley asked.

They told him about Michele's planner, the fact that she was scared of something to do with a job, and what she'd asked her professor.

"Sounds like it's a good possibility, then. What have you learned?"

"Before we fill you in on everything we've collected up to this point," LuAnn said, "I want to go over what I discovered today."

Everyone nodded.

"Good news on the tour front. The Boycrafts told me they helped Rosemary and Frank finish decorating the house. They showed me pictures."

"That's great," Tess said. "That was the last big concern you had about the tour."

"It was. The only thing I have left now is to perfect my portion of the lectures for each house, which I'll do tomorrow." LuAnn picked up her pen. "But that leads me to the mystery. The Boycrafts just gave me some information that I need to add to our clues. They confirmed what we already knew, and that was the Paglinos were having money problems. But now they've gotten a new business associate who has fixed the issues. That associate appeared in a couple of the pictures I looked at. And when I was there yesterday, I saw the same person drive up to visit Rosemary Paglino in a dark blue sedan."

"Uh-oh," Tess said. "And remember that Winnie said Michele helped them clean out their basement one time?"

LuAnn and Janice nodded.

Atley looked skeptical. "That could all mean nothing."

"Or everything." Janice shook her head. "I'd really hate it if their daughter was up to no good."

"Tell me about it. They're so sweet. And they just finished telling me how much they're looking forward to telling their friends about Wayfarers Inn." LuAnn sighed. "In addition, I visited Mrs. Brewster, who is Michele's next-door neighbor. She implied that there's 'riff raff' in her neighborhood. A few weeks ago, Michele helped Mrs. Brewster clean her house for free, which may or may not mean anything. She also reported seeing a fancy dark sedan, which doesn't mean anything, really. And then she claimed her boarder might have a gun."

"Oh dear," Janice said.

"And another dark car," Tess added.

"As I was leaving, Randy showed up to check Michele's house." LuAnn turned to Atley. "He's the same officer you saw at breakfast. He took the police report when the house was broken into." She also filled Atley in on the conversation Randy had overheard between Michele and the older police officer in the foyer of the police station. "Anyway, I mentioned Mrs. Brewster's suspicions to him. He said he didn't believe there was any immediate danger at Michele's. He did warn me to be careful."

"He's awfully concerned about Jerri and Michele to be showing up like he has been," Tess said.

Atley nodded. "I'd agree with that. What else do you know?"

LuAnn opened her notebook. "To recap, here are our suspects so far—people who know Michele and have businesses that could possibly lend themselves to money laundering. Boomer and Patsy Aldrich. They know Michele because she cleaned for them. Boomer owns a couple of Laundromats and he was acting weird. Protective of his desk. Michele could have seen something he didn't want her to see.

"Then, as I mentioned, there's Rosemary and Frank Paglino. They knew Michele from church. She's been in their home. They run a dry cleaners, and they were having financial troubles. Her parents said they've gotten a new business partner, and things are looking up.

"We have Fern McPherson and her son, Melvin. Michele cleaned their string of hair and nail salons, as well as their office. Those businesses could lend themselves to money laundering. Fern has been acting abnormally controlling and emotional lately, and we're not sure why. I also overheard an argument between the two of them. Melvin wanted to fire someone. Fern didn't.

"Oh!" Janice said. "Remember that Tishia came by the hospital today? She said Fern sent her to check on Michele. She even asked if Michele had some memory loss."

"I'd forgotten that." LuAnn added that fact to her notebook, then proceeded. "Then there's Michele's boss, Doria, who owns the cleaning service where Michele works, but I can't imagine how she or her business could be involved in laundering money. However, Jerri doesn't like her."

"And finally, I can add Mrs. Brewster's boarder." LuAnn made a note in her journal. "He's new in town. He wears cowboy boots and maybe carries a gun."

Atley laughed. "So big muscles or cowboy boots mean someone could be a bad guy?"

"It's always possible." LuAnn grinned.

Atley stroked Tom's head. "Anything else?"

"Michele's laptop is missing. We don't know what happened to it. And according to Jerri, all the pictures have been wiped from her cell phone."

"If she had been collecting information, she might have stored it on her computer," Tess said.

"I should also mention that Jerri found Michele's car trunk open the night of the accident," LuAnn said. "And Michele's house was broken into."

"You think someone stole her laptop?" Atley asked.

LuAnn shrugged. "That or she did something with it and doesn't remember."

"What now?" Tess asked.

"I guess we continue gathering information. Tomorrow morning Jerri is helping Patsy Aldrich clean her house to make sure everything is spotless for the tour on Saturday. Tomorrow afternoon Brad is driving Jerri around to the salons. Hopefully she can be subtle enough to find things out without pointing a finger at herself."

Atley's head jerked in LuAnn's direction, concern etched on his face. "Who is Brad, and are you sure Jerri will be safe at the Aldriches?"

"Brad is a friend of ours, and we can pray that she'll be safe." LuAnn shrugged. "We can't stop her."

Atley sighed. "I don't have kids of my own, but in a small way, Jerri and Michele are beginning to feel like mine. It's disconcerting."

"I feel the same way," LuAnn said.

"I can't imagine that Patsy is guilty of anything," Tess piped in, "and that's who Jerri will be with in the morning, if that's any comfort."

"Good point," Janice said.

LuAnn nodded.

"Okay," Atley said reluctantly. "Sounds like you've been thorough. I have nothing I can add at the moment. I need to hit the hay. Tomorrow I'm headed back to West Virginia, just for overnight. One of my good friends has a family member who is sick. I'll return on Saturday night."

"We'll fill you in when you get back if there's anything new," Janice said.

He took a business card from his back pocket and handed it to LuAnn. "Here's my number if you need to reach me."

LuAnn wrote the number down in her notebook. "Hopefully we won't need it, but we'll call you if something happens."

"Thank you. And please, stay safe."

CHAPTER TWENTY-FOUR

Friday night LuAnn was tucked in a chair in the far back corner of the parlor, next to the piano, going over her presentation notes for the Christmas tour the next day. Chores were done. Janice and Tess were Christmas shopping. Winnie had made all the Mary Todd Lincoln White Cakes. Wayfarers Inn sat in Civil War era Christmas splendor, waiting in readiness for its part in the tour event. Fern hadn't even called to complain about anything.

LuAnn tried to settle and enjoy the decorations as well as the contented murmuring of their guests chatting in the café and in front of the fire, but underneath, her chest hummed with anxiety. She didn't need anyone to tell her why. Most of it had to do with Jerri, Michele, and their mystery. She looked down at her lap. Beneath her clipboard of tour notes was her notebook. She had no need to go over the clues. She'd done it so many times, everything she'd written there was etched in her mind.

They seemed no closer to solving the mystery than they had been at the very beginning. She shook her head. There had to be a connection somewhere that she'd missed.

Jerri had texted her, explaining that she was later than expected collecting clues from the hair and nail salons and the Aldriches. She and Brad had grabbed some dinner, and she'd be in contact soon. Perhaps she'd have a clue that would help.

When the bell above the front door sounded, LuAnn got up and peered around the corner, but it wasn't Jerri. Instead, Brad came into view.

She waved, and he made a beeline for her.

"Are you just returning from driving Jerri around? She said you went out to dinner."

"I am, and we did," he said.

She looked over his shoulder, expecting Jerri to pop through the door. "Where is she?"

"I dropped her at Michele's house. She's going to the hospital."

LuAnn's stomach took a nosedive. "Oh."

"You seem disappointed to see me," he joked.

She smiled at him. "No, not at all. In fact, I'm glad you're here. I'm trying to relax, but this mystery is pounding away in the back of my mind. I was just hoping for more news from Jerri to add to my notebook. Is she coming by here?"

"Nope. But she gave me the assignment of telling you everything she learned."

"Oh, good."

She walked Brad to her quiet little corner. They both sat down.

"Are Tess and Janice around?"

LuAnn shook her head. "Christmas shopping."

"Jerri told me you have a famous guest staying here."

"Famous in certain circles," LuAnn said.

"I'll admit, I've watched him a couple of times. Can't say I would have recognized him out of the ring though. Anyway, are you ready for tomorrow?"

"I am. Surprisingly, I'm at peace about the tour. I've done everything I can to assure the success of the event. The houses are ready. My introductions for each speaker are memorized, not that they're lengthy."

"I wouldn't have expected anything less. And I've been praying for you. About everything going on."

"Thank you." She stared at him, but his face grew blurry. Lately there were times she'd suspected he was praying for her, and then she'd find out he had been. She felt protected somehow, knowing he cared enough to remember her before their heavenly Father.

Brad leaned toward her and gently waved. "Earth to LuAnn? Hello? Are you ready to hear the information Jerri gathered?"

She blinked, and his face came into focus. "I am." She set aside her tour notes and opened her notebook.

"Good. Because I think this information will help you." Brad pulled a piece of paper from his pocket and unfolded it with a quirky grin.

She recognized Jerri's neat printing, which filled the length of the page. "Looks like a long list."

"It is. One of her teachers somewhere along the line must have been a list-maker, because she's an expert."

LuAnn chuckled. "Guilty as charged."

He sat up straight, dramatically straightening his shoulders. Then he held the paper out in front of him, shook it energetically, and cleared his throat.

"What are you doing?"

"Following directions. Jerri said I had to be very precise. This is me being obedient."

LuAnn shook her head. "She's something."

"She is that. To tell you the truth, she might have missed her calling. Army general comes to mind." He cleared his throat again, his twinkling eyes intent on the list. "Jerri's insights and observations. Number one." He spoke slowly, in monotone, and lifted one finger. Then he paused, eyeing LuAnn with a grin over the top of the paper. "Just so you know, I'm reading this list verbatim, per Jerri's instructions."

"I gathered that, but a dry repetition of 'just the facts' will become tedious quickly. Would you mind summarizing for me? In your own words? And maybe with some verbal expression and extra description?"

He sat back in the chair, mouth open, affecting shock. "You're telling me to disobey a direct order?"

"I'll take full responsibility."

"Okay…as long as you promise." He pretended to shake with fear.

LuAnn held up her hand. "On my honor, I promise, if the topic arises, I'll explain to Jerri that I ordered you to tell me, in your own words, what she discovered."

"All right." Their shared laughter reminded LuAnn once again how much she'd miss him if he weren't around anymore.

Brad crossed his legs and put the paper on his lap. "The first stops we made were at the McPhersons' salons. Quite a few of the hairdressers, or stylists, as I learned they're called, know Michele. In fact, some of them have been to see her at the hospital, Jerri just didn't know who they were. That made Jerri's interrogation of them easier. And just so you know, I was in the car for these conversations. I didn't hear them personally. I thought it would be weird to follow her around like a bodyguard."

"It would have given them all something interesting to discuss after you left though."

"True."

LuAnn nodded. "Go on."

"A few of them are looking for other jobs. They feel like they aren't being taken seriously. The rest don't care."

"That would be typical of any company."

"It could be. But a couple of the hairdressers were irritated because the product order was messed up. Again. They called Fern, and she promised to fix it but hasn't done anything yet. And by the way, I don't know what 'product' is."

"Product is what they call shampoo and the like. And that doesn't sound like a big deal except that Fern is usually on top of everything."

"Gotcha." He glanced at the list in his hand. "A couple of the girls said that Melvin had been by the salons earlier today asking after his mother."

"Odd."

"And this could mean something. Jerri said 'mouse girl,' has been in several of the salons, doing some 'office stuff' for Fern. That only started recently."

LuAnn paused. "Mouse girl?"

"That's how Jerri referred to someone named Tishia." Brad shrugged. "I don't think I've met her."

LuAnn smiled. "She's the receptionist at the McPhersons' office. Not the nicest nickname, but it is apropos. Tishia acts like she's scared of her own shadow." LuAnn made some notes in her notebook. "Is that all?"

Brad shook the paper. "You see this list? I'm only a third of the way through."

"Good. I want more."

"And you shall have it. We took the liberty of checking out the Paglinos' dry cleaning business."

LuAnn inhaled. "You know what? That's something I hadn't even thought of doing."

"Well, your efficient student did. Their business venue, or should I say, their *old* business venue, was on the same street as a newer dry cleaner—competition, it looked like, which Jerri surmised could have led to a drop in income. We saw a sign on the front of their old building that said, 'TEMPORARILY CLOSED—RETURNING SOON AT TWO NEW LOCATIONS.' So we drove to both new locations, and low and behold, they are building brand-new dry cleaners inside two newer buildings in really good parts of town. Jerri went inside to interrogate the construction workers but got nothing from them except that they were under orders to work overtime to get things done, no expense spared. And if you were worried about Jerri's safety, I'll ease your mind. In my position of chauffeur-turned-bodyguard, I accompanied her to the buildings, where I waited, freezing, right outside. And from where I was standing, the workers inside just looked amused."

"Thank you for being her protector." LuAnn smiled and made some notes. "Sounds like the Paglinos have come into some money or investors."

"That's what Jerri thought. And we also drove by the offices of Sanders' Spotless Cleaning Service, however, Doria wasn't there. The girl who works for her said she was gone for a couple of days."

"It sounds like Jerri thought of everything. What else?"

He grinned. "I've saved the best for last. The following incident happened earlier in the day at the Aldriches'. I wasn't with her."

LuAnn leaned forward.

"Jerri was cleaning for Patsy, who at one point had to take a phone call. While she chatted in the kitchen, Boomer cornered Jerri and informed her that he wasn't keen about anyone cleaning for them. He wanted her to quit."

"Oh no."

"Oh yes," Brad said solemnly, but his eyes were smiling. "As you can well imagine, cornering Jerri is akin to cornering a wildcat. She comes back fighting, claws first. Or should I say, mouth first. According to her, Boomer panicked and shushed her, glancing at the kitchen as though terrified Patsy would come out, rolling pin in hand. Then he politely asked Jerri to come to his office for a chat."

"He didn't."

"Yes, he did. From what Jerri said, once they were in his office, she demanded to know, in her words, what his problem was. From her description, I suspect Boomer quickly realized that in Jerri he was up against someone of equal stubbornness and, uh, vocal volume as himself, unlike her more pliant sister, so he spilled the beans." Brad wiggled his eyebrows. "Things are rough when there are beans involved."

"Ha ha. Keep talking."

"Short story? He's not guilty. Long story? Boomer has been developing a business plan to add a new branch to his Laundromat empire. Self-service dog washes. It's supposed to be a surprise for Patsy, who has a plethora of dogs, as Jerri put it, that she loves like children. It will also be the first self-service pet wash station in Marietta. He had all the plans on his desk when Michele was cleaning there, and he was afraid she might see what he was doing and tell Patsy, or worse, tell someone else who would take his latest business idea and run with it."

"Self-service dog washes?"

"Mm-hmm. Like a Laundromat for animals where you can put money in and wash and dry your dog or cat, so you don't have to mess up your house or your bathroom."

"What you're saying is that Boomer isn't guilty of laundering money?"

"Probably not. In fact, he told Jerri to come and clean as often as she'd like until Michele returns. In addition, he offered

Jerri a spot in his company, if it grew. She told him she'd think about it after she has her doctorate, if she can't find a good job in her own field."

"Mutual respect of strength of personality there." LuAnn laughed. "Well, it appears we only have three suspects now, two of which are the most viable. I'm kind of leaning toward the Paglinos, but that makes me feel horrible because of the Boycrafts. And I have no idea how Mrs. Brewster's boarder fits in with this. If I could place him with the McPhersons or with the Paglinos that would work." She explained to Brad about the possibility that Kenley Ackerman carried a gun.

He frowned. "That doesn't necessarily mean he's up to no good. And Jerri didn't mention seeing anyone like that."

LuAnn sighed.

Brad folded the paper and handed it to her. "It's getting late. At the risk of sounding bossy, I think you should go get ready for bed and relax. Maybe read a good book. After you tell Tess and Janice all these details, of course."

"Of course."

"But my advice is that you don't sit up late tonight chatting. You have a long day tomorrow."

"That is excellent advice," LuAnn said. "I don't know if it's possible, but I can try."

"Oh, something else." He leaned toward her. "I have decided to give one more thing above and beyond the call of duty to the cause of the Marietta Christmas in History House Tour."

She frowned. "You've done so much already. You don't have to do anything else."

He held up a finger and chuckled. "Wait until you hear my offer, because I might have realized, like Jerri being an army general, that I've missed my calling."

She waited.

He put his hand on his chest. "I'd like to be your chauffer tomorrow. I'll drive you from place to place and stand guard at your side and protect you."

LuAnn had an overwhelming urge to hug him. "I'd love that."

CHAPTER TWENTY-FIVE

As promised, Brad chauffeured LuAnn all day long on Saturday, driving her from house to house, keeping her supplied with bottles of water. He seemed to sense when she needed to talk and when she needed to be quiet. When she had something to say, he listened intently as she spoke, occasionally nodding. Things seemed back to normal in their relationship; in fact, they seemed closer than ever.

"Penny for your thoughts?" Brad said as he drove toward the inn.

LuAnn turned to him, seeing his familiar silhouette against the window. "Too many to list. I guess I'm relieved that the first day of the official Marietta Christmas in History House Tour is over. Tomorrow's free house tours are the home stretch."

"I'd call it a resounding success. Jerri seemed to enjoy herself."

"She did. She's gotten quite chummy with Katie Mironoff."

"I noticed that," Brad said. "The only fly in the ointment, if you could call it that, is that Fern McPherson didn't show up. Don't you think that's strange?"

"On the face of things, yes, especially since the girls at the salon said that Melvin had been looking for her yesterday."

"Melvin said she left on a buying trip to some expo or something. He seemed slightly annoyed but acted like it was nothing."

"I noticed that too."

LuAnn fell silent again. In some ways, Melvin's explanation made sense. The hairdressers in the salons had said they were having problems with product delivery. But LuAnn would never have imagined Fern missing the house tour. Still, she had been acting erratic. The simple explanation could be that since she couldn't take charge of the tour, she turned her attention to the one place she could be boss—her business.

When Brad finally pulled into the parking lot of the inn, LuAnn felt like someone had pulled her plug. Soft snow fell, and the lighted inn had the appearance of a watercolor painting.

He turned the car off and faced her. "The hardest part of the tour is over."

"So it is." She laughed softly. Bags rattled in her lap. They'd stopped and picked up some sandwiches for a quick dinner. No one felt like cooking or even heating anything up. "Thank you for driving me around today. I knew I'd be tired, but I didn't expect this level of exhaustion."

"It's been a hard week. Between Jerri being here, the mystery of Michele, and the tour, I'm amazed you're still functioning."

"To tell you the truth, I am too. And I hope there's cake left over. After I eat my sandwich, I might even have two pieces. I haven't eaten a thing since breakfast."

"With all those desserts people served today? That doesn't seem fair somehow." He grinned at her. "I probably ate enough for both of us. You ready to go inside?"

"I am."

He got out and ran around to the passenger side of the car and opened her door. Flecks of snow fell on his face, melting on his cheeks.

Always the gentleman.

He took the bags from her hands and helped her out. Then he tucked her arm in the crook of his. "Don't want you falling. You have those fancy shoes on."

"Don't remind me. I'll never, ever wear shoes like this again when I'm going to be on my feet all day. I'm surprised I don't have bleeding blisters or a displaced vertebra. I'm too old for any kind of heel. From now on it's granny shoes for me. Lace-ups with rubber soles."

"Not a good look with a dress," Brad said with a sideways glance. "Perhaps moderation instead? A feminine shoe with a low heel?"

She narrowed her eyes at him. "And how would you know? Have you ever worn a feminine shoe? Men have it easy. You guys can wear loafers or lace-ups or boots in black or brown. The same styles all the time if you want to."

He threw his head back and laughed. "I can't argue with that. And I won't ever again say anything to you about shoes, especially when your feet hurt."

They both chuckled as he guided her carefully across the parking lot. His closeness brought her warmth. Just as Brad reached for the knob, the door flew open. Tess and Janice appeared in the doorway.

"At last!" Tess said.

"We've been waiting for you." Janice motioned for LuAnn to hurry.

"Wow. I didn't expect this kind of greeting. Are you guys that hungry? We came as quickly as we could."

"It has nothing to do with food," Tess said urgently.

Brad helped her into the foyer, concern wrinkling his forehead.

Anxiety constricted her chest. "Has something happened?"

"Yes, it has," Janice said.

"What is it?"

"Come inside and we'll tell you." Tess waved them in like a crossing guard.

Brad removed his scarf and coat, and LuAnn did too. She quickly hung them all up. Then Brad held her arm as she slipped off her shoes.

She looked around the room. "Surprisingly empty in here."

"Some of our guests checked out this afternoon," Tess said. "Those still here either went out to dinner or are eating in their rooms. And Winnie's finally gone home. She really worked overtime today."

"She did," LuAnn said, hugging her purse. "I need to use the ladies' room. Can this wait just a minute?"

Everyone nodded, but she saw the frustration on her friends' faces.

When she returned, everyone stood in a tight group looking down at Tess's phone. They all turned to face her. Brad's brows were drawn together in a frown, and he clutched the bags of sandwiches in tight fists.

"Someone left us a note," Tess said when LuAnn reached them.

"What kind of note?"

"Vaguely threatening." Tess handed LuAnn her phone. "This is a picture. We already called Randy, and he came by and picked it up."

LuAnn studied the photo of a piece of paper with printing on it. *Stop looking. It's none of your business.*

"A threat, but not really a threat," LuAnn murmured. "Where did you find this?"

Tess took her phone back. "Underneath the cake plate on the table. We didn't find it until we were cleaning up."

"And there's no way to know who left it," Janice said. "Too many people came through. At one point, the whole crowd was gathered around the table, oohing and aahing over the white cakes, as well as the table decorations that Winnie made."

LuAnn rubbed her temples. "I'm having trouble thinking."

"How about I go get plates for you ladies," Brad offered. "I've been coming here long enough to know where things are. I think LuAnn needs to eat something sooner than later." His tone was lighthearted, but LuAnn read the concern in his eyes.

"Good idea." Tess took the bags from Brad and pointed toward the furniture around the fireplace. "Go sit down,

LuAnn. Sorry. I was so upset by the note that I wasn't even thinking about how tired you must be."

Brad disappeared into the kitchen while LuAnn dropped onto the sofa, put her purse on the floor, and curled her legs under her on the couch. Janice and Tess sat on chairs opposite her.

"At least the main tour event went well. Tomorrow will be a piece of cake. Now we can concentrate on this mystery," Janice said. "Two of our suspects were here. Melvin and the Paglinos.

"I still don't understand why Fern went out of town like she did," Tess said.

"Me neither," LuAnn said. "I tried to call her cell phone to tell her how well the tour was going, but there was no answer."

"Melvin said she's okay," Tess said. "But he seemed annoyed or irritated or something."

"He did." Janice tapped the paper in her hand. "At least we know Fern didn't leave the note."

"Yes, but she could have ordered him to do so and then purposely not been here to throw suspicion off herself."

Janice frowned. "Bottom line, someone knows you're investigating."

"That's creepy," LuAnn said. "How did they find out?"

"It wouldn't be hard, really," Tess said. "Someone could have overheard something. Or maybe Jerri let the cat out of the bag."

"Or Winnie let on," Janice suggested.

"I guess any of us could have, just by coming across too obvious," LuAnn said.

Brad returned with plates and a tray holding glasses of ice water. "Wasn't sure what you wanted to drink, but I figured we could all use some hydration after a long day."

"We need to hire you," Tess quipped. "You have initiative."

Brad smiled, but his eyes were on LuAnn.

"Let's eat," she said. "I need to get my ability to think back."

Brad handed everyone plates and sat on the couch with LuAnn. They ate and tossed ideas back and forth, but even when the sandwiches were long gone, and LuAnn was stuffed with a piece of cake, they hadn't reached any conclusions.

"Back to square one." LuAnn stifled a yawn. "But I do think if anyone meant us immediate harm, he or she wouldn't have left this note."

"We're all too tired to think anymore," Tess murmured.

"Even I can't seem to cogitate coherently," Brad quipped.

They all laughed. LuAnn glanced at him with a fond smile. His humor was just one of the many things she appreciated about him. "I agree with you. And since none of us seems to be cogitating coherently, perhaps we should finish our hot chocolate, enjoy the last little bit of warmth from the fireplace, and call it a day. Tomorrow, as they say, is another day."

"Well, Miss Lu, I think that's a mighty fine idea," Janice said.

They quietly sipped hot chocolate until Atley strode through the door, frowning. But when he saw them, he forced a weary smile and joined them.

Brad stood, introduced himself, and shook Atley's hand.

"Would you like some hot chocolate?" Janice asked. "We could even scrounge up something for you to eat, if you're hungry."

"Thank you, but no. I grabbed something on the road." His smile deepened. "You guys are the best innkeepers, and I've stayed in some mighty fine places."

"They are that." Brad sat back down. "Care to join us?"

"I will for a minute." He sat on the fireplace hearth and looked around the room. "How was the historical tour? Looks like everything survived intact."

"I'd say the tour was successful." LuAnn glanced around. "Tomorrow we'll have the general public coming by to view things, but that's nothing compared to today."

Tess and Janice nodded.

"It's the note the ladies found when they were cleaning up that concerns us," Brad said.

"Note?" Atley knit his brows.

Tess handed him her phone. He looked at it, and his nostrils flared. "I was afraid of something like this."

All four of them straightened in their seats.

"What are you talking about?" LuAnn asked.

"I did a little investigating of my own. Because of the contact I have with prisoners in the correctional facility, I'm sometimes privy to an underworld grapevine. After meeting with the three of you the other night, I called a few people who know a few people who promised to look into things. I discovered some disturbing news. There's a criminal element slowly making its way into Marietta. Money laundering to cover some illegal gambling over in West Virginia."

"Oh no," Tess whispered.

Brad's body tensed. Concern creased Janice's face.

The news hit LuAnn like three shots of espresso. "I need to write this down." She reached into her purse for her notebook. "Do you really think this has something to do with Michele?"

Atley shrugged. "She was frightened by something. Her journal had the word laundering in it. She wanted to go to the police, but she was afraid. A young woman in her circumstances doesn't suddenly become afraid for nothing—do you agree?"

LuAnn slowly nodded. "I still wonder why she didn't just ask someone here to help her."

"Because she didn't know who to trust?" Tess suggested.

Brad leaned forward. "Or maybe she was afraid people would think she'd backslidden or gotten into something illegal?"

"All possibilities," Atley said. "She'd only recently turned her life around. Sometimes people are afraid their past will color their present in other people's eyes."

"So, who are we looking for?" Janice asked. "I assume people like that aren't going to look like gangsters in trench coats with bad James Cagney accents who hang outside speakeasies at night threatening people."

"Janice, you really need to lay off the movies," Tess said.

"That wasn't from a movie—at least not a movie I saw recently."

Atley chuckled, then grew serious. "No. They'll be savvy and take their time, building up contacts and looking for people to use. But what concerns me most right now is that all of you could be more involved than you think."

The tightness in LuAnn's chest increased.

"I don't know much more than that, and I'm too tired to speculate. I need to go sleep. That three-hour trip both ways is a lot of traveling in one day. I just wanted to warn you. Oh, and one more thing."

Everyone looked at him.

Atley stood. "Unfortunately, I have to return to West Virginia tomorrow. I came back tonight to pick up my laptop and the few belongings I left in my room. My friend's family member died. I have to be there." He paused. "I trust Jerri and Michele are in good hands."

"They are," LuAnn said, even though she wished he could stay. Having him here made her feel more secure.

Atley nodded at everyone, then headed up the stairs.

"Well the plot thickens." Tess broke the silence.

"This also adds to our concerns for Jerri, as well as Michele," Janice said.

LuAnn finished jotting the information in her notebook. "Especially since she's coming home from the hospital on Monday."

Brad rubbed his shoulder and looked at his watch. "I hate to say this, but I have to go too. Although I'm beginning to think I might need to rent a room here for the next week or so to stand guard."

"We'll have an opening tomorrow," Janice said. "Meanwhile, I'm taking the trash to the kitchen and heading for bed."

"We'll tidy up." Tess grabbed empty mugs and walked to the kitchen. "You go walk Brad to the door."

LuAnn was too tired to even roll her eyes at her friends' obvious attempts to leave her and Brad alone. And really, she didn't mind.

She walked him to the door barefooted. "Thank you for everything today."

"You're very welcome. It was my privilege to drive you around. I plan to do the same tomorrow."

"You did a fine job. So good, in fact, I'll take you up on that offer."

"Good, because I'm afraid I would have insisted." He gave her a quick hug. "Go on now. Get some rest. And please be safe. All of you."

December 19, 1857

Jason and Prudence stood at the door of their house, watching Herman Douglas help his sister mount the chestnut filly. Then he gently lifted Sarah to sit in front of her.

"Thank you," Sabina said to Prudence and Jason. "For everything. I'm relieved I can continue my journey now and no longer have to hide."

Herman nodded. "I'll be with her to protect her and Sarah."

"Will thy father seek thee?" Prudence asked.

"I'm sure he'll send someone to find us, but we will be safe by then." Herman smiled at his sister. "We will begin again."

Sabina looked down at her brother. "We don't need the wealth of our family to be content."

"I believe my sister has a Bible verse for that." Herman laughed. "She has a Bible verse for everything."

"I do. Paul said, 'I will be content in whatever situation I am in. I know how to be poor. I know how to be rich.'" She smiled. "In my own words."

"And none better," Prudence said. "We will pray for thee."

"Thank you," Sabina said.

As they headed down the path toward town, Sarah leaned around Sabina to wave at them.

"God's mercy is new every morning," Prudence said to Jason as they stepped back into their house.

CHAPTER TWENTY-SIX

LuAnn woke on Monday morning feeling like a new person. For the first time in weeks, she'd had a solid night's sleep. Now she felt ready to tackle the mystery of Michele with a mind unclouded by any other major responsibilities.

Sunday had passed uneventfully. No more semi-threatening notes had been left. And best of all, more people than LuAnn had anticipated came out for the free open houses, which led to more donations for the homeless shelter. All in all, the first Marietta Christmas in History House Tour had been a success.

After breakfast, LuAnn had called Fern to give her the good news, but there was still no answer. LuAnn left another message. Then she sat at a table in the café with a last cup of coffee and her notebook to check over her clues one more time before she headed upstairs to clean guest rooms. Tess was in the office, making a grocery order on the computer. Janice was finishing up some laundry in the basement.

The front doors opened and shut as people came and went, but LuAnn paid them no mind until she heard Jerri's voice.

"LuAnn!

She looked up. Everyone in the café turned around.

LuAnn put her finger to her lips and smiled.

Jerri bounded over to the table. "I have some things to tell you."

Tess came out of the office, chuckling. "Hello, Jerri. I would have recognized your voice from the third floor."

Jerri's cheeks reddened. "Sorry."

"I'm done with my work here. You two can have the office if you need some privacy."

LuAnn stood and crooked her finger at Jerri. Once they were in the office, she shut the door.

"Sorry about that. I'm trying not to be loud." Jerri sighed.

"I know you are. Now tell me what was so urgent. Does this have to do with our mystery?"

"Part of it." Jerri's body vibrated with excitement. "First, I get to bring Michele home late this afternoon. That's why I'm running around. I'm buying stuff like bottled water, Cheerios, milk, and ramen noodles. But the most important thing I wanted to ask you is can you come over to eat an early dinner with us? Like all of you? Like a celebration?"

"I'll see what I can do about Tess and Janice, but yes, I can be there."

Jerri's face seemed lit from within. "I don't know what we'll eat, but I'll look around the grocery store."

"How about I bring pizza?" LuAnn offered quickly, not wanting to chance Jerri's choice in food.

"That would be great. Two of Michele's close friends from church are coming by, as well as her pastor and Doria, who absolutely insisted she had to see Michele. But I asked them to come after seven. That will give the five of us time to think.

Michele's had a couple of pieces of memory return—at least we think that's what it is. And I'm hoping being at home will trigger more."

"What has she remembered so far?" LuAnn asked.

"Unfortunately, she remembers feeling really afraid. She remembers a loud voice and something about her car and driving fast."

"Did she feel threatened?"

Jerri shrugged. "She was afraid, but threatened? I don't know. She also remembers spreadsheets. That could mean nothing because she was studying accounting, but it could also mean she saw something she shouldn't have. They were on a desk."

LuAnn waited.

"That's it."

LuAnn felt a little deflated. She wanted some clear-cut answers, not bits and pieces.

"Anyway, I wanted to tell you. I have to get back to the hospital and make sure the doctors are doing what they're supposed to be doing. Michele has to take it easy. That means I have to make sure she's going to be fed, which won't be hard because Winnie arranged for meals to be delivered from their church starting tomorrow."

"How nice!"

"It's a good thing, because I can't cook. I eat frozen dinners at home." A smile played on Jerri's lips, but then it died. "As the days go by here, what you said to me about God and His mercy keeps coming back to my mind. How He uses people. Like there's you and Tess and Janice who have gone above and beyond to take me in and help me. And Atley, who actually turned out to be okay. I even kind of like him, although I still have doubts about my mother. And then there's Winnie and her church—they've all stepped up to help Michele *and* me. I'm someone they don't know, and I even tried to reject them all at first. I was obviously someone who turned her back on God. Worse, someone who had turned her back on her sister." LuAnn thought she saw tears glinting in Jerri's eyes. "Did you know that Michele and her church gang prayed for me regularly?"

"I believe it," LuAnn said softly. "You know, it's easy to blame God when people don't live up to our expectations, especially people who are supposed to protect us and love us, like your mother failed to do. People have free will and make their own choices, but if we allow God to, He'll bring in other people to meet those needs in us."

Jerri bit her lip in thought. "I can see that." Then she looked at her watch. "I gotta go. I'll see you at four?"

"We'll be there."

As soon as Jerri left, Tess came back to the office, followed by Janice with a handful of towels.

"So, spill. What was Jerri yelling about?" Tess asked.

LuAnn filled them in on what Jerri had said.

"That means there's hope Michele will recover her memory," Janice said.

"I think so. Meantime, how would you two like to help celebrate Michele's homecoming? Jerri invited us to come over this afternoon. I told her I'd bring pizza."

"That would be splendid!" Janice clapped her hands.

"I'm all for pizza," Tess said. "And I'll look forward to seeing Michele out of the hospital bed."

As LuAnn pulled her car onto Charles Street, light snow fell. Jerri would be arriving shortly. The aroma of pizza wafted from the passenger seat where Tess held three Over the Moon boxes. "I'm so hungry smelling the pizza, I could eat the cardboard," she murmured.

"Tell me about it," Janice said from the backseat.

"Do you have that flashlight?" LuAnn glanced in the rearview mirror. "Jerri said she might need it, although she thinks she has a light on her cell phone. I have one on mine."

"Yes," Janice said. "It's one I got from beside my bed. Small but powerful. Do you know why she wants it?"

"She didn't have time to say much when she called. Just something about a crawl space and Michele's memory. I'm not sure exactly what's going on. Jerri was talking really fast."

"And loudly, no doubt," Tess said.

They all laughed.

"Perhaps something is hidden in the crawl space," Janice suggested. "Maybe the laptop."

"That's what I'm thinking," LuAnn said.

Tess shifted the pizza boxes. "We can hope."

"Jerri said they'll be inundated with company later this evening, after seven. But we'll be done by then."

LuAnn was unable to park in front of Michele's house. Someone across the street was having a get-together, and they'd taken the parking. She found a space farther down the street. "We'll have to walk in the snow. At least it's not heavy."

"She should be here by the time we get to the front door," LuAnn said.

The three of them trudged up the sidewalk, pizza boxes in hand, when Jerri pulled into the short, narrow driveway. She hopped out of the vehicle with the vitality of youth, skipped around the front of her car to the passenger side, opened the door, and helped Michele climb out.

"She sometimes makes me tired watching her," Tess said. "Where does she get that energy?"

"Calories," Janice suggested. "Have you seen what she eats when she eats?"

"Yes, but she's skinny as a rail," Tess grumbled.

Janice nodded. "She must use all her food calories to bounce around. And any extras wear off through some sort of scientific osmosis thingy that totally bypasses her fat cells."

"Maybe we'll catch that scientific osmosis thingy from being in proximity to her, and we'll be able to eat all the Christmas cookies we'd like." Tess turned and grinned at her friends.

They reached the porch as Jerri unlocked the front door.

"Hey, you guys!" Jerri said as she pushed it open.

Michele smiled over her shoulder. "Thank you for coming."

Inside, Diesel danced excitedly at Michele's feet. She scooped her up. "Hello, my little girl. I've missed you." The dog licked her face, whining and wiggling in her arms.

"You need to sit down," Jerri said to Michele. "Let's go to the kitchen, and then Tess can put the pizza boxes down."

"Already bossing me around? It hasn't been thirty minutes since I left the hospital." Michele laughed and walked down the short hall to the kitchen.

"Trying to control the world is a hard habit to break," LuAnn said as the four of them followed Michele.

"Yeah, tell me about it," Jerri grumbled.

In the kitchen, Michele pointed at the table. "You can put the pizza there."

"I have water in the refrigerator. Paper towels on the counter. Dishes are in the cupboard. Ice in the freezer, obviously." Jerri turned to her sister. "Are you okay? Before I go investigate that crawl space?"

"I am, but I'm not made of glass. And I'm going upstairs with you."

For a minute LuAnn thought Jerri would argue, but she didn't.

"Here's the flashlight." Janice handed it to Jerri. "We're excited to hear what you think you've discovered."

"It's just conjecture," Michele said. "Because my memory feels like it's a series of small blurry snapshots."

"But it's a good possibility." Jerri edged toward the stairs off the kitchen. "We were reminiscing and talking about our bedroom in our grandmother's house. There was this crawl space where Michele would hide and read with a flashlight. As she talked, she remembered she had a crawl space in this house."

"And that's when I thought I remembered putting something in there," Michele said. "Could be nothing."

"But it could be where you put your laptop, for whatever reason." Jerri had one foot on the bottom stair. "The crawl space is in Michele's bedroom. You guys ready?" She didn't wait for an answer but disappeared up the stairs, followed by Diesel.

LuAnn tucked her cell phone into her sweater pocket, just in case they needed more light. Then she and Tess followed at a fast clip, leaving Janice and Michele to follow more slowly.

"I hope this gives us the answers we need," Jerri said from above them. LuAnn and Tess trailed behind her, breathless from trying to keep up with her.

"Maybe we should build a gym in the basement of the inn," Tess puffed at the top of the stairs.

"We could always just run up and down the three sets of stairs." LuAnn reached the landing and took a deep breath.

"Good point."

Jerri had already disappeared into a bedroom on the right when Janice and Michele reached the top of the stairs.

"It's always been like this," Michele said. "She never just walks, she rushes. When we were really little, our mother called her Little Miss Impatient."

"I heard that." Jerri's voice came from the bedroom. "Come on, you guys. If there was ever a time to be impatient, it's now."

LuAnn, Tess, Janice, and Michele joined Jerri in the bedroom. The traditional Cape Cod room contained a full bed with a flowered bedspread and a tall antique oak dresser pushed into the window dormer.

Jerri stuck her flashlight in her back pocket and then pulled at the dresser. It squealed on the wood floor as she maneuvered it into the middle of the room. When she was done, she clapped her hands. "Yes!"

There, on the left, was a tiny door leading to the crawl space that probably went the length of the front of the house.

Jerri dropped to her knees, flashlight in hand. "Ready?"

Michele picked up Diesel.

The rest of them pressed in behind her, trying to see over her shoulder as she opened the door.

CHAPTER TWENTY-SEVEN

"Eureka! A laptop! This is like a spy movie or something." Half of Jerri's body was in the crawl space, and her voice was muffled. She backed up with the laptop and handed it to LuAnn, who took it and stepped backward.

"I'm relieved. That laptop cost a small fortune." Michele rubbed her forehead. "I must have really wanted to hide it."

"There's also a bag here...like a great big backpack." Jerri crawled into the dark space again and then came out pulling the handles of a dark blue gym bag.

"That's the bag I carried to work with me with extra clothes and stuff." Michele's voice sounded thready.

LuAnn touched her shoulder. "Do you need to lie down?"

She shook her head. "Let's go back downstairs. I can sit there."

Janice took the dog from Michele and put her on the floor. "You're a little unsteady."

"I'm okay," Michele said. "I'm just...well...having a memory or something."

"You did have a nasty head injury," Jerri said as she shut the crawl space door.

Leaving the dresser right where it was, the group headed back down to the kitchen.

LuAnn put the laptop on the table. Janice guided Michele to a chair, and Jerri sat in the chair next to her, placing the bag on the floor between them. Diesel jumped up into Michele's lap.

"Are you sure you're up for this?" Jerri took her sister's hand and spoke in an uncharacteristically soft voice. "Do you want to eat?"

"I'm not hungry anymore. I need to know what all this is because this thing scares me bad." She kicked the gym bag, looking at it as if it contained wriggling snakes.

Jerri leaned down, and LuAnn heard her unzip it. Then she gasped and sat up, staring at Michele. "No wonder you were scared of this thing!" She began pulling stacks of money from the bag, placing them on the table.

"Goodness gracious goat!" Janice exclaimed.

"I don't think I've ever seen that much money in one place," LuAnn said. "Are those all twenties?"

"And hundreds." Jerri finished piling them up. "There's got to be tens of thousands of dollars here."

Michele put her fingers on her temples again, only this time her fingers trembled. "This terrifies me."

"Don't feel bad," Jerri said. "I'd be scared too. Just try to remember why you had all this."

"How about checking the laptop?" LuAnn suggested.

"Right." Jerri moved the bag, scooted closer to Michele, and pulled the laptop toward her, then she looked up. "The charger is on the counter. Please hand it to me?"

Janice got it for her and helped her plug it in.

"Your password?" Jerri asked Michele. "Or do you want to do this yourself?"

Michele shook her head, eyes wide. "Diesel#1."

"Seriously?" Jerri tapped the keys. "That could be hacked pretty easily."

"Like that's something to worry about right now?" Michele snapped.

Jerri patted her sister's hand. "Sorry. I'm intense right now."

"Yeah, I noticed," Michele said.

They all gathered around as Jerri leaned forward and waited for the desktop to appear.

"Okay. Here it is. Your programs. Pretty slim pickings. Does anything look familiar?

"Pretty much everything looks familiar. It is my laptop, after all."

Jerri rolled her eyes. "You know what I mean."

"Yes, I know what you mean, but you're making me feel like a dumb kid, and I'm already having trouble thinking."

LuAnn was tempted to stop their squabbling but let it go.

Jerri took a deep breath. "I'm scared, okay? It's making me more impatient than my normal impatience."

"It's okay. I understand we're trying to find information that I've hidden. But what if there's nothing to find?" Michele waved at the money, close to tears. "What if I stole all this or something?"

LuAnn walked over to where Michele sat and put a hand on her shoulder. "We don't believe that for a minute."

"Besides," Jerri said, "if this money was yours, wouldn't you have been using it? And why would you have hidden your laptop? It's not like the police were after you. If they were, they'd have already been at the hospital."

But why had Randy been driving by Michele's house so often? Did he know something they didn't?

Jerri manipulated the laptop touch pad. "What interests me is that all your pictures on your phone were gone. That's just impossible. I mean, who do you know who doesn't have a single photo on their phone?"

"I know some people who don't ever take pictures with their phones," LuAnn said.

Jerri and Michele looked up at her with identical expressions, like she'd sprouted another head.

"Your age is showing," Tess said to LuAnn.

"I guess it is."

The girls turned their attention back to the laptop.

"There!" Michele pointed at the screen. "Try that picture file." She gripped her head. "I think seeing that money is bringing back memories, but it's all just a mess in my head right now."

"Lots of pictures," Jerri mumbled. "Wait! Here's a file that says Tahitian vacation." She raised a brow. "Did you go to Tahiti?"

"Not that I remember."

As Jerri tapped her finger on the touch pad, picture icons appeared on the screen. Jerri tapped on one. A photo of a spreadsheet appeared.

"Whoa. This could be what you discovered." Jerri opened another photo. "It could be proof of money laundering."

"And that could be why you went to the police," LuAnn added.

The doorbell rang. Diesel jumped from Michele's lap, yapping, and ran to the front door.

"I told everyone else to come later," Jerri said, panic in her voice. "I don't know who that is." She glanced around the room, eyes wide. "You guys, put some pizza on paper towels or something. Make this all look normal." She stuffed the money back into the bag.

The bell rang again.

"I'll go get the door," Tess said as Jerri finished up.

LuAnn and Janice were laying pizza slices on squares of paper towels when Doria Sanders walked into the kitchen, followed by Tess.

Michele's fingers twitched. Tess returned to LuAnn's side.

"I didn't expect you'd have company already." Doria smiled, but tension narrowed her eyes. She stuck her hands in the pockets of her bulky wool coat. LuAnn noticed she wasn't carrying a purse.

"We didn't expect you to come so early," Jerri said. "I told you seven."

"I was eager to see how my favorite employee was doing." Doria's gaze went to Michele, and then it fell to the gym bag.

LuAnn had a very bad feeling about all of this.

The doorbell rang again, then the door opened, and a familiar man's voice called for Doria.

"That will be Melvin. He was parking the car." Doria called for him to come to the kitchen.

"Melvin McPherson?" LuAnn asked. "Why is he here?"

"We came together. We're engaged, didn't you know?"

The connection LuAnn had been looking for! And that's where she'd seen Doria. In pictures on Melvin's credenza.

Diesel kept barking as the front door slammed shut, Doria approached the table. "What is that?" she pointed at the laptop screen.

Jerri closed the laptop. "Michele's vacation pictures."

"Michele hasn't taken a vacation recently, and those didn't look like pictures of any scenery. They looked more like documents." Doria moved closer. "Care to show me?"

"No." Jerri moved her chair and blocked her way. "That's Michele's private stuff."

Melvin walked into the kitchen, followed by a still barking little dog. He stopped, mouth open, and his glance bounced from one of them to the other, then finally rested on Doria. "You said no one else would be here."

"I was sure there wouldn't be. Can you just keep your mouth shut?" Doria looked at Diesel. "Someone please shut that dog up."

Janice scooped Diesel off the floor and held her close.

"Yes, but now what will we do?" Melvin said in a whiny voice.

"We have to get what we came for and disappear." Doria's eyes fell on the gym bag again. "I'll bet that's still filled with the money that you stupidly put in her bag. Plus, the clever girl took pictures of the records you had on your desk. How careless could you be, Melvin? I trusted you."

"Why did you put money in my bag?" Michele asked.

"Because his mother was on a rampage, accusing him of dishonesty, and she was searching everywhere. The one place she wouldn't search would be your stuff. He obviously didn't think you'd leave before he could get it back. And he didn't tell me about it for two days."

"You were laundering money!" Jerri said.

"I was building a business," Doria snapped. "And now because of all of you, I have to drop out of sight and start over somewhere else."

While they were talking, LuAnn surreptitiously pulled her phone out of her pocket and pushed the number to reach Randy. Then she put it back in her pocket.

Jerri reached for her phone, but Doria pushed it out of the way and pulled a gun from her coat pocket.

Melvin gasped. "What are you going to do?"

"Whatever I have to do to get what's mine and to get out of here fast."

"This is getting ugly," Janice whispered. "We need to do something."

"No worries," LuAnn said quietly. "I just speed-dialed Randy, and I think I hear his voice in my pocket."

"Be quiet!" Doria ordered, waving the gun in their direction. "Melvin, get the gym bag."

He took a couple of steps toward the table, nervously glancing around the room.

"Did you break into Michele's house?" Tess asked in a loud voice.

Everyone turned to look at her.

"Why are you yelling?" Doria looked around with suspicion in her eyes. "It seems to me that it's obvious. I sent Melvin to find the money, which he failed to do."

Melvin reached for the gym bag.

"Jerri, give it to him, please," LuAnn said.

Before Jerri could object, a woman's voice yelled Melvin's name from the front of the house.

His mouth fell open. "It's my mother."

"What is your mother doing here?" Doria snapped.

"I have no idea. I thought she was out of town."

"I know you're in there," Fern roared, footsteps thudding down the hall.

"I told you to get her out of the way, didn't I?"

Fern stalked into the kitchen. "Melvin!"

He cringed and stepped away from Jerri and Michele.

"How did you know we were here?" Doria demanded.

"Tishia. She installed some sort of GPS thing on Melvin's phone when he wasn't looking."

"I told you to fire Tishia!" Doria said to Melvin through gritted teeth.

"I wouldn't let him," Fern said. "And I just got back from West Virginia. Tishia and I followed you, Doria. I watched who you met and what you did. We took pictures. I know about your little money-laundering plot."

Doria's face paled.

Fern turned and stuck her finger in Melvin's chest. "How could you let Doria—or should I call her Delilah—take you off the straight and narrow?"

Melvin stammered some incoherent words.

Fern pulled a cell phone from her purse. "I'm calling the police."

"No, you're not." Doria knocked the phone out of Fern's hand.

"I think we need to turn ourselves in," Melvin said. "We can't get away with this anymore."

Doria rolled her eyes. "Ever hear of 'take the money and run?' I have friends who will hide me. You can stay here and wimp out if you want to." She pointed the gun at Jerri. "Give me the bag and the laptop right now."

"Do it," LuAnn said to Jerri. "This isn't worth getting hurt over."

Jerri squirmed for a moment, and LuAnn thought she'd try to take Doria on, but she finally handed them both to Doria.

Doria snatched them from Jerri, then disappeared down the hallway.

"Are you going or staying?" Fern asked her son in a soft voice. The pain on her face made LuAnn want to cry.

He stammered what sounded like, "Sorry, Mom," and left the room.

They were all silent. In shock. Fern clasped her hands. Silent tears fell from her eyes. Somehow the lack of sound was worse than if she'd been sobbing out loud.

LuAnn spanned the gap between them and pulled her into a hug. "I'm so sorry," she whispered.

"I knew there was something wrong. I just hoped it wasn't true. LuAnn, I've lost my son. I'm losing my eyesight too."

Before LuAnn could ask what Fern meant, they heard Doria shriek and the sounds of scuffling. LuAnn let go of Fern. Jerri jumped up, ready to run down the hall.

"Don't," LuAnn ordered. "I reached Randy on speed dial. I'm pretty sure he or another officer is dealing with the situation. We're safer here."

Shortly, Randy walked into the kitchen, a wide grin on his face. He was followed by Mrs. Brewster's boarder.

"We got 'em," he said. "Good work calling me, LuAnn. I heard you loud and clear. Kenley here was just arriving when Doria and Melvin stepped outside." He motioned toward the man behind him.

"Mrs. Brewster's boarder is a police officer?" LuAnn asked.

Randy laughed. "In a manner of speaking. He's an undercover FBI agent."

Kenley nodded at the group with a smile. "We've been following Doria Sanders for over a month, but we needed more proof. I think this is it. Now, if you ladies will do me a favor and answer a few questions, we'd be grateful."

"I'm sure LuAnn has that notebook of hers." Randy grinned and glanced at the table where the now cold pizza slices lay on paper towels. "And maybe someone could heat one of those up for me? I was on my way home when LuAnn called. This drama interrupted my dinner. I'm starving."

CHAPTER TWENTY-EIGHT

Back at the inn, LuAnn sat in front of the fireplace, drinking hot chocolate with Tess, Janice, Jerri, and Michele. They'd decided to take over the seats and let their guests gather somewhere else for once. She'd showered, changed, and even applied some makeup. It was time to celebrate. Jerri and Michele were staying the night in the room that Atley had vacated, deciding that they wanted the company after the events in Michele's kitchen.

"Brad should be here in a while," LuAnn said. "I texted him and told him what happened. He's been tied up all afternoon."

"Oh?" Tess glanced at Janice, who sat right next to LuAnn.

LuAnn felt slightly peeved that Brad hadn't been able to rush away from whatever he was doing and make sure she was okay.

"Is that why you have lipstick on?" Jerri asked.

Janice and Tess laughed.

LuAnn ignored them all. "Our mysteries are about solved, I think."

"I feel sorry for Fern." Tess put her empty cup on a table. "Now we know why she's been acting grumpier than usual."

"Poor thing." LuAnn felt like crying just thinking about Fern's tears at her son's betrayal. "Not only was Melvin using their business to launder money, he was trying to force her to retire, and as grounds, he was using the fact that she's losing her sight. Now that I think about it, she was acting like she was having trouble seeing. And it explains why she couldn't read the committee's emails and thought she hadn't gotten the information."

"What did she call it again?" Tess asked. "Diabetic Retino something?"

"Retinopathy," Janice said. "I called Stuart. He explained it to me. She can halt the vision loss if she can get her diabetes under control. This also explains some of her erratic behavior. Uncontrolled diabetes."

"At least she has Tishia," LuAnn said. "Did you see that tiny woman come roaring up the road to take care of Fern?"

"Apparently the little mouse is a computer whiz," Jerri said. "She figured everything out for Fern. I wouldn't be surprised if she became a new partner."

"I'm amazed that Kenley was an undercover FBI agent," Michele said. "I met him at one of the salons when I arrived to clean. He'd just gotten his hair cut. We talked for a while, and he mentioned he was looking for a place to stay a couple of nights a week. I told him about Mrs. Brewster, and the rest is history."

The elevator doors opened, and the Boycrafts stepped out. For the first time since they'd arrived, they were dressed in semiformal clothes. They saw the group and headed over to join them.

"We have an announcement," Merrill said, a broad grin on his face.

Carleen grinned at his side. "We're going to be moving to Marietta."

"Really?" Janice said. "That's wonderful news."

Merrill nodded. "We invested in our daughter's dry-cleaning business, along with our bank. We now own a third. We wanted to keep it a secret until it was a done deal."

That explains the man in the suit, LuAnn thought.

"My mother left me a great deal of money." Sadness twisted Carleen's mouth. "But we're putting it to good use, and now we can be with family."

"And the kids can stop worrying that they'll lose their house, because we're moving in with them."

"That's wonderful," LuAnn said.

Carleen's face brightened. "It is, isn't it?"

"Now we're headed out to dinner with the kids and the other investor. We'll be returning late."

"Enjoy." LuAnn smiled. Their final mystery, solved.

As they opened the door to the inn, they almost collided with Brad. He apologized to them, exchanged some pleasantries, and then strolled across the open expanse with a bag in his hands. He seemed slightly out of breath.

"I'm sorry. I got LuAnn's text about what happened. I couldn't come right away, but I was concerned." His gaze zeroed in on her. "I assume since everyone is sitting here, drinking hot drinks, that all is well."

"Everything is," LuAnn said. "Would you like to sit?"

"Yes."

Janice jumped up. "Sit here." She pointed at the seat next to LuAnn. "Would you like some hot chocolate?"

"No thanks. My appetite is absent at the moment." Brad took Janice's place, and the bag rattled in his hands. "Care to fill me in on what happened?"

Between the five of them, Brad heard the whole story, including Fern's loss of eyesight.

"And now my sister is safe," Jerri said.

"Has your memory returned?" Brad asked Michele.

"Enough to give the police evidence," she said. "I'd seen some spreadsheets on Melvin's desk that looked off to me. I'm kind of ashamed to say, but I took pictures of them to study them later. I began to suspect things were weird when Doria kept showing up at the salons in the evening and doing things in the back."

"And you say Melvin put that money in your bag?"

"He did. The morning that Jerri arrived."

Jerri's jaw clenched. "And that's why she didn't answer my calls or texts that morning. She'd discovered the money, and she was terrified. She went home and hid it."

Brad raised his brows.

"That morning while I cleaned at the McPhersons' office, Melvin came and went. Then Fern arrived on a rampage. She careened around the office, going through everything. Apparently, she suspected Melvin of illegal activity, and she was searching for proof. He had already hidden the money in my bag, which was in my car. He figured that was one place she wouldn't look. But Fern ordered me to leave, so when he got back, I was gone."

"Melvin is the one who left the note under the cake," Tess said.

"He said Doria was upset about that," LuAnn said, "and you have to admit, it was kind of stupid."

"A panicked, last-ditch effort to fix the situation," Janice added.

Brad touched LuAnn's arm. "All I can say is that I'm relieved you're all okay."

"And we've had our answer about the Paglinos as well." LuAnn explained what the Boycrafts had just told them.

"You could write a book."

"We could," LuAnn said, thinking about some writing projects she had in mind.

"And poor Fern." Brad shook his head. "There I was, plying her with cookies the night of the committee meeting."

Janice shrugged. "Who knew? But people do need to take responsibility for their own health."

"True," Tess said.

Michele smiled. "Jerri and I have some news too."

"Oh?"

The two young women sat close to each other on the couch.

"We're going to go visit our mother at the penitentiary."

"Both of you?" LuAnn asked.

"I'm prepared to give her another chance." Jerri gave LuAnn a half smile. "And I'm *willing* to be willing to give God another chance too."

"Being willing is a good first step," LuAnn said.

"Would you guys like to sing some Christmas carols?" Janice suggested.

"That would be lovely," Tess said.

"I haven't sung Christmas carols and enjoyed them for a long, long time," Jerri said. "They've just been background noise at the mall."

Michele smiled and reached for Jerri's hand.

Janice went to the piano and began playing "Silent Night." Everyone joined in, even Jerri, whose singing voice was lovely. LuAnn felt weepy again and groped for the box of tissues on the side table. It was empty.

"I'll be back in a minute," she murmured to Brad. "I need to get more."

She took the empty box to the kitchen, tossed it in the trash, and then went to the storage room where they kept paper goods for the main floor. She grabbed a new box of tissues and wiped her tears.

When she turned around, she jumped. Brad stood there, waiting for her, with his hands behind his back.

"Sorry to startle you."

"That's okay." She tossed the used tissue into the trash and rinsed her hands. Then she smiled at Brad, feeling the warmth in her chest for him that had been growing exponentially the last few months. If he wasn't around anymore...if he met a woman and developed a relationship, she would lose this depth of friendship.

"You have a funny look on your face."

She shrugged and tried to set her expression back to "normal LuAnn." "Ignore me. I'm so emotional right now, it isn't funny." She held up the box of tissues then put it on the table. "I've spent the greater part of Jerri's visit on the verge of 'my eyes leaking,' as she would say. I'm surprised my nose isn't raw between that and the cold weather."

He chuckled and pulled the bag out from behind his back. "I have a gift for you, and I wanted to give it to you privately. I couldn't wait until Christmas."

"A gift for me?" The brown bag had handles made from twine.

"Yes." He handed it to her. "If you recall, last year I bought you supplies for the dog and cat."

"Yes, I remember, and it was very sweet." She took the bag and let it swing from her fingers. It had some weight to it. "I don't have a gift for you right now though."

"LuAnn, I expect nothing in return. Please accept this."

She heard the pleading in his voice. In a flash she remembered the times when she hadn't been receptive of his gifts. And she wondered if that was because she would have to admit she was attracted to him.

"Well? Are you going to make me take it back?"

"No, I'm not." She investigated the bag and saw a wrapped box about the size of a book. She pulled it out and ran her index finger over the gold foil paper.

Brad rubbed his hands together. "I hope you like it. Tess and Janice and I discussed it, and then I took it upon myself and ran with the idea."

"Tess and Janice are in on this?"

"And Jerri."

"Okay..." The normally sanguine Brad was acting so hesitant, she was eager to find out what was inside. But a suspicion already wiggled in the back of her mind.

"I've been all over the county to find this."

She looked up at him. "Is that what you've been doing all those times you were gone?"

"Yes. And I went to pick it up today, which is why I couldn't be here when I heard about what happened at Michele's. That about killed me."

She removed the bow, peeled away the tape, and undid the precisely wrapped paper. "Did you wrap this yourself?"

"Yes. That's why I was late tonight."

"Are you always this exact when you wrap gifts?"

"No. But this was important."

LuAnn glanced at him. He looked eager, grinning like a kid. She wanted to hug him.

"Well? Are you going to open it or not?"

She laughed. Underneath the paper was a bright red cardboard box like the kind greeting cards might come in. She put the paper and bow on the table and opened the box, pulled aside gold and white tissue paper, and gasped. Her suspicions were correct. There lay the most beautiful notebook cover she'd ever seen, with a perfectly tooled rendition of the inn on the front. The words "Wayfarers Inn" scrolled along the bottom in gorgeous script.

"Oh, Brad! I just don't know what to say. It's stunning." She stroked the cover and blinked back tears. Again. She looked up at him. "How can I accept this?"

"Just do it." He grinned, eyes full of light and joy. "I had it specially made for you. Do you like it?"

"I love it! Thank you." She dropped the box on the table and threw her arms around his neck.

He paused, then put his arms around her.

She meant for the hug to be brief. Like a church hug. But then something happened. She didn't want to move. Warm awareness started in her chest and filled all of her. She felt safe in the strength of his arms. She wanted to stay there.

The realization startled her, yet it didn't. It was like she'd always sort of known, and that's why she avoided the topic whenever anyone brought it up. Brad was a man who'd proven himself dependable. Godly. And protective.

She lifted her face and looked up into his eyes. Such kind, blue eyes, with crinkles around them when he smiled. He'd become an integral part of her life. She didn't want to let go.

"I'm really, really glad you love it," he said softly.

"I really, really do." Her gaze wandered around his face, which had end-of-the-day rough stubbles. She put one hand on his cheek, feeling the scratchiness under her palm. She knew then, for certain and for sure, she had fallen for Brad Grimes.

She stood on her toes and pressed her lips to his.

He stiffened for a second, then he pulled her tight to him. She felt the thump of his heart. The steady pressure of his arms.

When she finally took a step back, she felt breathless and ruffled. She smoothed her shirt and her hair. "My goodness. I don't know what just happened."

He chuckled softly. "I have a pretty good idea. I'll explain, if you'd like."

"That's not what I mean." A blush warmed her cheeks. "What I mean is that I've never done that before. It was presumptuous. I'm sorry. I don't know what came over me."

"Don't apologize," he whispered. "That kiss was not presumption. It was impulsive."

"That sounds worse."

"It's not, and it meant the world to me." Brad rested his hands on her upper arms and squeezed gently. "You, LuAnn Sherrill, organized list-maker extraordinaire, the woman I've admired since we first met, are rarely impulsive. In fact, I'd say the only time you are impulsive is when you're emotionally moved. That's what makes that kiss so special. Let me be frank. That was, hands down, the nicest kiss I've ever had. And if you haven't bought my present yet, you don't need to. That was the best Christmas present I could have ever wished for."

LuAnn closed her eyes against another bout of tears. She didn't know how to respond. She felt like a teenager in love for the first time. Joyful. Astonished. Like she was melting inside. And she really wanted to kiss Brad again.

She began to lean toward him when the sound of voices pulled her out of her dreamy state. The kitchen door swung open, and Janice walked in. "We want cookies and—oh." She stopped suddenly, glancing from LuAnn to Brad and back again.

Tess walked in behind her, almost slamming into Janice's back. She blinked at them in silence for a minute, then put her hands on her hips. "Did we interrupt something?"

LuAnn's face burned. She drew a breath and glanced up at Brad.

Brad smiled and patted her arms, then he turned to her friends. "I gave her the leather notebook. She was overwhelmed by happiness."

"I see," Tess said brightly. "I'm sure that explains everything."

Janice giggled.

Tess hit her arm with her elbow.

LuAnn reached for every ounce of self-control she had. She grabbed the leather notebook from the box on the table and waved it so they could see.

"Brad said you guys gave him the idea for the notebook." She was having trouble forming her words. "Thank you."

"You're welcome," Janice said. "It was really his idea."

"It was." Tess took a tentative step farther into the kitchen. "We discussed Fern's notebook and how much you liked it."

Janice sidled over to the kitchen counter. "We encouraged him to do it."

"He went looking all over the place." Tess took a few more steps.

"It's more gorgeous than we thought it would be." Janice opened a plastic container of cookies.

"Even nicer than the notebook Fern was banging all over the table at the meeting," Tess added while she grabbed some napkins.

Her two friends were chattering like nervous birds.

The kitchen door swung open again, and Jerri bounded into the room. "I came to see if you had any hot cider mix." She skidded to a stop. "What's going on?"

LuAnn looked up at Brad again.

His lips twitched.

LuAnn held up the notebook cover again. "He gave me my Christmas present early."

"Really?" Jerri narrowed her eyes and stepped closer to them. "And that would be why Brad has the remnants of lipstick around his lips?"

LuAnn hadn't noticed.

Tess shook her head furiously at Jerri. "Shhh!"

Janice giggled again.

Brad grabbed a tissue from LuAnn's box and wiped his mouth, then looked down at it with a fake frown. "Well, what do you know? Look at that. And it's not even my shade."

Jerri snorted.

Tess burst out laughing. Janice joined in.

LuAnn finally sighed and grinned. "What can I say?"

"I say, if you can't beat 'em, join 'em. But we might want to consider a color that's better for my skin tone." Brad chuckled and smiled down at her with affection that made her heart beat faster. "I've suddenly got my appetite back. I'm ready for hot chocolate. And cookies. And I want to sing some songs. Celebrate all the good things we have to celebrate, including God's gift of love and mercy. It is, after all, the Christmas season."

"A time of miracles." Janice piled cookies on the plate.

"Many miracles," Tess murmured.

"Multitudinous miracles," Jerri said, grinning from ear to ear.

"Well, Jerri, that word wins the prize!" Brad gave LuAnn one more smile that made her feel warm to her bones. "Hand me some cookies. I'll take them out there. And LuAnn, I'll save you a seat. Right at my side." He disappeared from the room.

"I have some ideas for Christmas songs," Tess said. "Something slightly romantic. 'Let it Snow,' perhaps?" She ducked out the door before LuAnn could reply.

Janice opened a cupboard and pulled out some hot cider mixes. "There's already hot water out there, so I'll take these out there for you, Jerri. I think I need to sit down. It's been an astonishing and enlightening day. And things just keep getting better." She swirled out the door, leaving it swinging behind her.

LuAnn heard sniffling. She turned. Jerri was crying.

"Come here." She pulled Jerri close. "Why are you crying? If anyone should be crying, it should be me, embarrassed to my toenails, caught kissing a man in the kitchen."

Jerri wiped her cheeks. "You have no reason to be embarrassed. Brad is a very nice man. He likes you a whole lot, and that's been obvious since I met him. It's time you admit to yourself that you like him. You deserve that kind of happiness after everything you've been through." She grinned, face still wet with tears. "But I would like to know who initiated the whole thing."

"That's my little secret, cheeky youngster."

Jerri laughed and cried at the same time.

"But you haven't answered me. Why are you crying?"

"I'm overwhelmed with emotions, I guess." Jerri took LuAnn's hand. "You know what you said about God's mercy?"

"Yes."

"I looked it up. One of the meanings is 'a blessing that is an act of divine favor or compassion.'"

"Yes, it is."

"And that's exactly what's happened for me this Christmas. It's like God had the whole thing arranged, from beginning to end, out of compassion just for me."

"Like the 'Mercy Song,'" LuAnn said.

"Yes. Just like that."

Dear Reader,

I first became familiar with Secrets of Wayfarers Inn as a reader, not an author. I had already fallen in love with these gentle, faith-based mysteries when I was given the opportunity to write *Mercy's Song*.

Writing a book is never easy. Any author worth their salt will tell you that. However, after writing five traditionally published cozy mysteries, I jumped into writing this book with the confidence that I knew what I was doing. I quickly discovered that was not the case. Despite my surface familiarity with the Wayfarers Inn series, stepping into a well-established setting and continuing the development of the character of LuAnn (as well as the other characters) was a challenge. To complicate matters, I needed to move the romance between LuAnn and Brad Grimes forward. That had to be realistic and within character for both of them.

Then came Prudence's story. Although those portions of the book might seem small compared to the contemporary mystery, I quickly discovered how much I didn't know about abolition and the Underground Railroad.

I spent a lot of time in prayer about this book, and God was faithful to help me. When I was done with the final edits, I felt I had a book that contributed to the growth of a series I dearly love. I hope you, my reader, have enjoyed my addition to Secrets of Wayfarers Inn.

Candice Prentice

ABOUT THE AUTHOR

Candice Prentice is the author of ten books, mostly cozy mysteries. She lives in the semi-suburbs of Maryland with her husband and Jack the dog. When she's not writing, she enjoys quilting, sewing, and scouring the web, books, old newspapers, and old magazines for cool historical facts. She loves Bible study and intercessory prayer. She's also a bit of a health nut. Visit her website and blog at www.candiceprentice.com. You'll find a list of her other books there.

CHARLES FINNEY

When I began to research the historical portion of this book, I was interested to learn that revivalist Charles Finney stood among the many Christian men and women who opposed slavery. I read many comments about him, some negative but most positive. He was an imperfect person, as we all are, but God used him mightily. Once Charles Finney turned his heart to God, he never looked back. He was a prayer warrior. He loved lost people. And he was passionate that all humanity be treated equal in Christ. He refused to segregate his churches. He was so convinced slavery was evil, he denied slaveholders participation in communion at his churches.

In addition to being a revivalist and abolitionist, Charles Finney was a professor at Oberlin College in Ohio and then became its president in 1851. Oberlin College was among the first colleges in the United States to open its doors to African Americans and women. Finney, and the Oberlin, Ohio, community, like the community of Marietta, played an important role in the Underground Railroad.

Roasted Sweet Potato, Onion, and Carrot Soup

Ingredients

- 1 tablespoon butter (or ghee)
- 1 garlic clove, minced
- 1 cup roasted carrots, onions, and sweet potatoes (mash into measuring cup with fingers)
- 1 cup liquid (water or broth as you wish)
- ¼ teaspoon ground turmeric (or to taste)
- ¼ teaspoon ground ginger (or to taste)
- ¼ cup milk, cream, or milk substitute for a creamy texture. If you have none of those on hand, just use more broth or water instead.
- Salt and pepper
- A handful of herbed, roasted pumpkin seeds (pepitas) for topping (optional)

Directions

In a Dutch oven, melt the ghee. Add minced garlic and cook for 10 seconds, until fragrant. Remove from heat.

Place roasted carrots, onions, and sweet potatoes in a food processor. Add the garlic then the liquid. Process just until blended (if you double the recipe, you'll have to process in batches). Return the Dutch oven to medium heat. Add the carrot, onion, and sweet potato mixture to the Dutch oven. Stir in turmeric, ginger, milk, and salt and pepper to taste. Heat, top with herbed roasted pumpkin seeds if desired, and serve.

Read on for a sneak peek of another exciting book
in the Secrets of Wayfarers Inn series!

There's No Place like Holmes
by Roseanna M. White

Tess Wallace slid the awkward box into the back seat of her car and then debated for a moment. She just ought to hurry back to the inn with it. That was the logical thing to do, and it was going to be a weekend of logic.

But it was also going to be a weekend of fun, and she just couldn't resist an early peek. Brandishing her most jagged key as a small knife, she sliced open the tape, folded back the flaps, and grinned in pure delight at the assortment of items Emma at Antoinette's Closet had been helping her find used and cheap.

A gust of wind tore down the street, slicing right through Tess's heaviest winter coat, but she ignored the shiver and reached inside the box. Emma, as always, had come through. Tess pulled out a deerstalker hat in red and tan tweed and put it on.

She felt Sherlockian already. And the assortment of fabric in the box proved that Emma had found other hats in a variety of colors. Browns, grays, a black, even one in pink-and-gray check. Chuckling a bit, she reached for a cherrywood pipe.

Now, there also ought to be...yes! There on the bottom, the glint of old-fashioned magnifying glasses.

"Tess!"

She spun around, pipe still in her hand, unable to place the voice that shouted her way. Her brows drew down a bit when she spotted Sylvia Weber jogging toward her, hand waving. Her fingers were enveloped in purple gloves, and a matching ear-warmer headband held her waist-length blond hair back.

Tess waved with the hand not holding a pipe. Oh, heavens, she must look ridiculous. Her fingers fell to the hat covering her hair—though when another icy blast of wind whipped down the street, she was tempted to simply untie the flaps so they could protect her ears rather than take the thing off.

"I'm so glad I saw you! I was going to give you guys a call as soon as I got inside." Sylvia, all smiles, came to a halt a few feet away. "We just got the coolest donation in at the museum, and I knew you and LuAnn and Janice would want to see it right away." Then, of course, she narrowed her eyes, and her smile twitched. "Um...have I interrupted you on your way to a Sherlock Holmes convention or something?"

Tess laughed and swiped the hat from her head, wind or no wind. "Actually, yes. Well, sort of. We're hosting a little event at the inn this weekend. My uncle's club. The Sherlock Society."

Sylvia raised her eyebrows. "Your uncle runs a Sherlock Holmes club?"

"His lifelong passion." Tess nestled the hat and pipe back into the box and closed the flaps. Then she checked her watch and pressed her lips together. She'd be lucky to make it back to the inn before the society pulled in, but she shouldn't be rude to Sylvia. Though the Inn Crowd hadn't exactly gotten off on the right foot with this woman and her husband, Sylvia had been making a real effort to prove them worthy of the trust Maybelline had placed in them, handing over the reins of the Underground Railroad Museum this month while she was away on her honeymoon.

Tess fastened a smile in place. "He's a professor of English Lit at Oberlin. He started this club... oh, heavens, I don't even know when. A long time ago. Thirty or forty years, maybe."

"No kidding." A glint—interest?—lit Sylvia's eyes. "I've always been a bit of a Sherlock fan myself. Is this event at the inn open to the public?"

"I'm afraid not, no." Tess closed the rear door of her car but kept her smile in place. "Uncle Harold and his crew have booked the whole place, even though they only needed six of the rooms, to guarantee quiet and privacy."

And frankly, she and her friends were looking forward to the quiet weekend too. Oh, there would be some heated debates going on in the parlor, no doubt. And an endless supply of hot water for tea and coffee would be required. But with only eight guests who probably wouldn't even leave the inn until they checked out on Sunday, it might be their easiest weekend all year.

And she'd get to see Uncle Harold. A pang of guilt struck her square in the stomach when she counted back and realized it had been a full two years since she'd hugged her favorite uncle. Her only uncle left, now, after Uncle Charlie passed away three years ago. The last of her father's generation, of the five Westerfield brothers, and the one she'd always most enjoyed spending time with, other than her own father. Harold was a special one. An odd one but a special one.

"Well, I shouldn't keep you then, if you have to get back to the inn to get ready for him." Sylvia backed up a step. A gust of wind snagged a strand of her long hair and deposited it directly into her mouth. She peeled it away with a comical glare. "Hope they make it in before the snow comes."

"Oh." Tess waved that away. "I really doubt we're going to get much of anything. It seems the meteorologists have become sensationalists lately—every storm's the biggest one of the century, according to them."

Sylvia chuckled. "Too true. Well, I'll get in touch later about that donation you guys will want to see, all right?"

Donation? Tess had to blink twice before she remembered that Sylvia hadn't just hailed her to say hello. She'd begun with something about a donation to the museum. "Sure, that sounds great. Anytime, really. You have our number?"

"Yep. Have a great weekend with your uncle, Tess."

"I will. Thanks." Lifting her hand in a wave as Sylvia turned, Tess pulled open the driver's door and climbed in. There were a few snowflakes in the air, already drifting down, swirling here and there when another gust of wind went by, but they didn't look particularly ominous.

Even so, she whispered a prayer that any weather would hold off while her eighty-four-year-old uncle was driving the three hours from Oberlin. Because they all knew he wouldn't turn the wheel of his ridiculous van—painted with the famous Sherlock silhouette and the titles of each and every one of Sir Arthur Conan Doyle's popular stories—over to anyone else.

Man, she'd missed him. After checking traffic, she pulled out onto the street and pointed her car toward home. Her responsibilities at the inn had made it a bit hard to get away for a weekend lately. And she didn't exactly encourage Uncle Harold to drive this far very often. Frankly, she'd feel a whole lot better if he limited his driving to around his own town, during daylight hours.

But there was no convincing him of such things. Good grief, the man still taught two classes a semester! Retirement, he'd claimed twenty years ago, just didn't suit him. And since he remained one of the most popular professors at Oberlin, apparently the college hadn't argued with him.

At any rate, she was so glad he'd had this idea for a getaway for his club. They had a lot of catching up to do. And she'd planned a big family lunch for Sunday—Lizzie and Michael and the kids were coming over, and Jeff Jr. They hadn't seen their great-uncle in even longer than it had been for Tess.

A few minutes later she was pulling into the inn's parking lot, noting a distinct absence of Sherlock-themed vehicles in the lot. Good—she'd beaten him here. Claiming her box of goodies from the back seat, she hustled into the inn's kitchen entrance.

Winnie looked up with a smile from her place at the counter. "Success?"

"Emma, as usual, outdid herself. I have no idea how she found all this stuff for next to nothing, but I'm grateful." She smiled at the rows of unbaked Cornish pasties on cookie sheets. "I see you've outdone yourself too."

"You know me—I love an excuse to try something new." Winnie grinned as she crimped the edge of a meat pie with a smooth maneuver. "The fridge is packed with classic British foods for the weekend for the society. I've left instructions on heating them, in case I don't make it in with the snow."

"I seriously doubt it's going to snow that much. But thanks." Tess aimed herself toward the café, and from there toward the front desk.

She found Janice behind it, the phone clamped between shoulder and ear as she clicked the computer's mouse. She wore a tight smile and a frown in her eyes. "Uh-huh. Yes, I totally understand, Mrs. Kelly. We do extend our cancellation policy in such cases, I assure you. Just give us a call on Sunday morning, and we'll be happy to let you know how the weather's looking." Janice typed something in then shifted so she held the phone in her hand. "Uh-huh. You too. Goodbye now."

She ended the call with a loud exhale and looked to Tess. "Yet another Sunday guest concerned about whether they can cancel if we get a blizzard."

"All this hype—we'll probably be lucky to get an inch." Tess shook her head and deposited the box behind the front desk. "But as long as Uncle Harold doesn't cancel."

Laughter sounded, not just from Janice, but from the parlor, and LuAnn joined them at the desk a moment later. "You know very well that nothing as mundane as a snowstorm could keep the professor from a weekend of mystery-solving." She motioned toward the sitting area. "I've got the corkboards and whiteboards set up for them, as requested."

"And I've been dusting off my violin skills." Janice made a face. "Goodness gracious goat, but they're rusty! I need to practice my other instruments more often instead of always turning to the piano."

Tess slid the box onto the desk and grinned. It was true that they always took care to make sure their guests were comfortable, but this was more than that. This was her friends going above and beyond for her, and for the uncle they knew she'd missed. "Thanks, guys. Guess I'd better take care of all this stuff." She patted the box.

Her friends chatted while she unloaded the hats and pipes and magnifying glasses, making predictions about the weather, the state of the rooms after the last guest checked out this morning, the lunch crowd at the café. And then Janice asked, with a teasing note in her voice, "So where's Brad taking you for dinner tomorrow?"

Tess glanced up from her arranging of pipes just in time to see the pretty pink flush in LuAnn's cheeks. "Spagna's, I think. We're both in the mood for Italian."

Tess was tempted to add a bit of teasing of her own—she couldn't be happier that LuAnn and Brad were finally exploring the possibilities of something more than friendship—but when she glanced up, her gaze snagged on the giant Sherlock silhouette slowing in front of the inn, turn signal flashing. "They're here!" It came out a little squealing, a little girlish.

But her friends clapped, looking nearly as giddy as she felt. "I'm going to go help them in."

"I'll man the door," Janice said.

LuAnn picked up the cardboard box. "And I'll get rid of this."

The cold wind bit again the moment Tess stepped outside, but she ignored it and zipped up the coat she'd not yet gotten around to taking off. She hurried toward the lot, getting there just as the van stopped, snug in one of the many parking spaces.

Her beeline for the driver's door hitched when the passenger door opened first, and her uncle's lined face emerged, wreathed in a grin. "Tessie!"

A pang followed the hitch. He hadn't been driving? Confusion warred with her relief, both of which she covered with a grin as she rushed into his open arms. "Uncle Harold!"

He gave her his signature hug—both arms squeezing tight until she gasped, a chuckle in her ear—and then he set her back, hands on her shoulders, as he'd done for as long as she could remember. "Well, my girl, I'm sad to report that you've not grown an inch since last I saw you."

She laughed—as she'd been doing every time he said that since she was fourteen. "As long as I'm not shrinking."

"Did you get the gift I sent you for Christmas?"

In answer, she lifted her foot and tugged up her pant leg a few inches to show off the socks he'd sent—tan, with dark brown Sherlock silhouettes, complete with deerstalker and pipe.

"I couldn't resist when I saw them," he said with another chuckle. "And who better to send them to than my sleuth of a niece? Graham, did I tell you how this young lady and her friends have actually solved a few mysteries lately? Does a heart proud."

The sliding door of the van had of course opened by now, and Tess turned to see which of the collection of literature lovers within answered to Graham. She'd met quite a few of her uncle's club members over the years, but they came and went as their lives took them to and from the college. She'd never met Graham.

He was apparently a thirty-something fellow with curly hair and glasses. Brown eyes twinkled behind them. "You may have mentioned it a time or ten on the drive here, Professor."

"When you weren't shouting at me to turn the wheel." This came from a feminine voice that sounded a bit testy. A moment later, the owner of said testy voice rounded the van.

"Matti!" Tess held out her arms for the woman she knew was one of Uncle Harold's best friends—a professor of Classic Languages at Oberlin, and a few years younger than Tess. They'd met quite a few times over the last thirty years and had always gotten along like cousins. Appropriate, given that Matti had claimed Harold as a father.

Matti's smile was stiff though, as was her hug. "Hey, Tess. Good to see you. I hope you have a medal ready for me, for actually convincing this lug to let me drive."

Tess grinned. Maybe Matti was just stiff from what could have been a stressful drive. "How about a cup of something hot?"

"Even better. Come on, crew. Bud, can you get our bags?"

"Already got 'em, honey." Bud, Matti's husband, had opened the back doors and was handing out luggage to the half-dozen other Sherlockians who had climbed down from the van.

"I've got yours, Professor," another unfamiliar man proclaimed.

"My gratitude, Tom." He hooked an arm around Tess's shoulders. "Lead the way, Tessie."

She did, and Janice held the door open for them as promised as they neared, the group of eight—nine, counting Tess—entering with banter enough to prove them all good friends, despite the sixty-year age range between Harold and the youngest member, who was a student at Oberlin.

Once inside, Harold let go of Tess so he could hold out his arms toward LuAnn, who was covering the desk. "CC!"

LuAnn laughed and came around to hug him.

Matti, just behind Tess, sighed. "I thought her name was LuAnn."

"It is. CC is for—"

"Carbon Copy," Uncle Harold said, tweaking LuAnn's nose. "This one is just like me, aren't you, my girl? An English teacher, a lover of mysteries and stories of all varieties, and even a confirmed bachelor."

"Actually," Janice put in from the door she was just closing, "she's seeing someone."

Uncle Harold splayed a hand over his heart. "Ah, she cuts me to the quick! Abandoning our brotherhood!"

LuAnn rolled her eyes and returned to the desk. "Let's get you all checked in, shall we?"

There was a bit of chaos as they checked everyone in, let them all pick hats and pipes, much to their delight, and then got them settled in their rooms. Tess and her friends turned to the café while the visitors were upstairs, prepping the tea and coffee and a few snacks that Winnie brought out.

The crew was tromping down the stairs again en masse when the front desk phone rang. Being closest, Tess picked it up. "Hello, Wayfarers Inn, how may I help you?"

"Hey, Tess. It's Sylvia, from the museum. I just wanted to check and make sure Jim got there okay."

"Jim?" Tess turned to survey the group of mystery lovers. There was a Tom and a Hiram and an Ollie, but no Jim that she could recall. "I'm sorry, Jim who?"

"Jim Sutherland. I sent him over with the chair."

Her brows drew together. "With the what?"

"The chair—that donation I started to tell you about on the street? I wanted to make sure he got it unloaded okay before the snow hit."

Tess looked up, out the windows, and gasped. Those few little flakes swirling around had apparently decided to invite their friends. The world outside was now a blur of racing snowflakes, and the ground and trees and shrubs were covered. "Oh goodness! When did that start?"

"About fifteen minutes ago. But Jim should have had time to get there and get it unloaded. I was expecting him back by now."

Tess turned to LuAnn and Janice, who had apparently been drawn her way by the incredulity in her tone. She lifted her brows. "Has anyone seen a delivery man with a chair?" she asked the room. After receiving nothing but blank looks and shaking heads, she turned back to the phone. "Did you send him to the rear door, Sylvia?"

"That's where I told him to go, yes. You have a loading dock there, right?"

Janice hurried off to check with Winnie, who would have seen anyone coming toward the loading dock, but soon reported that no one had arrived at the inn save the Sherlock Society.

"Weird," Sylvia said in reply. "I wonder where he could have gone. He was in a truck, so he shouldn't have had any problem in the snow. Man, I hope he's not out in it with that chair in the back!"

Tess switched the phone to SPEAKER so LuAnn and Janice could hear. "What exactly is this chair, Sylvia?"

"An antique. A local bought it from an estate sale and was going to have it reupholstered but donated it to us instead. As we dismantled it, we saw a stamp on the bottom for Quaker Inn Station. Do you know of it? An inn out in Chester Hill during the Underground Railroad days—they were very active in the UR. Anyway, there was also a bullet lodged in the thing, and a rolled-up photograph in a hollowed-out leg that had Prudence Willard in it. I knew you guys would want to see it."

Tess looked up to meet the gleam in her friends' eyes. "We definitely would, yes. But why did you send the whole chair instead of just the photograph?"

"Because it's a chair with a bullet in it! How cool is that?" Then Sylvia's tone grew serious. "What in the world could have happened to Jim though? He's not answering his phone."

And the roads, despite being treated, were covering fast. "He has to be somewhere between the museum and the inn—it's not that far. Want us to help you look for him?" Not how she'd planned to spend her evening, but there were worse things than a twenty-minute walk in falling snow.

"You'd do that? Oh, that would be great. I'll start at this end. Jim's about thirty, fair hair, gray eyes, and he was in a 1980s Chevy truck. Gold. Hideous thing, but it goes great in the snow."

"Okay. We'll head out now from our end and see if we spot him." She disconnected and spun, intending to reach for her coat and hat.

She found her uncle holding both—and wearing his own, along with a grin of pure mischief.

Tess sighed and took her coat from him. "Thanks. Now you go get your club started. You've got a lot to talk about, don't you?"

"Don't be ridiculous. You know how I love walking in the snow. And this?" He motioned toward the phone and pulled the wool hat Janice had knit for Tess onto her head for her. "You're not going off sleuthing without me, young lady. If you three are out on another adventure, the Sherlock Society is coming along."

This Jim fellow being late was surely no great mystery—but that wouldn't stop Uncle Harold from turning it into one. Tess zipped up her coat and surveyed the all-too-eager collection of society members poised behind him.

So much for a quiet weekend.

A Note from the Editors

We hope you enjoy Secrets of Wayfarers Inn, created by the Books and Inspirational Media Division of Guideposts, a nonprofit organization that touches millions of lives every day through products and services that inspire, encourage, help you grow in your faith, and celebrate God's love in every aspect of your daily life.

Thank you for making a difference with your purchase of this book, which helps fund our many outreach programs to military personnel, prisons, hospitals, nursing homes, and educational institutions. To learn more, visit Guideposts Foundation.org.

We also maintain many useful and uplifting online resources. Visit Guideposts.org to read true stories of hope and inspiration, access OurPrayer network, sign up for free news-letters, download free e-books, join our Facebook community, and follow our stimulating blogs.

To learn about other Guideposts publications, including the best-selling devotional *Daily Guideposts*, go to ShopGuideposts .org, call (800) 932-2145, or write to Guideposts, PO Box 5815, Harlan, Iowa 51593.